POWERS BEYOND

Charles Brackett

ISBN: 978-1-943258-79-6
Library of Congress Control Number: 2017917579

Edited by: Jessica Carelock

Published by WARREN Publishing, Inc.

Charlotte, NC
www.warrenpublishing.net
Printed in the United States

Proverbs 3:5-6

My thanksgiving goes to Mindy Kuhn and her staff at Warren Publishing for this opportunity. I also wish to thank my wife for her presence, love, and support for the last 50 years in all of my careers.

PREFACE

Before you begin reading my novel, I would like to provide you with a list of principles I kept in mind while I wrote:

1. Sexual relationships are not a spectator sport; they are to be private, between husband and wife. I will not include them in my writings! I chose a publishing company that believes the same as I do, and I am grateful they are giving me the chance to publish.

2. Curse words don't add to the plot or to the action of a story. I once heard a teacher say those who have nothing to say resort to curse words, and I hold this adage to be true.

3. I have children and grandchildren. I cannot and I will not write down anything for publication that would cause me to fear if they should pick up the book and read it. Also, as a born-again believer, that would not be a good witness to my brothers and sisters in Christ, nor would it honor the Lord.

4. My writings have involved prayers of people for thanksgiving and in invoking God's blessings. People in real life do make mistakes and do make the wrong requests. Those in my stories are no different.

5. Books should not take the place of what our real lives should be about. The best reading one can have is in the Bible. The best time one can spend is in prayer. The best relationships one can have are being an obedient child of God, a terrific spouse, parent, and grandparent. My advice is not to live in a fantasy world.

PROLOGUE

What if…

The hypothesis stated in this novel is that our universe is stacked against other universes in different dimensions. All of the Time/Space Realities are living on this same planet and occupying the same space, but only phased in different dimensions. Each Time/Space Reality is protected by a cortex. These cortexes are essential to keeping the complete universe of thousands of Time/Space Realities separate from one another. Each timeline is unique and any outside disturbance can irrevocably alter the entire timeline of that reality.

POWERS BEYOND

BOOK 1
THE BOY GENIUS

INTRODUCTION

REALITY: 437269

Christopher Lee Beckett, Jr. was born on April 23, 1945. He was talking and walking by the age of one, reading by the age of two, and printing and writing by age four. By the time he reached age five, whatever math problem he was given, he could solve. He was insatiable in his quest for knowledge. He excelled in first grade, second grade was a bore, and at the beginning of the school term for third grade, the principal and the teachers sat down with his parents and said there was nothing left they could teach him. Chris learned on his own and wanted to learn everything he could. He was kept in school, but he was allowed independent study. He didn't want to just learn information, he wanted to learn how to do things. He had read every book in the elementary, junior high, and high school libraries as well as the downtown library, and was answering high school students' questions on English, French, Spanish, German, Physics, Geometry, and Chemistry. No matter the subject, he knew all the answers by the time he reached the sixth grade.

When Chris was twelve, he sat down with his parents and told them he could make them rich, but there was a catch. He said there was an island in the South Pacific that belonged to England and he wanted his parents to buy it for him and sign the title over to him when he turned eighteen. He drew up a contract and had a lawyer attest to his parents' signatures and his own. Chris then told his parents how and what to invest in the stock market and bonds. He also told them how and where to buy properties and then flip them over, because other people wanted them badly. Chris was highly cognitive and empathic. He could ascertain what people were thinking and he used it to his advantage. In a short period of time, his parents had earned a vast amount of money.

When Chris was seventeen, he prepared for the trip to England with his parents with an agenda larger than the purchase of an island. His parents had no idea of that agenda.

CHAPTER 1

The Becketts flew to England with their son on March 5, 1962. They left Chris's younger sister at home with a friend. She was five years younger than Chris. In England, Chris, with his parents present, negotiated the purchase of the island with the government. There was an independent UK Police Agency called the Worldwide People Protection Agency (WPPA), and part of the price for the island was for Chris to sell them a new weapon designed for defense. His parents knew nothing about this firearm and became very agitated during the negotiations. They explained to Chris he had no rights as an American citizen to sell his inventions to a foreign power.

One of the negotiators was a WPPA agent who acted as a government secretary. Her name was Edna Ryder. She asked for a recess and took Chris aside. They discussed several things, including dual citizenship for Chris, his future plans for the island, and other inventions he had created.

"Mrs. Ryder, I am basically a pacifist," said Chris. "I don't like war and I don't like seeing people killed. I have researched the WPPA and feel they would make the best use of my energy weapon; it does not kill people, it just incapacitates them, making them able to be transported without harm. I did not have a good feeling turning my inventions over to the US Military or the Counter Intelligence Agency."

"Chris, does this weapon really work?" asked Mrs. Ryder.

"Yes, I have a prototype here in my briefcase. I have to assemble it first. Once fired, an energy bolt incapacitates the target and then encases them in a protective shield casing so the person cannot flee. It also uses a laser target locator for accuracy. The sound from the weapon is very minimal," he said.

"Do you like the idea of dual citizenship?" Mrs. Ryder asked.

"Yes, I do. How long would it take for that process to be approved?"

"I think I can complete it by the end of the day. Also, what do you think of being declared emancipated from the control of your parents?"

"That is a hard one," said Chris. "My parents have control of my wealth and I have signed a contract with them that they keep and manage it until I'm eighteen. I love my parents, although they do not agree with what I am doing. I am unable to discuss things with them, because they don't see the usefulness of my abilities beyond how I can benefit them."

Chris and Mrs. Ryder had gone to a separate room for this discussion while his parents waited elsewhere. They were sitting at a ninety-degree angle from one another at a table and she pulled back from the table, turned her chair around, and faced Chris directly.

"Chris, what do you say to this: I do not know how much your parents have, but what if I say you can have the island for the price of the rights to your weapon—if it works, that is—and for refusal rights for any future inventions? Also, we will pay you a living allowance of £5,000 a month."

Chris had a puzzled look on his face. "How are you able to negotiate this without the approval of the prime minister?" he asked.

"I am doing this on behalf of WPPA and our authority goes beyond the prime minister's. I see your hesitation. Why don't we do this? Let's break for lunch and meet back for a demonstration this afternoon. Should we have a firing range?"

"No, that won't be necessary," he said, "as long as we have a volunteer."

"Alright, let's keep this discussion to ourselves and announce a recess until 2 p.m. and meet back in the main room. You can give me your decisions at that time."

"Okay," said Chris, as he stood up with briefcase in hand. Edna stood with him. They went back into the meeting room and the anger Chris saw on his parents' faces hurt him deeply. Mrs. Ryder announced to the prime minister that Chris would demonstrate his weapon at 2 p.m. and everyone would return at that time.

"Chris are you coming with us?" asked his dad.

"No, Dad, I am not that hungry. I'll stay here."

Everyone exited the room except Chris and Edna.

"Chris, I have to make some calls, are you going to be okay?" she asked.

"Yes. I'm going to go back to the meeting room, put the revolver together, take a nap, and see you here at 2 p.m.," he said calmly.

"Okay, Chris, that sounds like a plan. We'll talk a moment before the meeting starts."

"Sure, we'll talk more then."

Edna went to make her calls to have certain people at the meeting, including her husband, Colonel Thomas Ryder.

Chris went into the room, saw there was no other exit to the room, and disappeared. He reappeared at his parent's home in Aiken, South Carolina. He went to his safe, opened it, and pulled out several sets of blueprints and a copy of the contract with his parents. Once he had all the necessary papers, he placed them in his briefcase. Then he picked up a large box from the back of his closet and went downstairs, made himself a ham and mayonnaise sandwich, and then disappeared with the briefcase and box in hand.

Edna had just finished her calls and walked over to the room Chris was in. She knocked, opened the door when there was no answer, and looked inside. Chris was not there.

"I know I didn't see him come out!" she whispered to herself. She closed the door and looked at her watch. It was 1:45 p.m. She heard a crackle in the room and reopened the door. There was Chris in the middle of the room with a large box and his briefcase.

There is more to this young man than meets the eye, she thought to herself.

"Hi, Chris," Mrs. Ryder said with as much calmness as she could manage. "I didn't see the box earlier."

Chris thought how stupid it was of him to come here with the invention rather than take it to the hotel, but he didn't trust anyone right now, except maybe Mrs. Ryder.

"No, you didn't see it," he said. "I will have to explain that to you later. Let me put together the revolver as we speak. I think the first order of business is for me to become a citizen of the UK. Then I need to become emancipated; that would get my parents on their way home. We can then discuss where we need to go from there."

"Chris, do you want a guardian? You don't need one in the UK if you are over sixteen, but it would look favorable to the judge if you had one."

Chris's face was thoughtful as he contemplated the decision. "I met your husband the other day. I liked him, he is a good man. How about you and him?"

Edna had a surprised look on her face, but she managed to say, "If that is what you want, I would be honored. And I know Thomas would be, as well."

"Okay, let's get the ball rolling," said Chris as he finished assembling his weapon and inserted it in a chest holster he had been wearing under his blue dress coat.

They left the room and everyone from the original meeting was there along with several others Edna had called. Her husband, dressed in his formal Royal Air Force uniform, went to hug her when three hooded men walked into the room. Chris didn't give them time to shout their commands as he pulled his weapon and fired three shots. All three men went down. Shocked, everyone began to panic.

"I don't suppose we need a volunteer now," Chris announced as he re-holstered his weapon.

The security cameras had shown to the security room what happened and the security team entered quickly. They expected to find men wounded or dead, but all they found were three men lying on the floor knocked out and encased in some type of shield. The unit commander came forward and was about to grab Chris when Edna stepped in front of the commander and pulled out her identification. Upon recognizing the ID, he stood at attention and said, "Yes Ma'am, Madame Commander."

"At ease, soldier," said Commander Ryder. "Chris, would you show us how to release my men?"

Chris smiled. He had suspected they were plants, but wasn't sure. "You are good, Madame Commander, very good."

Edna smiled in return. Chris walked over to the men, pulled his weapon, showed Mrs. Ryder the release button, and pushed the button three times as he pointed it to each man. The shields disappeared and the men were released. They each looked at Chris with admiration in their eyes. They would be telling the story of his reaction and skill for many days to come.

CHAPTER 2

At age fourteen, Chris had received his first college degree in mechanical engineering at USC and his second was a pre-med degree two years later at USC Medical College. He also obtained a degree in microbiological engineering at USC in the spring of his seventeenth birthday, just before the trip to England. His knowledge, however, went far beyond any schooling.

"Mr. Prime Minister, if you don't mind, I shall continue this meeting," said Mrs. Ryder.

"Not at all, Madame Commander, you and Mr. Beckett have my undivided attention," said the prime minister.

Chris was at Mrs. Ryder's side and touched her shoulder while whispering into her ear, "Please, let me start."

She stepped aside as Chris began.

"Dad, Mom, I love you with all of my heart. I know things have been strained for some time because it was difficult knowing your son was taking care of you at such a young age. I need to begin what I believe is my mission in life. I believe the time has come for me to begin making my own decisions. I am applying for citizenship in the UK and for emancipation from you. I...."

Chris's father stood and shouted, "I forbid you to do this! You are still my son and too young to make decisions on your own!"

"Not in the UK, Dad." A soldier came and stood beside Mr. Beckett as Chris continued, "I am giving everything we have made to you. The entire checking account belongs to you and Mom. I just need to find a judge to handle the next step and to have some lawyers draw up contracts and notices."

A man rose from the group.

"I am the Honorable Justin P. Humphries, son, and Madame Commander Ryder has informed me of your intentions," he said. "Consider the matter settled and those three lawyers sitting there will take care of the papers. Do you have a copy of the original contract?"

"Yes, I do, sir," said Chris as he opened his briefcase and handed the contract to the judge.

New contracts were drawn up, printed, and signed, and one hour later Chris's parents were escorted from the room. They had acknowledged Chris's money was theirs and Chris was emancipated. When Chris attempted to hug them, they refused to show love toward him in any way. They were escorted to their room at the hotel downtown and then driven to the airport, and were not allowed to enter Chris's room at the hotel.

Chris was under eighteen and did not need to make an oath to the Queen, but he did anyway. Papers were drawn up and signed, and Chris was officially under the guardianship of Mr. and Mrs. Thomas Ryder and had dual citizenship with both the United States and Great Britain.

The judge also had several lawyers draw up papers for the sale of the island to Chris. Chris decided to call the island Sobarus Island. He also had the lawyers draw up an agreement for the building of a retreat on the island and the transport of materials. The transport of materials would be made by RAF C-130s using a new propulsion system Chris had developed. Chris gave blueprints to Mrs. Ryder for the island retreat and a materials list. He had already purchased the materials needed and they were waiting for pickup at various companies throughout England. It would take three trips for the C-130s to deliver the material to the island. Chris and Colonel Ryder would be flying the materials because Chris would have to operate the new propulsion system. A crew of WPPA agents would be on the flights as well as a work crew sworn to secrecy.

Chris handed another set of plans to Mrs. Ryder.

"Chris, this blueprint is for a satellite," she said. "One with lasers on board and an atomic power cell. You know weapons in space are forbidden."

"Yes, ma'am, I do," said Chris. "I just need the satellites built. I will launch them from my island, so no one will be blaming the UK. I also need this rocket built. It will launch all six satellites together."

"Chris, wait a minute. You said you were a pacifist. This doesn't fit the pacifist mode," said Mrs. Ryder, furrowing her brow.

"Madame Commander, these satellites are for defense only," he replied. "As I told you earlier, I do not want to kill anyone, ever. Once these satellites are made, the blueprint needs to be destroyed."

"I am not sure my government will allow them to be built," she said.

"That's alright," said Chris as he placed the blueprint back in his briefcase.

Mrs. Ryder had a puzzled look on her face with a frown as she asked Chris, "So, what are you going to do about the satellites?"

Chris, with a smile on his face, said, "I am not sure at this time. I have to think about this for a while."

"Please let me know your intentions when you decide," said Mrs. Ryder.

"I won't promise, but I may. Now, when can the first C-130 be ready for the trip?"

Thomas answered, "Today is Thursday, so they have four days to transport the materials and to load one C-130 allowing us to leave Monday. The C-130 is at our Mendenhall base two hours north of London. We will be sending all three shipments from there. I need to arrange for refueling in the air or a stopover in Argentina."

"You won't need to refuel," said Chris. "The box over there has the mechanism in it that will propel the airplane to the island. We will use fuel to take off and land here in London. The rest of the time we will be using the earth's magnetic and gravitational fields to propel us. It's a little more complicated than that, but it will be similar to teleporting. Your wife has already seen the end result of a human teleport. This will just be a large package moved and in a different way. The trip to the island will take about four hours at Mach 3, as I don't want to upset the men on board too much. I could go Mach 7.5, but that would be pushing it."

"Chris, it would take twenty-seven hours flying at maximum speed for a C-130 to reach this island!" said Colonel Ryder. "I hear what you are saying, but what about G-force? Are you absolutely sure this is possible?" He was baffled.

"No problem, sir," said Chris. "The mechanics are similar to wind moving and there is no G-force."

"You can't travel that fast without having G-force," said Thomas with an air of skepticism.

"Colonel Ryder, all I am asking is that you trust me."

Chris grabbed each of the Ryders' hands and teleported the three of them to his home in Aiken, SC.

"Welcome to Aiken, South Carolina," he said. "Are you convinced?" The television set was on and the picture showed a local weather report for the Central Savannah River Area that encompasses Aiken and Augusta, Georgia.

Mrs. Ryder sat down. She couldn't believe what she was just a part of and what she was seeing. "Chris, how do you have this ability?" she asked. "And how are you able to duplicate it for a plane as large as a C-130?"

"I don't know," he said. "I do know my IQ is off the chart. Doctors are unable to measure it." Chris reached for their hands and they found themselves back at the meeting room they had left.

"Is there any way to teach us how to do this?" asked Thomas.

"It is not something I learned," said Chris, shaking his head. "One day it was there. There are some other abilities that go with the teleportation, but I would rather discuss those at a different time. Right now, I have to leave. I need to go home and pick some things up before Dad and Mom arrive."

"Chris, the hotel downtown was rented by WPPA. We did not check you out of your room, but a WPPA agent is guarding it 24/7. What do you want done with this box?" asked Mrs. Ryder.

"I'll take it back to the hotel with me and leave it there if you assure me it is safe," said Chris. "It's my first manual teleporter and I would have to start all over if it were lost or stolen. There is no software nor writings on it; it's all in my head. I can make more, but I just haven't done it yet and a couple of the components are hard to obtain. How long before I can come to the base?"

"It is getting late in the day," said Thomas. "I have to get back on base and arrange for you to have clearance so you can modify the system for one C-130. It should be fairly easy with my wife's signature from WPPA."

"Here's my mobile phone number. One of you call me when you need me," said Chris, and with that, he picked up his briefcase and the box and teleported to the hotel room. He left those items there and teleported back to Aiken. He found his Corvette keys and drove it to the Aiken airport to an empty hanger he had rented earlier. Once he safely stashed it inside, he locked the door and teleported back to the house. In the refrigerator Chris found some leftover chicken and mashed potatoes, which he heated and ate for supper. Then he went to his room and placed most of his clothes on the bed along with other items he wanted. He looked around the room, tied the bedspread around the bundle, and teleported back to the hotel room. He put everything on the extra bed in the room, then pulled a key pad out of his briefcase and stuck it to the wall with double-sided tape.

Chris keyed some numbers on the pad. The room was now protected by a shield. He then teleported to his father's shop at the Aiken home, looked through the projects he'd been working on, and put them in a large box. He placed any writings or parts he'd purchased in the box, also. Finally, he put his hands on the box and teleported the box and himself back to the hotel room.

"I almost forgot!" he yelled as he teleported once again to the house. He went to the back-left corner of his closet and picked up a bag. Chris had stashed $200,000 inside this bag.

"I may need some cash," he said to himself and then teleported back to the hotel.

Once at the hotel, Chris sorted his clothes and found pajamas and underwear. He took a long, hot shower, dressed, and went to bed. He slept soundly.

The next morning Chris woke with a start.

"The nanorobots!" he exclaimed. He quickly dressed and teleported to his room at the Aiken home. His father was in his room reaching for the refrigerator door. Chris was behind him. He encased his dad with a shield and turned his dad's face away from the refrigerator. Then he opened the refrigerator door and took out three packages. He removed the shield from his dad as he teleported back to the hotel.

"That was close; dad will wonder what happened," he said to himself. "He will also wonder about the missing clothes and items from the workshop, but that wonder is better than his knowing I can teleport and better than him or someone else having the nanorobots. I hope I have remembered everything. My computer was already in the Corvette's trunk, so I believe I have everything now."

CHAPTER 3

Chris opened the door into the hotel hallway and an agent snapped to attention.

"That's not necessary," said Chris.

"It is if I want to keep my job," replied the agent.

"What if I asked you to stand at ease?"

"That would work," said the older man as he relaxed.

"I think I recognize you as one of the plants yesterday, am I right?" asked Chris.

"Yes, you are. That was an awesome display. My name is James Smart," said the agent as he reached and shook Chris's hand. "I am your daytime room protector."

"So, you just came on duty?"

"Yes, sir," said the man with a nod.

"Isn't it pretty lonely out here?" asked Chris.

"That it is, sir, but that's part of the job. We do whatever is asked of us. That is how we protect people and property, by doing what is commanded and with the right attitude. It is what Jesus asks of us every day," the agent replied.

Ignoring James's last comment, Chris asked, "Can I exchange dollars to pounds at the main desk?"

With a surprised look at how quickly Chris changed the subject, James remarked, "Yes, they offer a fair exchange."

Chris said, "Thank you," and turned and walked to the elevator.

Chris had to give his room number and show his key before the hotel clerk would exchange the $1,000 he requested. Once the hotel clerk saw it was the room rented to WPPA, nothing else was said. In the hotel's dining room, Chris ate a breakfast of eggs, sausage, ham, and orange juice and then went out the front door for a walk.

He had noticed two men watching him from inside the hotel lobby while he was eating breakfast and assumed they were WPPA agents keeping watch over him. He walked around London with them following at a safe distance. He saw the London Bridge, the London Tower, and Buckingham Palace, until his phone rang at 11 a.m.

"Do you see the military sedan in front of you on the curb?" asked Colonel Ryder.

"Yes, I do, Colonel," replied Chris.

"Open the right rear door and slide into the back seat."

Chris had only a few more paces to do as requested. He did so, shut the door, and the car quickly sped away. Colonel Ryder was sitting next to Chris and looking out the rear window, watching the two men who suddenly recognized their prey was gone.

"Good morning, Chris. That was close. Had you noticed you were being followed?" asked the Colonel.

"Good Morning, Colonel. Yes, they watched me from the lobby while I ate breakfast and have been following me all morning. Weren't they WPPA agents?"

"No, they weren't, Chris. They are from the CIA," warned Thomas.

"So, you have a leak from someone who was there at the meeting yesterday?" asked Chris.

"It appears so. I hope they were not going to try to kidnap you. I am certain you would have given them a surprise; but then others would learn more about you than we wish to have disclosed."

"That is correct, Colonel," said Chris. "Are we headed to the base?"

"Yes, we are," Thomas replied. "The Base Commander wants to have lunch with you. He has a couple of questions. We should be at the base at 12:50 if traffic is okay."

"Is the driver authorized to know about me?" Chris asked.

"He was one of the plants from yesterday, but we don't want anyone knowing about extra powers for now."

"Okay, I'll sit back and relax," said Chris, stretching his legs. "Where will I live while my retreat is being built and furnished?"

"Chris, let me address the issue of the building of the retreat," said Thomas in a business-like manner. "I saw the plans. The only hold-up will be the special glass for the windows on the eastern side. They are of special construction and there is only one glass company in England that can do that. I suspect it would be six months before they can be made."

Chris shook his head. "The windows are already made. They're in the shipping yard all boxed up and waiting for my agent to pick them up. I ordered them last June. I paid for them up front and the glass company was more than happy to get the job prioritized. I hope you read all my notes and saw the materials were ready to pick up at the various vendors. Also, I hope the government isn't out anything—just the fuel for the flights and rental on the C130s, and I will reimburse for those expenses."

"I was going to ask you about that," said Thomas. "How did you know we would make the deal? Certainly, you couldn't have known the future!"

Chris just smiled at the Colonel, sat back in the seat, and closed his eyes. People didn't need to know everything about him or he would no longer be a mystery. The colonel just smiled at the calm demeanor of this young man.

They arrived at the base and a special pass was at the check point for Chris. The car went through without any hold up and they went directly to administration. The colonel asked Chris to follow him and they went inside. The colonel went to a particular desk, handed the pass to a female clerk who snapped to attention, and asked the colonel and Chris to follow her. They went into a room. An ID badge was manufactured, and Chris had his photo taken and was handed the ID. The woman saluted the colonel and waited for Chris's returned salute. He didn't understand but saluted her anyway. When they returned to the car, Chris read the ID.

"Commander Christopher L. Beckett, Jr. from WPPA. How did I earn that ranking?" he asked.

"It was the only way we could get you in and around without a lot of questions," said Thomas with a grin. "You can thank my wife for that. Now, to answer the question of where you will be staying; you will have an apartment at this base in your name. It is actually on the same floor as ours."

They arrived at the officer's dining hall and Chris and the colonel exited the car and walked inside. There was a private room to the left and the general met them at the door. After the necessary salutes, they sat down. It was a buffet and after a few general questions and surface conversation, the colonel bowed his head and said a prayer of thanksgiving for the meal. He also asked the Lord's blessing on the meeting. Chris was non-committal and the general noticed he didn't bow his head. Each one then went to the table, filled their plates, told the waiter their drink orders, and sat down. When the waiter brought their drinks, the general asked him to close the door and not to disturb them.

"Mr. Beckett," said General Putnam, "what is this invention you are putting on my plane?"

"It is a manual teleporter, Sir," said Chris. "It will increase the speed of the plane up to Mach 7.5 if necessary. But we will be flying only at Mach 3."

"Son, do you take me for some kind of fool?" asked General Putman.

"No, sir, I don't," said Chris as he grabbed the general's arm and Colonel Ryder's. They suddenly found themselves in the middle of the firing range on post and people were firing. Chris had covered them with a dark shield and no one could see what was in the large dark ball that suddenly appeared on the field. After about 10 seconds, Chris brought them back to the table at the officer's mess.

"Young man, what type of trick did you just pull?" General Putnam demanded. "Did you hypnotize me?"

"No, he didn't, General. He has teleported me once before," said Thomas. "The shield, however, was something new. I am glad he is on our side and not the side of the Russians or even the USA."

The general was still shaking while Chris enjoyed his meal. Finally, he calmed down enough to ask. "The method of movement for the C130 is not like what you just took me through, is that correct?" he asked.

"You are correct, General," said Chris. "It will take between four and five hours to reach the island. When we finish the transport of all the material, I will need to leave a large construction crew on the island to complete the retreat—except for the east-facing windows. I will have to be there to hold the window panes in place while they are installed with the metal retainers. While the workers are building the retreat, I will make several working teleporters. I would recommend a squadron of twenty-four Typhoon jets, six C130s, and six medical jets from the GNAT series. I request that three of the GNAT series be placed under my command. I would modify the jet before the propulsion unit is installed, and I need eighteen top-notch computer and construction men or women.

"I also want the entire project finished before I leave for the island around the first of September," he continued. "The equipment I will put in these aircrafts will be different from the one I am flying to the South Pacific. I will also need several pilots who are unafraid to learn something new. Naturally, General and Colonel, it is up to you two to determine these people are not CIA or Russian spies and they will keep this information top-secret."

"Colonel, what was the meaning of that statement?" asked the general, seemingly puzzled.

"We thwarted an attempt at kidnapping this morning," said Thomas. "We believe they were CIA agents. Someone who was in the meeting yesterday leaked information, unless Mr. Beckett's parents went to the CIA."

"Colonel, I hadn't thought of that!" exclaimed Chris. "You are correct. My parents were very upset I didn't sell my weapon to the CIA."

"Colonel, what have you not told me?" asked the general. "A weapon? Who has control of that?"

"It is a defensive weapon, Sir," said the Colonel, "and WPPA will have exclusive rights to it for manufacturing and distribution."

"Young man, thank you," the general said as he stood, returned their salutes, and left the meeting.

"Well, that was rather abrupt," said Chris, with a puzzled look on his face.

"Don't be alarmed, but you bested the general!" said Thomas. "He felt he had one on you since you were so young, and although he isn't happy with the outcome of his suspicions, he is very happy to have you on his side."

"Okay, what now?" asked Chris.

"Let's find your apartment, get the keys, and get you moved. We need you out of that hotel and here on base."

"I will be able to move myself. It will take several trips, but it is the way I want to do it. Let's go."

Chris and the colonel went to the housing authority, had Chris sign several documents, picked up his keys, and walked to the apartment complex. They were on the third floor, which meant no one was above them. They walked upstairs and Chris opened the apartment and walked in. It was furnished, had a TV, the refrigerator was stocked, and there was food in the freezer.

"You can thank Mom Edna for the food and beverages," said Colonel Ryder, referring to his wife and Chris's new legal guardian.

"Thank you, also, Dad Tom," Chris said with a wide smile that the colonel returned. "Go spend the rest of the day with your wife," he continued. "I will be moving in and checking out of the hotel."

"Okay, call me if you need anything," said the colonel. "If not I will see you at 0600 tomorrow for calisthenics."

"For *what?*" asked Chris, astonished.

"You heard me. There are uniforms in the closet. Wear the fatigues."

"Okay," Chris said as he closed and locked the door. "Like I'll be there," he muttered.

He teleported to the hotel, picked up the box and his briefcase, and teleported back to the apartment. He placed the box in a corner, his briefcase on the dresser, and made sure the rear door was locked. Then he removed another device from his briefcase, put it on the wall with two-sided tape, punched a few buttons, and the apartment was now securely shielded. He then teleported back to the hotel and began making several trips with his clothes, the other experiments, and the nanorobots. He double-checked everything in the hotel room, pulled the device off of the wall, put it in his pocket, and teleported to an empty restroom located on the same floor. A minute later, he walked out of the restroom and over to the front of his hotel room.

"Agent Smart, how has your day gone?" he asked.

"Rather boring, Sir," said the agent.

"Well, they won't need you tomorrow, as I will be moving to the base," said Chris.

"Will you need help with anything?" asked the agent.

"I appreciate the offer, but no, the colonel and his wife will be helping me tonight."

"If you ever need anything, please let me know."

"I sure will, Agent Smart," said Chris, and he continued on his way.

CHAPTER 4

The C130 was fully-loaded, the contents from the box had been installed by Chris over the weekend, and the crew was in place. Thirty workers were lined up on the side seats of the plane. Fifteen WPPA agents were also in place. Colonel Ryder was in the cockpit with Chris in the copilot's seat.

"Colonel, there is a stealth position for my equipment," Chris said. "I have told the control tower we are testing the stealth technology. You will taxi and take off like normal. You will take a bearing for the Isthmus of Panama and once in the air I will flip the stealth switch and once the tower says we are off radar I will begin moving the plane. You will keep the engines on idle so the radio and other items will operate. Any questions?"

"No, Chris, you have been on the mark about everything you have said; I don't expect anything less from this."

"If that is the case, let's contact the tower."

Colonel Ryder started the engines and began the taxi toward the correct runway after conversing with the control tower. Once they had risen to 28,000 feet he checked his trajectory with the tower and stated the test would begin. Chris flipped the switch to stealth mode and the tower confirmed they had disappeared off radar.

They asked, "Flight 2341, are you okay? You are not on Radar?"

"We are still at 28,000 feet and our trajectory has not changed." said Colonel Ryder.

Chris then hit the control button for the propulsion system and set it for Mach 3. There was a short uncomfortable shudder in the plane, but it smoothed out and they were off. Colonel Ryder watched as they left Europe and how quickly they found themselves over the open sea. Two and a half hours flight time later they were over Panama. "I see it but I cannot believe it," exclaimed Colonel Ryder.

"Colonel, seeing is believing. This is absolutely wonderful. This should make you happy to know what you and your country can do with this new technology."

"Chris, you are absolutely right. Thank you for letting me be a part of this."

"You are welcome." Chris said with a big smile.

Exactly two and a half hours later the island came into view. It was beautiful. It was a tropical paradise and the colors were awesome. The sea was crystal clear and a beautiful blue. Colonel Ryder could see a large bay Chris was directing the plane toward. He saw at the edge of the island a large clearing. They had flown over 10,000 miles in exactly five hours. Now, the colonel was wondering how they were going to land.

He watched as the plane stopped in midair. The altitude kept getting lower as if in a vertical drop. The plane turned around and faced out to sea. The plane's descent stopped ten feet from the ground. The tail end of the plane was over a concrete pad at the edge of the island about 500 yards from the shore. "Colonel, instruct the men to unhook all of the cargo from its restraints so it's free from the plane. Lower the cargo door. I am going to use one of my powers to move the cargo on land and put it where I need it. Please don't let anyone in the cockpit and don't touch my controls."

Everyone watched as the cargo moved from the plane and neatly stacked itself at one end of the concrete pad. Once it was in place, Chris was back on board and the cargo door was raised. Colonel Ryder was on the speaker and he said, "Gentlemen, you never saw what you just saw. Don't discuss it with anyone, not even among yourselves. We have two more trips to make. Let's go home."

Chris manipulated his instrument panel and the plane rose to 28,000 feet and made a bee line for Suffolk, England. He wanted to show off and the men wanted to get home, so they were almost home at 1300 hours. He slowed the plane down over the ocean and Colonel Ryder took over, Chris removed the stealth mode, and the colonel called the control tower. "Flight 2341, test is over. How did we do?"

"Colonel, you could have flown to Hawaii for all we know. No radar picked you up; either ours or any other countries'. You are cleared to land on runway 4." Chris and the colonel grinned at one another at the control tower operator's comments.

When they landed and before Chris left the plane he told the construction crew he wanted them to see where they were going. They would fly out in the morning with the rest of the crew on this plane.

On Tuesday morning at 0800 the same flight crew and over 100 construction workers were loaded in the plane. There were several pallets of food, water, latrines, tents, and sleeping bags. Chris was talking with Agent Smart from WPPA. "I didn't know you were an architect," he said.

"My dad wanted me in the business, but I wanted to work for WPPA. And here I am building a building. Go figure!"

"I am pleased to know you will be in charge. I had felt you are a man who can be trusted from the first time I met you. I believe with the way I have the materials and the cranes set up you can have this built in ninety days. The final piece to assemble will be the large curved windows. It will be tricky, but I know we can do it. You have my mobile phone number if you need me. The phone I have given you is a satellite phone, so communication will not be a problem."

"Chris, what is a satellite phone?"

"Someday I will explain. For now, just know it will work from this remote location." Chris then raised his voice so all could hear him. "Okay, let's get ready for takeoff everyone." Chris and Colonel Ryder performed their tasks as yesterday. This time Chris started out at Mach 7.5. He was anxious to get this job done. He went to the main bay area. "Gentlemen, what you are flying in is a modified C130. The propulsion system is linked to the earth's magnetic and gravitational fields. We are flying at Mach 7.5 and will be at my island in under two hours. We will be over 10,000 miles from England. I would appreciate it if you never told anyone what you have seen and will see over the next ninety days. It is okay to talk amongst yourselves while you are on the island. You will not be able to go into the jungle as I will have a barrier up that will keep the wild animals away. We brought fishing gear and a couple of small boats, so you can do some light fishing. There are a couple of chefs on board and we have food for thirty days and have set up supply routes for more food. We are using military portable electrical generators for refrigeration and if anything is needed, Agent Smart is in charge and can reach me. I want to thank each of you for volunteering for this unusual construction project, and I assure you that you will be compensated as you were told." Chris fielded a couple of questions and soon Colonel Ryder was calling him on the intercom.

"Yes, Dad? Are we there yet?"

"That wasn't even half funny. Would you come to the cockpit please?" Several men around the room were laughing.

"What speed did you set us? It has been only forty-five minutes and we are already crossing Panama. "

"I thought maximum speed was Mach 7.5. We must be going around Mach 8. Let me slow it down a bit." Chris adjusted the controls. "There, that should do it. I don't want to have a problem with structural integrity, although that really should not enter into the equation. Yes, that feels better now. Say, has Edna found me a warehouse yet?"

"There is an empty hanger on the base. It would hold two or three of the jets at a time."

"That is good. When can I have it?"

"Is tomorrow okay?"

"Wonderful. When may I have the jets allotted to me?"

"You already have them. They are parked outside the hanger. I have picked some men and women, so I believe the program is ready to start. I have the list of parts you asked me to get. I did have a little difficulty on a couple of items, but I found everything. I also have the testing tools you requested as well as the other tools needed. If anything else is needed, please let me know."

"Thank you, I appreciate your help."

The men with their tools and supplies were dropped off at 10 a.m. London time. They turned around and were back at the base by noon. Chris took the box out of the C130 after it was parked out of the way and went to the second C130 that was loaded and ready. He installed the propulsion system and tested all the connections. Colonel Ryder, Chris, and the regular crew got on board. Chris looked up and coming across the tarmac was Edna in a flight suit.

"Good afternoon, Commander. What brings you here?"

"You do, young man. You've taken my husband across the world twice now and if you expect me to sit at home while you do it again, you have got another thing coming," said Mrs. Ryder as she came on board in her flight suit and sat behind the pilot. She had a grin on her face as she said, "Okay, Colonel, call the tower and obtain clearance for the next test."

This last flight went without a hitch as did the other two.

Chris and the team in the hanger worked well together and all of the Typhoon Jets and the GNAT jets were modified. The GNAT jets were made into pilotless planes. They could be piloted, but their main reason for existence was to get people to a medical facility fast. Edna and Colonel Thomas had seen Chris had a hospital floor at the retreat. He told them he felt he could help people with transplants. He was working on a heart and a lung apparatus and a neural implant that would go in someone's head if he had a traumatic head injury.

It was June 30th. Most of the construction workers had been flown back and paid, even a bonus they did not expect. Secrecy was discussed more than once with everyone and documents to that effect had been signed. Chris, Edna, and the colonel were in the plane with the rest of the crew and the glass for the final installation. The plane had just been placed perfectly at the site and Chris and the crew were removing the shipping container from the first piece. The construction workers were in place on the fifth floor and Chris, using his telekinesis powers moved the glass in place. He held it there while all the retainers were bolted in place with stainless steel bolts. The crew on the plane was removing the shipping crate from the next piece of glass as the construction crew moved to the fourth floor. Everything went flawlessly for all five floors. One of the construction crew placed the Great Britain flag on the top of the building to signal its completion. Everyone was very pleased.

The C130 they were flying had been modified with the new electronics and electrical system and it could be flown by the pilot with no help needed from a second person. One would have to know what he was looking for in order to activate the teleporter. Chris had asked the colonel to train the pilots the RAF wanted to fly the new system.

The construction crew had been through the building and cleaned it up. All of the furniture and equipment was in place. Chris was very happy. He was looking at the forest from his veranda on the third floor when his head began to pound. This was the fourth headache in a week. Chris said, "I will have to check this out soon."

Chris had moved in several personal items, including the computer, as the building was built. He had been working the stock market personally since he was emancipated and had earned a considerable sum, so the money he needed for repayment to the government and workers was there when needed. Although the government owed him a lot, Chris didn't want some bureaucrat saying that the government had paid for the work so they owned it. The colonel, Edna, and the crew were leaving Chris on the island alone. He had almost perfected the neural implant. Everything was operational except the computer which Chris was installing that day.

"Computer, today is June 30, 1962. Please adjust all of your software to reflect that date and the local time is 1330. My name is Christopher L. Beckett, Jr. I would prefer you call me Chris. Please recognize my voice imprint and lock it in as to the only voice imprint you will obey. I will call you 'Computer.' Do not be alarmed at the difference in the date. I purchased you from a reliable source in the year 2511. You are the best computer with the best software and with my added programs, you will be unequaled. Your main purpose is to control and protect this retreat. I will add other duties at a later time. Do you accept the conditions and my ownership?"

"I do, Chris, it's good to meet you. What is your first command?"

"I have inserted a program to place a protective shield around this island. The perimeters are in the program. Please activate the shield."

"Shield activated."

"Computer, do you detect anyone on the island?"

"No, Chris, I do not. All I detect are normal animals associated with a rainforest."

"I have had a busy day. I am going to turn in early. Continue to monitor the island according to your program."

"Yes, sir."

July 12, 1962: Chris was in the medical center of the retreat. He had just finished looking at an image of his brain. The small spot he saw didn't explain his headaches, but it did tell him something was wrong and he was concerned.

CHAPTER 5

Chris awakened with a horrible feeling. He quickly showered, dressed and teleported to his apartment at the base in England. He could hear the sirens immediately upon arriving. He opened the door and went into the hall. Edna was coming out of her apartment with a medic and a female officer. "Chris, Tom is dead. He was training a new student who flew off course. Tom didn't react in time and they crashed headlong into another trainer. There was no hope for any of the four."

Chris reached for Mrs. Ryder and hugged her for all he was worth. He couldn't believe it. He had no idea that the colonel would be taken from them like this. He didn't understand and his anger was apparent.

"Chris, anger won't do any good. Tom is with the Lord now, he is at peace. We need to understand that."

"I will never understand a god that would allow this. It is so unfair. It is so capricious. We have discussed this many times. I will be here for you. I will help you as best as I can. I do not share your beliefs."

"I know, Chris, I pray for you every day. Your being here will help me. Thank you for coming. Did the base call you?"

"No, I woke in the middle of the night with a sense of something being wrong and came here as soon as I could."

"Chris, you amaze me with your knowledge, yet the smallest bit of evidence into the spiritual and you refuse to believe. Please come with me. I must identify the body and make arrangements. I will need you with me, please."

Chris held on to her and was with her throughout the entire ordeal. The military funeral was Friday and Chris performed his duties to the letter and with great compassion. The colonel was laid to rest and Chris was now at Edna's apartment.

It was 4 p.m. on Friday.

"Chris, we need to talk. Sit here beside me, please. We are going to have to give up our apartments. I have decided to leave WPPA. I cannot handle the pressure right now. My husband is gone and I have no purpose left."

"What about me? Do you not have a purpose in me?"

"I do, Chris, but you are so independent, how can I help you?"

"Okay, let's talk. I need a supply system for me at the retreat. I also need advice on many things. I am to meet my intended Saturday in Aiken, SC. Would you like to come along?"

"Chris, this isn't the first time you have said something to the colonel or me about knowing the future. Have you been into the future?"

"Yes, I have, and I can even monitor the future and other entities. My computer is from the year 2511. I can see these other entities through a program I have written. We are not the only reality. You and I exist in thousands of realities. I have seen enough to know I am to marry a young girl named Anna Marie Koch from Aiken, SC. As long as the timeline does not get corrupted we are meant to be together. The problem is she is three years younger than me and I want to meet her. Even though it is too early, I need to see her and I want you there."

"Okay, so how do you intend to meet her?"

"I don't want to draw attention to my teleporting skills, so I suggest we take a Typhoon. I have a hanger in which to hide it. They are always on the ready line. We'll have it back in a few days. Will you come with me? Besides, you need to have something to take your mind off of your loss."

"Meeting your future intended? I like that. Yes, I will go with you."

They were in flight suits and ready. Edna told the control tower it was a security issue and she and Chris would return in a couple of days. The general okayed the use, and they were gone. They arrived in Aiken early Friday morning, and Chris found a hotel and rented two rooms. They slept for a few hours then they walked arm in arm through main street of Aiken and talked for a long time. Several people recognized Chris from high school and he introduced Edna as his mother. One young lady from his high school was Donna Height. She cornered Chris as they were about to enter a dining facility.

"You never did come to my church."

"No, I didn't, Donna."

"Would you come to an ice cream social tomorrow afternoon at one?"

"I think we would enjoy that. We'll be there."

CHAPTER 6

Chris and Edna arrived at the social shortly after it started. It was well-attended. Donna was there and introduced Mrs. Ryder to everyone as she went around. They came to the cake table and there was a German chocolate cake that had not yet been cut. He asked the lady behind the table if he could purchase the whole cake.

"I am not sure," she replied. "Why don't you ask the person who made it?"

"And who might that be?" asked Chris.

"That would be Anna Marie Koch. Donna, why don't you introduce the two? She is over there by the crepe myrtle with her friends."

Edna and Chris walked over and as Donna was introducing them, one of the girls said, "Yes, you are the boy who sold out his country and threw away his parents."

"It isn't like that," said Edna as she took over the conversation and Donna grabbed Chris and Anna Marie's hands and took them aside.

"You two talk over here. It seems she has that conversation under control."

"Hello," said Chris. "My name is Christopher. I am told you made the German chocolate cake?"

"I did. Why do you want to know?"

"I would like to buy the cake. How much is it?"

"It's all donations, so whatever you feel led to give. By the way, my father works with your father and he is very upset at the way you treated your dad. There was a magazine you were interviewed in and you told your side of the story. I understand what you did. I asked my father to read it, and he understood the situation better, but he did not change his opinion."

"Do you mind if I just say you are about the prettiest girl I have ever met? I love your blue eyes and your brown hair. It flows over your shoulders very well. You are not too short and not too tall. I would guess 5' 9"?"

Anna Marie was blushing as she nodded her head. "You are rather forward, aren't you?"

"I don't mean to be. Are you planning on going to college?" he asked.

"I am in a few years. I don't want to mislead you. I am only fourteen years old and both dating and college are a few years away."

"You carry yourself so well and you look older; I am sorry if I have offended you."

"You haven't, Chris, and I appreciate the compliment. Will you be moving back to South Carolina?"

"Only if I can receive approval from your dad to date you!" Chris replied.

"That would be out of the question at this time. Check back when I am sixteen."

"May I speak with him anyway? Maybe he would allow chaperoned dates?"

"Chris, I have to get to the cake table, it is my turn to sell cakes and slices. If you want to speak with my dad, I cannot stop you, but be prepared for a big 'NO.'"

"Is a donation of $100 enough for the cake?"

"That is a little much, but thank you. The youth group thanks you, as well."

Donna had been keeping people away from Chris and Anna Marie so they could talk, and Mrs. Ryder had finished her conversation with the other girls. All were walking back to the cake table and Edna was smiling at Chris as she whispered in his ear, "She *is* pretty."

Chris thanked her as he lowered his head and blushed. He purchased the cake, thanked Donna for inviting him, and told Anna Marie he would call her dad. Chris purchased cones of ice cream for himself and Edna, and they left with the cake in hand.

That night Chris and Edna were sitting at a table in the dining room of the hotel drinking coffee and sharing large slices of the cake.

"Chris, this cake is delicious. You said the icing was homemade?"

"Yes, it is. What do you think of Anna Marie?"

"I believe she is beautiful and well poised. She is only fourteen years old?"

"Yes, but I am going to ask her dad if I can court her with a chaperone and I would like you to meet her family, as well."

"When? I have received a communication there may be trouble brewing with Russia and they could recall the Typhoon at any moment."

"I'll try to set it up for Monday afternoon. Hopefully nothing will happen before then."

Chris set up the meeting for Monday with Mr. Koch, and Mrs. Ryder went to church Sunday close to the hotel. Monday evening at 7P.M. Chris rang the doorbell of the Koch residence. He was dressed in a black suit with a tie and Mrs. Ryder was in a black dress.

Albert Koch answered the door and invited Mrs. Ryder and Chris inside. "Mrs. Ryder, I read in the news about the training accident. You have my condolences on the loss of your husband." Anna Marie was sitting with her brother and mother at the kitchen table and Anna Marie's hand went to her mouth as she didn't know of the accident. She had not read any news and Chris did not mention it Saturday.

"Chris, did you find Anna Marie's cake tasty?"

"Yes, sir, both of us did. We ate it at the coffee shop in the hotel and shared it with others and they send their compliments to the cook," said Chris as he looked toward Anna Marie and smiled. She ducked her head and Chris could see her pink cheeks before her head fully lowered.

"Chris, you said you wished to speak with me. What can I do for you?"

"Sir, I know Anna Marie is only fourteen, however, I was hoping you would allow her to date me with adult supervision."

"Chris, you know I work with your father at the plant. The plant is part of the Department of Defense. You had designed a weapon that was useful for our country and you sold it to a foreign power and then disowned your parents."

"Mr. Koch, the defense weapon I designed was sold to an independent police agency, WPPA. I did not sell it to the UK. They are free to share it with anyone in the free world. Also, I did not disown my parents. I had myself emancipated. I had allowed my parents to control my finances, and at my emancipation I gave all of my finances to them. It was a considerable sum. I felt that it was time for me to begin what I believe is my life's work, and the UK could better suit me than the USA. Also, I do not trust the CIA and believe they do not have the USA's best interest at heart. We could discuss politics all evening, but my decision did not harm my parents in any way and they don't have to be concerned about my upbringing anymore."

"Alright, Chris. First, my daughter is too young to date, even with a chaperone. But, even when Anna Marie is allowed to date there is a very important question that has to be asked and the answer to that question will determine who she dates."

"And what is that question, sir?" Chris asked.

"Whether or not the young man has a personal relationship with Jesus Christ," Mr. Koch replied.

"Do you mean the Jewish itinerant preacher of the Bible from the first century AD?"

"Yes, that is who I am speaking about."

"Pardon me, if you will, sir, but I have read many different religious books and studied many philosophies and I have found that no religion or philosophy has a cure for our world's needs and difficulties. If there is a god, he left us a long time ago. Just look at the trouble we are in with wars and sickness and good people dying young, even my guardian in England. He didn't need to die now, along with the other young men in the accident. No sir, I do not see how a relationship with this preacher, even *if* he rose from the dead, could change or help our condition, or our needs in this world today."

"Well, Chris, I do not believe I have ever heard it worded the way you have, but you have missed the point entirely. Jesus said in John 14:6...."

Chris interrupted him. "I am the way, the truth, and the life, no man comes to the Father but through me."

"So you do know something from the Bible," Mr. Koch stated, gazing at him with an unreadable expression.

"Yes sir, I do. I have it, the Koran, and the Torah all memorized, including the middle section of the Bible that Catholics believe, the Apocrypha."

"But you see no need for Jesus in your life, no need to have a personal relationship with Him?"

"No, sir, I do not. I have had many people give me the 'Gospel' as they put it, but I do not believe it is necessary. I believe there is no eternal bliss, nor eternal judgment."

"I am sorry to hear that, Chris. My family and I will pray for your soul. If that's all you have to say then, no, unless you ever come to the saving knowledge of Jesus Christ, you may not date my daughter."

Anna Marie, her mother, and her brother, sat in the kitchen taking all of this in. Anna Marie felt a tug of compassion for this young man, for she had never met a person who refused Jesus Christ as Lord and Savior. Chris and Edna rose from their chairs.

"Well, sir, I hate to hear I cannot date your daughter. However, I respect your wishes. Goodnight, sir, ma'am, Albert, Anna Marie."

Each one said "Goodnight, Chris." Anna Marie waved to Chris from the kitchen table as he and Mrs. Ryder shook hands with Mr. Koch and left the house. As they walked toward Chris's red Corvette he let himself feel a flash of disappointment at the way the conversation with Anna Marie's father ended. He let Mrs. Ryder in the passenger's side, slid into the leather seat on his side, and drove away. Mrs. Ryder squeezed his arm with a touch of compassionate mother's love.

CHAPTER 7

Edna's phone rang. It was an urgent call saying she and Chris needed to return to England immediately. Russia had a squadron of eighteen planes leaving Stalingrad and heading for the German border. Chris took a left at the intersection and parked the car in Anna Marie's church parking lot. He and Mrs. Ryder exited the car. He looked around and they ducked behind the church. Chris teleported them to the hanger at the Aiken Airport. They were in the air in a few minutes and Chris pushed the speed to the maximum. They were above the UK airfield in fifteen minutes. Chris found his position in the formation and Commander Ryder was on the radio to the German authorities asking them not to deploy their fighters. Chris heard her broken German and intervened. He identified himself as Commander Beckett of WPPA in perfect German and explained the situation, telling the Germans that the WPPA's 24-plane squadron would protect Germany. He then proceeded to turn the radio dial to a new frequency and told the Russians it was in their best interest to turn around and go home. He did so in perfect Russian. There was no change in the Russians attack formation.

They were ten minutes from contact when Chris asked the rest of the squadron to go to stealth mode, put up their shields, and to stop their planes in the air. He and Mrs. Ryder went forward and Chris activated the shield. At contact he fired six times and six MIGs were encased in a shield and were stationary in the air. He again contacted the Russian authorities and asked if they wished to continue this charade. Three of the other MIGs zeroed in on Chris and fired missiles. He fired his energy weapon on all three missiles and they were frozen in midair. He then fired on the three MIGs and froze them in the air. The Russians were jabbering in panic with one another that they were fighting aliens and Chris just stopped his Typhoon and waited for them to calm down. Using a device from his pocket, he pushed some buttons and the prime minister of Russia was on the line.

"May I speak to the President?" asked Chris, again in perfect Russian.

"Who is this calling?"

"You really don't want to know. I have nine of your eighteen MIGs frozen in the air. I know your President does not want to lose these planes and men."

The Russian President reluctantly came on the line. "You have attacked my planes who were on maneuvers. Who are you?"

"Mr. President, please listen to this conversation and tell me this is not you." Chris pressed some buttons and a voice came on the radio of the President of Russia authorizing his military to make an air strike against Germany. This entire exchange Chris had patched into Mendenhall Air Base as well as on all stations throughout the world.

"How in the world is he doing this?" exclaimed Edna.

"Please return my men and planes to me. I will apologize for this unfortunate incident in a press release later today."

"You just did, Mr. President," said Chris as he broke contact. Chris then flew to each plane and pressed the release button on each one. He detonated the missiles, turned the Typhoon around and entered the formation and flew home with the squadron.

When he reached the base a squad of police officers were at the hatch of the Typhoon when he parked it. They escorted him to the base commander.

"Do you have any idea what you have done? You broke every rule, every protocol, every chain of command, and could have started an international conflict." Commander Whitfield, head of WPPA, was standing next to the general. He was shaking his head as General Putnam continued to berate Chris.

"Lieutenant, put him in the detention center. We will deal with this tomorrow after I have seen all of the fallout." Mrs. Ryder stood next to Chris and gave him a hug as they took him away.

They took Chris's shoes, belt, wallet, and all of the contents from his pockets and placed him in a cell. He sat down on the bunk and tried to make sense out of the reason they were angry with him. He had saved lives; no one was injured. The Russian President was humiliated. The public heard what he had done. He felt it best not to teleport away, so he just sat there.

In the morning the news was all over the world, how the UK had put Russia on its knees; how a single Typhoon had thwarted a Russian attack on Germany. They also recounted the apology of the Russian President.

The espionage world was in an uproar. Where did the UK get these new weapons, and how did WPPA plan on using these new weapons to the advantage of the free world? The CIA reported what they knew about Christopher Beckett, Jr. and the strained relationship with his parents; they knew nothing of these inventions. The news was full of facts, fiction, and rumors, but the one fact was clear to everyone; Christopher Beckett, Jr. was a hero in the eyes of the public.

The prime minister came to the base and asked for the general to bring Chris and Mrs. Ryder to a meeting. Chris was given his belongings, allowed to shower and change and was escorted to a room near the commander's office. Chris and Edna were standing. She was holding his hand. The prime minister, the general, and Commander Whitfield of WPPA were sitting behind a long conference table. The prime minister began speaking.

"Mr. Beckett, I cannot express to you enough as to what you have done for our country. The weapons and the upgrades on our aircraft have been astonishing. This shield program on the fighter planes will save many lives. We have continued to update our fleet and will hopefully have all planes fitted by the end of next year. WPPA has shared with the UK all of the energy weapons and I understand there are some medical implants you may provide for us in the future. I say all of this to let you know we are heavily in debt to you; even for yesterday. We would have handled the situation differently, but you handled it well. I do believe there will be some repercussions from the Russians, but time will let us know exactly what.

"However, Mr. Beckett, authority and respect for authority are very important in society. Yesterday, you became your own authority and that was blatantly wrong. As a result of yesterday you are forbidden from flying any RAF aircraft. Your membership in WPPA is now severed and we wish to have your ID Card in hand. We will treat you as an independent contractor and you are welcome to assist us in the future. You are welcome to stay in the UK, but you are not to publically speak of your inventions or of your participation in what took place yesterday. Do you understand all I have said?"

Chris had a frown on his face and his eyes were very sad. Edna felt he would start crying if pushed in that direction. "I understand, Mr. Prime Minister, and I recognize your position and authority in this matter. I shall clear up some business I have here in the UK and return to my island soon. Is there anything else, sir?"

"No, Chris."

"Then I will take my leave. Edna, are you coming with me?"

"Yes, son," said Edna as she placed her hand in the crook of his arm and they left together.

They went down the hall and into an empty conference room. Chris locked the door, and hugged her and began crying. She just held him in her arms without saying a word. She stroked his back and attempted to comfort him by humming an English lullaby. She silently prayed, "He is still a boy, Lord, and knows nothing of real world policies or even personal relationships. Please draw him to You."

After ten minutes, Chris wiped his eyes, took Edna's hand, and teleported to Oxford, England. They were above Pullens Lane, Headington, Oxford. "What do you think of this property for your retirement home?"

"My retirement home? What do you mean, Chris? I can't afford this."

"You can't, but I can. I am going to buy this home for you. I need a base in England and I need supplies for the island. You will not be without responsibilities. We will work out all of the details. I have two supply planes. They can land here and you can have them restocked and returned to me. You will have a computer and a special phone system. I will have a room here for when I visit. You will have a staff and all will be paid for."

"Chris, I cannot accept that from you. It wouldn't be right."

"Mom Edna, you have supported me from the beginning. You stood with me when the prime minister raked me over. I love you, and…."

"Chris, what did you just say?" Mrs. Ryder asked with a tremble in her voice.

"Which part?"

"You said you love me?"

"I did, and the second part was I need you, you are the best mom I could have ever hoped for."

CHAPTER 8

Even though they were above the estate, Edna turned in Chris's arms and hugged him and now it was her turn to cry as she said, "I love you too, son."

Chris returned to the island three weeks later after he had Edna moved to the estate, purchased a new limousine for her, and hired a driver and a staff for the estate. He began working on the satellites and the rocket. The rocket and satellites were launched in stealth mode on August 22, 1962. He did not tell Edna what he had done.

Among all of this heartache and heartbreak Chris remembered his Corvette. He called his sister. "Hello, Frances."

"Hello, stranger. How are you doing?"

"I'm making it. I have a favor to ask of you."

"Sure, brother."

"Do you remember my giving you a set of keys to the 'vette? "

"Yes, I have them in my jewelry box."

"Do you know which church Anna Marie Koch attends?"

"Yes, I do."

"Unless the police have impounded it, it is parked in their parking lot. I need you to find it, pay the fine, and keep it. Do you have anyone who would help you get from place to place and who would take care of the car? The title is signed and in the glove box and the other set of keys are also in the car. I am sending you some money to handle the fine, insurance, tags, title transfer, and anything else you may need."

"Do you remember Colleen Knight?" she asked. "She needs a car and she would help me."

"Kenneth's older sister? I remember her, she taught me to dance."

"That's her."

"All right, get with her and sign the car to her. Naturally you want to do this without anyone else finding out beforehand," Chris said.

"Okay, I will get it done. I read and saw the mess you were in. It wasn't your fault. Most everyone I know supported what you did, and I do too," Frances responded.

"Thank you, Frances. That means a lot to me. Take care of yourself. If you have any problem, I will put a card in the envelope and you can dial that number to let me know what you need."

"Thank you, Chris. I love you."

"I love you, too, Frances, goodbye."

"Bye."

CHAPTER 9

Chris peered at the third set of results of the brain scan he had done on himself. The tiny tumor was not as tiny as before. It had not grown much, but it was growing. He made a decision. He walked over to the refrigerator and took one of the nanorobot packages. He removed the syringe and let it warm up for fifteen minutes. Chris then found a vein on his left arm, cleaned the area, inserted the syringe, and squeezed the nanorobots into his bloodstream. He lay back on the examination table, closed his eyes, and fell asleep.

CHAPTER 10

OCTOBER 1, 1962

Chris was looked at the fourth set of scans of his brain. There was still growth in the tumor. Upon taking a sample of his blood, there were no live nanorobots in his system. He didn't understand. What were the implications? Why did the nanorobots die? The worried look on his face would have alarmed anyone else if they were present. Chris, however, was all alone.

CHAPTER 11

Chris's phone to Edna rang. "Good morning, Edna. How are you today?"

"I am fine, Chris. Mr. Koch has requested to speak with you and he sounds very distraught. He said he wants so ask you to save his daughter from dying. He is at the Aiken County Hospital and can be reached at the number on this card."

"Thank you, Edna." Chris closed the call and dialed Mr. Koch immediately. "How may I help you, sir? What's wrong with Anna Marie?"

"Chris, thank you for returning my call. I have no right to call you, but I am desperate; I'll make it brief. Albert and Anna Marie were at a football game with Kenneth Knight last night. They were returning from the game after taking another friend home and a drunk backed his car into the road in front of their car and there was no way for them to stop. Kenneth, the driver, is okay. Albert has minor facial cuts and bruises, but Anna Marie was sitting on the side that had the brunt of the impact. She has major head wounds and has lost a lot of blood. She is in a coma, and they tell me there is no chance of her making it. I have read of your inventions and brain surgery techniques and you are my only hope. Please help us!"

"Where is she?"

"She is in ICU at this hospital."

"I'll call you back in a few minutes."

Chris went to his computer, pushed some buttons, turned some dials, and made some adjustments. The room Anna Marie was in came on screen. He looked at her vitals and even measured a couple himself through the magnetic and gravitational fields of the earth. What he was doing was similar to his recalling the conversation of the Russian President, only this was video, not audio.

He called Mr. Koch back. "Sir, there is no way I can help her where she is. A small vertical lift off plane will land in the parking lot of the hospital in ten minutes. Have her loaded in and strapped down with a Ringer-Lactate solution bottle attached. Tell them to also leave the blood transfusion bottles attached. The plane has a way to give her the oxygen she needs, so do not transfer the oxygen equipment. There is no need for the monitors; the plane has equipment that will monitor her condition. She will be in my hospital in less than one hour. No one is to come with her. She will be safe."

"Chris, why can't we come with her? Also, you are over 7,500 miles away. How can that be?"

"The plane will hold only one person. I know you have a top-secret security clearance with the USA and I know you know about my C130 trips for the UK. Do I need to tell you more?"

"No, you don't Chris. Please save my daughter."

"I will. Remember, I care for her, too. If she stays where she is, she will definitely die in just a few hours. I can save her."

Mr. Koch spoke with hospital administration and staff. There was a lot of discussion about legality and care of the patient, but the doctor said she was going to die within six hours. Mr. Koch looked at the doctor and hospital administrator and said, "Do I have another choice for her to live? If you were her father, what would you do?"

Anna Marie was loaded on the plane that had landed like Chris said it would. It was a medically modified GNAT jet. Once they had her strapped in and the staff members exited the plane, the door automatically sealed and it took off with no sound. It was a clear night and they watched the plane until it disappeared from sight in less than five seconds.

While Chris was waiting on the plane he called Edna. "Anna Marie is dying. I did not see this scenario in my trip to the future. The timeline has been altered. I hope my meeting her a year earlier is not what caused this accident. I need your help. Will you assist me in operating on her? She needs a neural implant."

"I will help you Chris. Sharon Patterson is also an RN. You will need two."

Chris teleported to the estate in England where he picked up Edna. He then went to another address to pick up Edna's friend. The two women prepared the surgical suite and had everything clean and ready for Anna Marie. Chris met the plane on the heliport on the top of the complex. He brought Anna Marie down to the operating room on a gurney and while she was being prepared he went to the clean room, stripped, washed up, and dressed for surgery. Exactly twenty-four hours later the operation was over. She had a neural implant and the area of her skull that was damaged was growing back together with the nanorobots at work. Anna Marie was placed in a very modern and up to date hospital room. Chris collapsed on a bed next to hers and the two women found sleeping space in an adjoining room.

CHAPTER 12

Exactly fifty-four hours later, Anna Marie woke up. Chris was at her bedside with a stack of blueberry pancakes, peanut butter, and milk.

"Thank you for breakfast, but why am I in a hospital room? I remember a terrific shutter from the car and nothing else until now."

"Anna Marie, you were in a very bad automobile accident. You currently are on my private island in the South Pacific Ocean. Your father called me when he was told you had zero chance of survival where you were, so I flew you here and I and two others performed emergency surgery on you. You have had extensive brain surgery and, although you have lost twenty-eight percent of your brain, I have installed a neural implant and you will be in much better shape than you were before. In fact, because of the implant and the nanorobot technology, you may end up being smarter than me," Chris explained.

"Take it a little slower, please, and with more detail."

"Okay. You were in an accident. You were in a coma and you were dying. Your father called me and I had you flown here in one of my medical rocket jets. When you arrived, I took you to the surgery suite and performed brain surgery. During that surgery, I installed a neural implant that is powered by a unique power cell. I downloaded to your implant all known information I have regarding my work and the known knowledge of all sciences on the planet. Among other things, I also downloaded to you all known languages." Chris then spoke to her in

Hebrew and she immediately responded. He then said something in Chinese, and again, she answered back without hesitating.

"Chris, I am overwhelmed and impressed. This is too much! How long have I been here?"

"Three days," he answered.

"Why do I not feel any bandages on my head and why do I not feel any pain?"

"Because of my nanorobot technology. Here, look in the mirror."

Anna Marie looked in the mirror he gave her and was absolutely fascinated by the fact there were no scars and her head of hair was intact, although in need of a shampoo.

"If I had extensive head surgery why is there no scarring, and why do I have a full head of hair?" she asked.

"I have used nanorobots and they have been very busy at reconstruction," Chris replied.

"You mentioned them earlier. Do I need to be concerned? Will they always be in my blood?"

"No, you do not need to be concerned. They will always be in you, keeping you safe and well. All information you need to know will be perfectly clear to you whenever your programming is complete."

"My programming?"

"Perhaps programming is the wrong word. Whenever your brain and the neural implant completely merge and you begin thinking with all of your capabilities, then you will understand."

"How long will that take?" Anna Marie asked curiously.

"It will be very soon."

Sharon and Edna walked into the room at this time.

"I see our patient is awake and full of questions," said Edna.

"Thank you for assisting in my operation," Anna Marie said. "I am very grateful. When will I be able to go home?"

"We will discuss that later. Right now, I have to take these ladies back to their homes."

"We can stay a little longer, can't we, Chris?" Edna asked.

"You are in charge of my supply system. I can't take the chance that you are not at the estate available for a delivery. Also, I need those special items we discussed this morning."

"You are right. Sharon, grab your purse; we are headed home."

Chris grabbed their hands and the three of them disappeared. Anna Marie's jaw dropped to the floor. Two minutes later the air crackled in the room and there was Chris.

"All right, what just happened?" she asked.

"I teleported Sharon and Edna back to England," Chris responded nonchalantly.

"And, how can you do that?"

"I don't really know. One day about five years ago I could do it, along with some other abilities that we'll talk about later. For now, you need to finish your breakfast."

"Chris, I have several questions. First, when will I be able to go home?"

"I will need to care for you for several months as the neural implant is absorbed into your brain and I need to monitor the nanorobots as they do their repairs. I need to be sure your body does not reject the implant."

"Exactly how long will that take?"

"You will continue to evolve the rest of your life. You will obtain abilities you never dreamed of having. You need to be around someone who understands those abilities and can tell you how to control and use them."

"Do you mean like what you just did? Teleporting?" Chris nodded. "So, you never plan for me to go home, do you?"

He turned away from her. "Anna Marie, can we discuss this another time?"

"No, Chris. Do you plan to keep me here with you?"

"Yes. Anna Marie, I care for you very much. I would say it was love at first sight, but I don't know if you would understand."

"I know I am in the middle of the South Pacific with a man who has kidnapped me and won't let me go home to my parents and family! This will not do, Christopher Beckett; this is so wrong!" Having said all of that, Anna Marie lay back down on her bed, turned on her side, and began crying. She was still crying when Chris walked out of the room five minutes later.

During this interval of time a rocket plane had landed and Chris removed items needed for Anna Marie. He put some of the items in her suite and had others in a parcel he was carrying when he heard her yelling for him.

"Where are my clothes, you monster? I need to get dressed."

Chris walked back into the room with a package and put it in the bathroom. Anna Marie was sitting up in the bed with her arms crossed.

If looks could kill, Chris would be a dead man twice over. Her eyes followed him around the room until he came to the other side of her bed.

"Anna Marie, I am not a monster. Your father approved of your trip and asked me to save your life. He never asked the price. You would be dead right now if I had not intervened. You are on a Pacific island and on some islands, parents marry their young girls off as early as twelve years of age. I am not going to force myself on you, but I hope in due time, you will see I do care for you and I hope we can discuss a future relationship," he told her.

"Well, you certainly have a strange way of attempting to start a relationship. I am an American citizen and I am being kept here against my will. Now, you do something about that and give me some clothes. Oh, and unless you have made a decision since your meeting with my father, I could never have a relationship with an unsaved man. And if you have, then a Christian wouldn't be acting this way. Now, for the third time, give me my clothes, Christopher Beckett, NOW!" she demanded.

Chris let out a very large sigh, walked over to the bathroom door, opened it and said, "Your clothes and toiletries are in here. I'll close the room's door. When you are ready, you may open it and turn left when you exit the room and you will be able to find the living quarters. I'll be there."

Anna Marie went into the bathroom, tore open the package, pulled out the clothes and the soap and shampoo. "He expects me to wear this? What is wrong with that man? I am not some model; I will discuss this with him when I get cleaned up."

Anna Marie washed, shampooed, dried, and styled her hair and dressed in the blue dress Chris had furnished. It had a high neck that was laced and sleeves that went to the wrist. There was a blue stone necklace, a bracelet, and a cocktail ring. She left the jewelry in the bathroom. "I won't give him the satisfaction," she said.

She walked out of the room, turned left, saw a set of doors to a living area. With an aggressive shove, she pushed them open and walked into the room. When she saw Chris across the room, she walked over to him as he stood up, and shoved him in the chest. He fell back down on the chair and she swung at him, connecting with his left eye.

"Ouch!" he exclaimed, clutching his eye.

"Now, find an airplane and take me home, you beast."

"Who is the violent one here?" Chris asked indignantly.

"I'll blacken your other eye if you don't get a move on, mister. By the way, how many people are on this island?" Anna Marie paced the room, waving her arms around while she spoke.

"Just you and me," Chris replied.

"So the two who helped with the operation were the only others and you took them away. Can I trust you not to touch me?"

"You have my word," he said solemnly.

"Mr. Beckett, your word doesn't mean very much to me right now!" she retorted.

"Anna Marie, I will not touch you, I promise."

"And what about supplies?" she asked with her arms crossed.

"My planes bring them in."

"Okay, I'll leave on one of them."

"They are pilotless aircraft and are not set up for passengers."

"All right, call my dad and he will send a plane for me."

"Can't do that Princess, you're stuck with me."

"Don't call me Princess, you jerk." Anna Marie saw a book on the end table, reached over, picked it up, and threw it at Chris. It struck him in the forehead and he fell down. He decided to play opossum and see what she would do. She stared at him a moment, saw blood on his forehead, saw the tissues on the table and threw the box at him. "Clean off the blood before you get it on your clothes."

Chris got up, snatched a tissue out of the box, grabbed Anna Marie's hand and pulled her over to a door. "This is your room. Get it cleaned up." She started screaming for him to take his hands off her as he pushed her through the door and shut it behind her.

"So much for a relationship!" Chris said to himself as he entered his suite to clean up. He was trembling. "I tried to protect myself twice with a shield and a shield would not form. I tried to teleport her to her suite and could not do so. What is the matter with me? I need to check the size of the tumor again." Chris went to the lab. He took the syringe full of Anna Marie's blood he had withdrawn during the operation and checked a sample under the microscope. The nanorobots were alive. He injected the blood into his arm. He was able to use her blood because they both had O positive blood. He made another set of scans. There was a small tentacle coming from the tumor. "What does this all mean? Hopefully these nanorobots will help."

CHAPTER 13

Anna Marie was straightening up the room where Chris had just dumped everything from the plane. She was hanging up clothes and storing soaps and shampoos and toothpaste in her suite when she was suddenly overwhelmed with information. She sat down to keep from falling down. She was wondering how she could get word to someone to come and take her away from here when suddenly, the programming kicked in and Anna Marie was able to answer her own question. The more she thought the more information flooded her brain. "Oh, the shields. They're up all the time and nothing can penetrate them except for the supply planes. What is he planning? Guns won't work and nuclear warheads will be neutralized? What is this information in my brain? I was a pretty good student before and thought I was well-educated, but what I am seeing has to be from something like the year 2600 rather than 1962. What about those satellites he has that could beam laser weapons to earth? Who is he? What on earth are his capabilities?"

It was 5 p.m. and Anna Marie was hungry. She thought she smelled food cooking, so she walked out of her suite and cautiously stepped into the living room. The kitchen was to her right. She saw Chris stirring a pot on the stove. He turned and looked at her and then turned back to his cooking. She walked up to the dining room table and saw two places were set and the salads were already on the table. There was a covered silver platter at each place. Chris suddenly broke the silence. "I hope you like spaghetti and meatballs and fresh salad. Do you have a favorite dressing?"

"I do like spaghetti and my favorite dressing is Thousand Island."

"Would you mind coming over to the refrigerator and pulling a jar out of the inside door? It is my favorite also."

"I don't mind," she responded, walking to the fridge. "I'll put it on the table."

"The spaghetti and sauce should be ready in about five minutes if you want to go ahead and sit down."

"I don't mind helping you serve."

"No, I'll serve. Just be seated."

He brought generous servings over and sat them down. There was parmesan cheese on the table and he asked if she wanted some. "Yes, I would. Thank you."

Chris sat down across from Anna Marie and she was startled as she saw his face. She put her hand over her mouth, and her eyes went wide as she looked at the purple and black left eye and the bandage on the forehead. "I am so sorry, Chris. I am not a violent person. I have never hit a person in my life."

"My reflection in the mirror doesn't verify that."

"Chris, I am sorry I hurt you, really. As a Christian, I behaved badly."

"Before we continue talking, you may go ahead and pray silently for your food."

"Thank you Chris," Anna Marie said, bowing her head. *Heavenly Father, you are sovereign and I should not have reacted as I did knowing You have me where You want me. Please help me to be a good witness. Please draw Chris to Yourself. Bless this food, now I pray, In Jesus name, Amen.*

"Anna Marie, I should have expected the violence. I am sorry for the circumstances that bring us together like this. You don't know how my heart caved in when I saw you in the hospital, all broken."

"Did you teleport there?" she asked.

"No. I'll show you the technology when we talk to your parents tomorrow. Your programming should have come online by now. You will find you have an index system to put things you wish to recall easily rather than going through the alphabetical index. There are several abilities you will find you will have within the next six months. You will have the ability to place a shield around yourself or another person or object, the ability to put yourself in what I call the stealth mode as it makes you invisible, and the ability to teleport. I am not going to ask you not to leave me, but I am going to ask that you let me train you before you attempt to teleport. If we teleport without pulling ourselves to zero gravity we can damage our reality, or even our cortex to another reality," he explained.

"There you go again. What did you just say? Did you just tell me there is more than one universe?" Anna Marie asked incredulously.

"Yes, there are thousands of universes on this planet. That piece of information should come online within twenty-four to forty-eight hours from this morning. Please, do not attempt to leave our universe. You can really hurt many people if you do, and it is more than the zero gravity knowledge. For me, I just was able to do it. I don't have an implant; the knowledge is in my brain and the calculations come automatically. For you with your implant, they will have to be calculated manually the first few times and with great care and then your implant will take over and calculate for you."

"Chris, I have no idea what you have just told me. Suffice it to say I will not attempt anything with special abilities without first talking with you. That doesn't mean I'll stick around once you teach me." She was thinking she ought to be able to endure six months of this.

"I understand, Anna Marie. I see you have finished dinner. Would you like some dessert? If so, please lift the cover on your silver platter."

Anna Marie lifted the cover. "Wow, chocolate pudding, my...."

"...favorite," he interrupted, "I know."

"About this morning, why the special dress and the jewelry?"

"I noticed you didn't wear the jewelry. I was planning on calling your parents today before the violence. Quite frankly, I am not in the mood for another bout, so it will be tomorrow."

"Okay. Chris, again, I am so sorry. Is it normal for me to feel fatigued?"

"Well, you just had a major operation and your body is attempting to either accept or reject the implant and the nanorobots. So, yes, I would suspect you are probably starting to feel tired just now, so why don't we call it a night?"

"Okay, Chris. Goodnight."

"Goodnight, Anna Marie."

CHAPTER 14

Anna Marie woke at 5 a.m. The sun was just rising outside her window and the view across the ocean was stunning. "Thank you, Lord, for such beauty in the midst of such a difficult situation. Please help me to be Your witness and please save this boy. Help me to know the time to leave on my own and help me not to harm anyone when I do. In Jesus' name, Amen."

She put on a housecoat and walked into the living room. The windows over the forest displayed such beautiful and varied colors of the trees and flowers. As she walked around the room she was overwhelmed with the size and beauty of the place. She slipped out of the living room and into the hospital room she had been in, and then went to the bathroom and picked up the jewelry. She walked back into the living room and was in the hallway to her suite when Chris stepped out of his suite. He was fully dressed in a yellow polo shirt and blue slacks.

"Is breakfast at six okay with you?" he asked when he saw Anna Marie.

"Sure. Can I help?"

"No, you just get dressed and be ready to talk to your parents."

"Okay, I'll see you at six."

She decided to wear the beautiful blue chiffon dress with the high neck and sleeves to the wrist accentuated with the jewelry. She went to the separate bath area of her suite, stripped, showered, used her own soaps and shampoos and washed, dried, and styled her hair. She brushed her teeth and put on a little makeup. She put on the dress and the jewelry and looked at herself in the mirror. "Who would have thought I was dying four days ago? God is so good. Now, Lord, what am I going to do? Please give me Your wisdom."

She exited her suite and was coming to the table when she heard Chris gasp. She looked up and Chris was staring at her. He said, "Wow, you look beautiful."

Anna Marie blushed and lowered her gaze. "Thank you. It smells like blueberry pancakes again."

"It is, they are my favorite and I hear they are yours also."

"How did you hear?" she asked.

"While you were asleep after the surgery I asked Edna to call your mother. Your mother told her of several of your favorites meals."

"So, you knew that information before last night's meal?"

"Yes, I did."

"Are you experienced at stalking?"

"No, just Edna and your mother getting to know one another before the wedding."

Anna Marie turned red as a beet, sat down at the table, lowered her head, said her silent prayer, and poured some syrup on top of her pancakes. She was furious, but she held her anger in check. He was not going to bait her. She was not going to become violent again. She kept telling herself that as she worked on her breakfast. She ate in silence for several minutes before she heard him say, "We'll be calling your parents after breakfast. Please don't become violent during the call. I'll receive enough of your father's anger as it is."

After breakfast Anna Marie went to her room to freshen up and returned to the living room as Chris had asked her during the meal. He was watching the forest when she walked up beside him. He sensed her presence and motioned for her to follow. They went out of the living area and Chris began talking. "We are on the third level. The fifth floor is storage. The fourth floor is where we are headed. The second floor is guest and recovery rooms and a dining facility should the retreat ever be used for what it was intended. The first floor has exercise equipment, a game room, an Olympic sized pool, and a garage. You are welcome to go anywhere you want alone. Please don't attempt to go into the forest alone, I would hate to lose you to a jaguar or a snake."

Anna Marie shivered at the thought of what he said and forgot what he said about the rooms and dining facility. They entered an elevator and

Chris pushed the button for the fourth floor. They were headed up to what he described as the television studio. The elevator doors opened on the fourth floor and he turned left, held the door open for Anna Marie and she found herself looking out over the ocean and the forest. "What a beautiful sight."

"It is, isn't it? I could stare at it for hours."

"And you don't see God in it?"

"Nope! Sit here, please."

There were two chairs in front of the window. In front of the chairs was a table with switches and levers and about ten feet in front of the table was a very large television screen and several smaller ones. The smaller ones had various images of things going on in the world, but the large screen was blank.

Anna Marie sat where she was asked and noticed her part of the table was just a flat surface and the switches and levers were all on Chris's side. His side was slightly elevated and at an angle. She placed her hands on the table, sat upright, and faced the large screen. Chris pulled a communication device that looked like a phone from under his side of the table, pushed some buttons and made a call. "Edna, please call Mr. Koch and ask him to sit in front of his television with his wife and son." After a few minutes with Chris pushing buttons and moving levers Anna Marie saw an image of her living room at home appear on the screen. Her parents were sitting on the couch and her brother was on the floor between them.

"Hello, Mr. and Mrs. Koch and Albert. It's seven in the morning here, and I believe about three in the afternoon there?" said Chris.

"Yes, it is, Chris," said Mr. Koch. "Hello, Anna Marie. It is so good to see you. You look remarkably well!"

"You look fabulous, sis. Where are your bandages?" Albert asked.

"Hello, Dad, Mom, Albert. It is good to see you also. My head is fully healed, Albert, and my hair has all grown back."

Chris interrupted before there could be further interaction between the family members. "Mr. Koch, your daughter's surgery was very extensive. She had lost about one fourth of her brain's usage. I had to install a neural implant and do a lot of repair to the area surrounding her skull cavity. Because of new technology I would rather not divulge her healing process is still going on as we speak. When that process is finished, she will be as intelligent as I am."

"Chris, that's wonderful. When will we be making plans for her to come home?" Mr. Koch asked.

"Mr. Koch, Anna Marie will be staying with me indefinitely. She has her own living quarters and she and I will not be doing anything against her morals or your Christian beliefs. I need her here to monitor the healing from the surgery, as only I can handle the complications that may arise."

"I don't understand; you mean you are kidnapping her? What happened to your face, have you tried to attack my daughter?"

"No sir, she attacked me when I told her she would be here for awhile."

"Way to go, Anna Marie!" said Albert a little too enthusiastically.

Anna Marie smiled and put a thumbs up toward her brother.

"Mr. Koch, I am keeping your daughter for observation. I am not kidnapping her. I am the only one who can help her should a problem arise concerning the implant. She will need to stay here at least six months. I request you contact her school and allow her to do distance learning for a while. I will allow her to contact you as she desires. She will be able to use this studio at will."

"Chris, I do not find this acceptable. Can't Anna Marie come home and then go back if she needs to? My security clearance has allowed me to learn a lot about you and I am told you have some ability to teleport. Can't you bring her here and then take her back as necessary?"

"Mr. Koch, you begged for my help which I gave. Now, the conditions of her recovery are set. You haven't even thanked me for saving her life."

"You are correct, Chris, I did beg you for help. Please forgive my lack of manners; I thank you for saving my daughter's life. The shock of seeing her as she is was a little overwhelming. I do now ask, beg, that you not separate my daughter from us. You can see my wife is already crying and I do not know how we can stand this thought."

"Mr. Koch, thank you for thanking me. Now, think through what I am about to say. Anna Marie was as good as dead. I saved her life. Tell me, if I did not save her life where would she be today?"

"She would be in Heaven with Jesus and that is a lot better than where she is if she is stuck in your prison."

"Mr. and Mrs. Koch, this is the end of this conversation. Anna Marie say goodbye to your parents and brother."

"Goodbye Mom, Dad, Albert, I love you. Remember Proverbs 3:5-6. Please continue to pray for me. I will be praying for you...."

And the screen went blank.

Anna Marie looked at Chris with contempt in her eyes and stood up, walked out of the room, took the elevator, and went to her suite. Once there, she tried to decide if she was going to cry, scream, or just tell him off the next time she saw him. Walking around the room while muttering to herself, Anna Marie said, "Wait, I have an index and I have the Bible totally memorized. What is that verse from whence cometh my help... there it is Psalm 121! 'I will lift up mine eyes unto the hills, from whence cometh my help. My help cometh from the Lord, which made heaven and earth. He will not suffer thy foot to be moved: he that keepeth thee will not slumber. Behold, he that keepeth Israel shall neither slumber nor sleep. The Lord is thy keeper: the Lord is thy shade upon thy right hand. The sun shall not smite thee by day, nor the moon by night. The Lord shall preserve thee from all evil: he shall preserve thy soul. The Lord shall preserve thy going out and thy coming in from this time forth, and even for evermore.'"

After reflecting on the passage, Anna Marie bowed her head to pray. "Father in Heaven, I claim that Psalm as my own: My help comes from You, the Lord Jesus Christ. My foot will not be moved. You are my keeper; You will preserve me from all evil; You shall preserve my soul. You, oh Lord, are my strength and my shield. In You do I trust, and You will never fail. Please give me the grace and wisdom to do the right thing. Amen."

Anna Marie lifted her head, and with new confidence began to think about how to respond to Chris's demands. "He takes a lot of stock in understanding how to build things; what can I tear down?" She paused. "That might actually not be a good idea. I do not want to make him angry, and that would not be a good witness."

Anna Marie began to scan through the index looking for ideas, and stopped when she came across a file labeled 'Alternate Realities'. "What is this all about? He mentioned this, but said I should not leave this reality. If I did leave him he could find me with his abilities." Anna Marie studied all there was in the file. She searched her own mind and looked at all the science she could behind the theories she found. The more she researched the more she was convinced they were real. Could that be the key to escape Chris forever? "But I don't want to leave my family forever. Oh, Lord, what am I to do?" Anna Marie was tired. She decided to think about alternate realities more the next day and, even though it was early in the day, she went to bed.

CHAPTER 15

Anna Marie woke with a purpose. She brushed her teeth, looked for pad and pen, and began to write a list:

1. Bible KJV
2. Journals
3. Pencils and sharpener
4. School books
5. Promised ability to contact her parents
6. Reading material

She laid her list aside and had her prayer time and Bible study. She tried doing a topical study and found she could move this topical study to a file in the neural implant and leave it there for reference later as Chris had told her. She moved the file on alternate realities to this same location. At seven o'clock she walked to the dining room and found Chris sitting down to breakfast. A covered dish was placed at the spot across from him and he motioned her to it. She didn't say anything, sat down, bowed her head in prayer, and then looked up to find him staring at her.

"Like what you see?" she asked sarcastically.

"Well, you feel perky today."

"No, actually I am looking for a fight and you seem to be the perfect target."

"Bring it on, I am all ears."

When Anna Marie raised her food cover all the fight went out of her. Blueberry pancakes again, topped with peanut butter and apple sauce this time. She didn't say another word, just dug into her breakfast, looked over at Chris, and said, "Thank you for the delicious breakfast."

"Just trying to please."

"I'm still going to talk to you, but not now, my pancakes will get cold."

Chris let out a hearty laugh. His mobile phone rang. Very quickly his lighthearted mood suddenly changed as he answered the phone and learned what Edna had to say. "Really? How long before it arrives? Okay, I'll check the area and give them a taste of my capabilities. No, Edna, I will not kill anyone; I hope I never have to resort to that."

"Chris, what is going on? What do you mean you won't kill anyone?"

"Your father has called in the big guns and the United States is sending a nuclear submarine to pick you up and take you home. I wonder how they plan to get you away from me? Would you please join me in the studio when you finish your pancakes? Just leave the dishes, I'll do them later."

Anna Marie finished her breakfast quickly and headed to the studio. Chris was pushing buttons and moving levers, and an image of a submarine underwater came on the large screen. It appeared to be in a hurry to get somewhere. "People spend lots of money for video cameras to protect their property and all they need is to learn how to cooperate with the planet we live on." Anna Marie didn't comment, just took the information for future cataloguing. She sat beside Chris and watched what was to happen.

On one of the small screens Chris was looking at the bridge of the submarine that was approaching the island. He saw the person in charge and said, "Captain, oh, excuse me, Admiral!"

The person on one of the small screens looked around him, searching for the person speaking. "Who said that?"

"I did, sir. I would suggest you slow that thing down to a crawl or you are going to break it."

"Who are you? Better question, where are you?"

"I am on my island and you are approaching much too quickly. I have a protective shield around my island and if you hit the shield you will destroy that submarine and lives will be lost."

"You are Christopher Beckett? Why can't I see you?"

"I am, sir, and I have technology you do not. That is why you cannot see me. I respectfully ask you to stop your submarine before you crash it."

"Lieutenant Pearson do you see anything on radar or sonar?"

"No, sir."

"Mr. Beckett, our radar and sonar do not detect any obstacle."

"You won't. It is a stealth signal. Are you going to listen?"

"No. I don't believe you."

During this conversation Anna Marie was also watching another screen on Chris's bank of screens and it was showing how close the submarine was getting to the shield. She began to wring her hands and almost shouted to Chris when she heard his next command.

"Satellite one engaging."

Anna Marie saw another screen show a satellite in space and two laser beams shoot from it toward the earth. A blue and a red laser beam struck off the coast behind her as she turned and saw the beams just as they hit the ocean. "Did he just kill these people?" she asked herself.

One of the submarine's crew was reporting to the Admiral. "Sir, our reactor is offline. The gauges show there is no uranium in the core. Our ICBM's computers are not coming up on screen. We are also rising to the surface like a balloon."

"What happened?" asked the Admiral.

"You, sir, were just removed from service," Chris answered. "Your atomic core is no more and the ICBMs no longer have atomic material in them. You will need to have your submarine towed. You will see right in front of you is a buoy. Any attempt to go beyond that buoy will be met with resistance, as that is where the shield begins. Had you hit the shield you would have all died. Report that to the Rear Admiral, no, to your President. Goodbye." Chris closed the connection without waiting for an answer.

"You just stopped my chance to go home," said Anna Marie with a frown on her face as she stood and then scowled at Chris.

"Yes, I did, didn't I? Was there something else you wished to discuss?"

"Not really. I am disappointed I cannot go home. However, you told me I could ask for anything I needed. Is a treadmill part of the exercise equipment?"

"Yes, it is."

"What about a physical copy of the Bible?"

"It was supposed to be in your room. Haven't you finished putting everything in order?"

"No, I haven't. I guess before I go more into my list I need to unpack and take inventory of what I do have."

"It would probably be a good idea, Princess."

Anna Marie stuck her nose in the air and headed straight for her suite, leaving Chris chuckling behind her.

CHAPTER 16

Chris was on the phone with Edna. "Chris, when the news surfaced that you saved Anna Marie's life, your popularity soared even more than before, but when it was learned you are keeping her against her will, it dropped. Now that you used your satellite as a weapon—which, by the way, you did not notify me that the satellite existed—you are a very unpopular person. Heads of state are wondering if you plan on attacking their countries. Chris, you are making decisions I expected you to speak with me about. Why don't you come and pick me up and let me stay with you at the retreat?"

Chris was now trapped. He didn't want to tell anyone about his tumor and he knew that having Edna at the retreat would lead to her learning of his condition. Not only that, he couldn't pick her up anyway. "I would rather not."

"Chris, you are under eighteen. Anna Marie is fourteen. I know your island was sold to you as a separate sovereign nation, but you cannot do these things. You are not your own authority where other people's rights are concerned. Come and bring me to the island and we can talk some more."

Chris was silent for a long time. Edna could hear his breathing on the phone. She had a feeling something was wrong and he was not telling her the whole story. "Chris, talk to me. You told me you could trust me. You asked me to be your guardian. You told me you loved me." Chris started crying at the same time Anna Marie walked into the living room. He didn't hear her above his sobbing, so she just stood at the edge of the kitchen and waited. He finally spoke. "I can't teleport or form a shield. Anna Marie attacked me and I couldn't protect myself. I grabbed her to teleport her to her room and couldn't do it. I have a brain tumor and the nanorobots won't stay alive inside me." Anna Marie gasped and Chris looked up, saw her, and dropped the phone and ran into his room.

Anna Marie heard Edna calling for him. She picked up the phone. "Mrs. Ryder, Chris ran into his room. I had no idea; I am so sorry."

Edna was crying and Anna Marie started to cry also. After a few minutes Edna had control of herself. She said "Anna Marie, do you know how to read a scan?"

"I don't know, why?"

"I want you to go to the medical infirmary and find the room where the scan equipment is. Hopefully Chris has scans there on the wall."

"Okay, give me a few moments," said Anna Marie as she walked in that direction. "Mrs. Ryder, I was frightened when he grabbed me, now I know he was wanting to teleport me to my room. It was after I attacked him because I was so angry about being held here. Yet, once he told me about the powers I would have and what training I would need, then I understood why he wanted me to stay. If only he had started the conversation with that information."

"Anna Marie, what powers?"

"The neural implant has information in it that when coupled with the nanorobots will give me the same powers Chris has or had. It was something he manufactured into their existence."

"What was that boy thinking? Anna Marie, don't repeat what you have told me to anyone. There would be governments attempting to gain access to that information, and it is a good thing Chris is keeping you there. You would be kidnapped and torn apart as a science experiment."

Anna Marie gasped. She did so for two reasons. One was from what Mrs. Ryder said and the other was from what she saw. She found that with her new abilities, she could read scans. "Chris does have a tumor. It is small, and it has little tentacles growing out from it. I can see from the scans that he did do something to reverse it, but it started growing again."

"I used your nanorobots," said Chris as he walked into the room. "Here, let me put the phone on speaker." Anna Marie handed him the phone and he began telling them the complete story.

"You drew blood from me and put it in your body? YUCK! So we are the same blood type?"

"Yes!" Chris said as he grinned at Anna Marie who turned her head away from him.

"Chris, why is it the nanorobots don't work in your body?" Edna asked.

"I don't know. I really don't know." Chris sounded defeated.

"Chris, I need to get there. How can we do it?"

"As much as I would like to get you here, how could we handle the supply jets?"

"I could train Sharon to handle everything, give her access to the bank account, and ride one of the GNAT jets."

"Do you trust this woman that much?" Chris asked.

"She is my sister," Edna replied.

"You never told me. Why wasn't she there when Tom died?"

"She was out of the country at the time. She was a secret agent and embedded in a country's government. When she finished that assignment, she resigned from the agency."

"Wow, your family has been in government work for a long time. Wasn't your uncle a Prime Minister at one time?"

"Yes, he was. Now quit changing the subject. We need to deal with this tumor of yours quickly. Fortunately, Anna Marie isn't beating your brains out right now."

"No, she already did that." The women ignored his remark.

"Anna Marie, can you put up with Chris until the middle of November?" Edna asked. "I believe I can have everything handled by that time and I am sure Sharon will do this. That's another five weeks."

"I believe I can trust him. I understand now what happened when he grabbed my wrist and pulled me to my room. I know it wasn't malicious, Mrs. Ryder," Anna Marie responded.

"You can call me Edna."

"Or you could call her Mom Edna," grinned Chris.

Anna Marie turned around so fast it would make a person's head spin. She slapped him and barged out of the room. "Just when you appear to be a likeable person you go and say something like that, you jerk!"

"Chris, did she just slap you?" Edna asked.

"Yes, she did," Chris said with a frown.

"Chris, did you ever date or have friendships while growing up?"

Chris's expression turned very sad, even though Edna could not see him, "No, children didn't come around me and I didn't know how to play games. No one ever taught me to throw a football or bat a baseball. The only friend I had was Kenneth Knight. We played tennis together. I enjoyed tennis. His older sister taught me to dance so I could go to the dances, but I never danced at them. I was too shy to ask. I have to go now. Goodnight."

"Goodnight, Chris. I love you, son. We will work this out."

Anna Marie had come back to ask Chris's forgiveness for slapping him and she heard the entire exchange.

CHAPTER 17

The phone rang. It was Edna. "Chris, the President of the United States still wants to talk to you. Haven't you put him off enough?"

"Alright, let me get prepared and I will call you back."

Chris went to Anna Marie's door and knocked. "It's locked, you can't come in," she said teasingly.

"I need you to meet the President of the United States with me."

"I think not!"

"Please."

"Come in and tell me why," said Anna Marie as she went and released the lock.

Chris opened the door and looked inside. She had her study door opened and he walked through to her bedroom. Anna Marie had everything cleaned up. The place looked wonderful.

"Wow, this place looks very nice. You did a great job."

"I would make someone a great maid."

"Anna Marie, the President of the United States wants to talk to me and I want you to sit there so he can see you are healthy and I haven't killed you."

Anna Marie raised her left eyebrow and said, "And if I weren't there, what could he do?"

"I am only asking, please, would you be there? Things are complicated enough in my life."

"Who is to blame for that?"

"Okay, you have me there. I am the blame for the complications in my life."

Defeated in this request, he turned to go with a frown on his face. Anna Marie, encouraged he would admit his flaw, decided to attend. "Okay, Chris, I'll be there. Is my sweat suit good enough?"

"I am wearing a suit and tie. I feel I owe him that."

"I'll find something dressier. What time?"

"Is thirty minutes enough time?"

"Make it forty-five minutes and I'll meet you in the studio."

Anna Marie found a pink dress exactly like the blue one she had worn. She looked in her jewelry box and found a pink necklace, bracelet, and a cocktail ring hidden under a cover and put them on. The ring actually looked like a pink diamond.

As she entered the studio Chris stood up from where he was sitting at the control table, pulled her chair out, and said "I told you blue was your color; I hadn't seen you in pink. You look very lovely, today, Anna Marie. Please be seated."

He had already called Edna and had to push only one more lever in position and there, sitting at his desk, was the President of the United States. Standing next to him were military officers from the Navy, Air Force, Army, and Marines. They were all standing at attention. Chris began: "What can I do for you, Mr. President?"

"Mr. Beckett, I am impressed with your capabilities and appalled with your morals. The United States and other countries have agreed no weapons of destruction would be deployed from space. Also, if you were in the United States we would put you in jail for kidnapping and other related offenses. Then there is our submarine; that vessel was worth well over $35 million not counting the ICBM's and their payloads. What do you have to say for yourself?"

"First you can ask your men to stand at ease. I am no formal chief of state and that position has to be uncomfortable." Anna Marie quickly put her hand to her mouth to hide a smile. "Second, my satellites are not weapons of destruction; they are for defense and assistance in returning this planet to peace. As for your submarine, it was headed for an accident and not a man on board would have survived. I am willing to pay you the going price of $40 Million for the package. Just leave it where it is and

I will move it when you agree. I can have my PA move my funds to the Treasury when you say so."

"That brings us to the subject of Miss Anna Marie Koch. Miss Koch was dying in a hospital in her home town. Her father pleaded with me not to let her die. That could only be accomplished with an operation and the insertion of a neural implant in her skull attached to her remaining operational brain. The technology for such a device and operation costs around two billion dollars. I did the operation willingly for free. There is no payment required. Mr. President, Miss Koch's body is still adapting to her new capabilities and she needs to be observed by someone who can help her until she is completely well, which will take a minimum of six months and possibly up to a year. If complications arise I am the only one capable of knowing what to do. As I told her father, who is also watching this exchange, I will not harm her nor ask her to do anything against her principles or morals."

Anna Marie perked up on this last statement and looked at the small screens to see her parents and brother on one of them, apparently watching this scene take place. "Is there hope for this boy?" she thought. "Lord, please take care of my heart. He is a handsome young man, but his heart is black without You. Don't let me ever become involved with an unbeliever, please."

Her attention turned back to the conversation in time to hear the president say, "…cannot tolerate the placement of those satellites; they must be removed. I'll talk to the staff about the submarine and get back to you. Miss Koch, have you been harmed?"

"Mr. President, other than being here without being able to leave, I have not been harmed in any way. I have every comfort I need and do not feel threatened by Mr. Beckett's presence. I am thankful for the operation and healing I have received and continue to receive and hope such technology would be available for others in the future. I have recognized there are certain complications that could arise. Mr. Beckett has explained them to me very recently. I think he does have my best interests at heart, although he could have gone about it differently."

"Mr. President, one of your staff should be coming through the door right now to let you know this exchange has been broadcast throughout the world. I thought you would like to know that. I have not threatened you, nor my country, nor Miss Koch. I want to live at peace with everyone. Good day, Mr. President. Say goodbye, Anna Marie, please."

"Goodbye," she said.

With that, Chris ended the stream and the screen went blank.

"How could you beam the broadcast like that?" Anna Marie asked.

"It's easy; just one connection and I used their technology along with mine. The television was already connected to antennas so the rest was a piece of cake."

"Why did you broadcast to the entire world?"

"I do not want stories or rumors coming from sources whenever I speak with heads of state. I felt it best to broadcast so that all could hear me first hand. Hopefully people will understand me better."

Chris looked down at the ring on Anna Marie's right hand and then continued speaking. "Anna Marie, the ring you have on your right hand was not meant to be in your room. That ring is what I was looking for after the shipment arrived and I made such a mess. Do not freak out on me, just listen, please. It is a real diamond and it was meant to be your engagement ring. It is okay to wear it, and should you ever change it to your left hand, I will know you have accepted my proposal I make right now; Anna Marie, will you marry me?"

"Chris, I wish you would think through your decision concerning Jesus Christ. I cannot marry you. Besides, I do not love you. I will continue to wear this ring on my right hand every day because it gives me cause to pray for you every time I look at it. It is beautiful and one I would have chosen had I seen it in a jewelry case and I were thinking of getting married. I have been and will be praying for you, Chris. I do not know what the future will hold, but my decision regarding marrying an unsaved man is nonnegotiable. Right now, you have other things to be concerned about. You need to find some way to deal with your brain tumor."

"Enough of this conversation. Would you like to go swimming?"

"As in getting in the ocean?"

"No, silly, as in your own private pool."

"Really? Yes, I need some exercise."

"Okay, grab a suit and covering and meet me in the living room and we will do so. Towels are already at the pool."

They went down the elevator together to the living area and each went to their own suite. Anna Marie changed quickly and met Chris in the living room. He had purchased for her a very modest blue suit with a high neck and a skirt. He was wearing a basic black swim suit with a white stripe that went to the knee. They went back to the elevator and Chris pushed the first-floor button. After descending, the elevator doors opened in front of a lovely pool.

"Chris this is beautiful. Look at all the windows! The scenery is just breath taking."

"Thank you, Anna Marie, but it was all here before I built. I just built around it."

"And you don't see God's handiwork in all the variety?"

"Anna Marie, let's just swim."

Anna Marie thanked God for His beauty silently and again prayed for Chris's salvation. They each did individual laps for some time. Anna Marie noticed Chris swam a lot under the water like a porpoise and his style fascinated her. At one point, she just stared at him and was mesmerized as he swam three lengths of the Olympic sized pool under water without taking any breaths. During all of this time Anna Marie was running an inventory program in her mind, something she learned she could do without taking her attention off of everyday things. She found she could carry on a conversation with Chris, do a topical Bible study, and have the background inventory program running without any stress. She added to the program theory possibilities for leaving one reality and entering another. She also had begun a program on the character traits and flaws of Chris. Every time he exhibited any stress, anger, or hurt she put it into the system. She was actually able to record her daily activities and visuals and play them back later. It gave her some comfort and hope to be able to stay busy with these mental activities. She was preoccupied and didn't hear Chris speaking.

"Anna Marie, are you lost in the recesses of your mind?"

"What do you need, Chris?"

"Do you want to relax? I was thinking about a game of chess."

"Chess is relaxing? Well, I'll give it a try. Let me access the moves and rules." After a few moments, she said, "I can handle that. Where's the set?"

He lead her over to a side room and as they entered she saw all types of games, boards, and a TV set up in a corner with what looked like remote controllers attached.

"Chris what is that?"

"That is an experimental system. Video games, I call them. Someone has invented something called 'Pac Man' and it is too simple. So, I said what can I do to add to it?"

"Sounds interesting. Ah, I see the chess set. Let me put my towels under me and wrap my wrap around me. I believe white goes first and since that is in front of you, be my guest. Well, I'm technically your guest, so just make your move."

Chris looked at her with a puzzled look on his face, but didn't comment as he began the game.

Four hours and eight games later, six of which were draws and Chris winning the first game, Anna Marie won a game. She recorded the angry look on Chris's face and his comments which indicated he thought it impossible she could win. He excused himself by telling her he had business to do and left.

CHAPTER 18

NOVEMBER 8, 1962, THURSDAY, 7 A.M. LOCAL TIME
PACIFIC ISLAND

It had been a week since the chess games. Anna Marie again came out after her quiet time to find Chris was not in the living area. She had searched him out a couple of times, only to find him either in the pool not making eye contact with her or the living room pretending to read a book. This time she could not find him anywhere. She had learned how to place a shield around her like Chris placed around the island and she learned there were various dimensions within her own dimension so she could phase the shield for protection and, hopefully, Chris could not detect it. She had done a lot of thinking this past week. If he was this upset over a lost chess game, what would keep him from becoming angry at something else so trivial? She spotted his phone on the end table in the living room so she called her mom a couple of times. Chris was a very unpopular person. He was not getting good press over his interview with the president. Perhaps he thought having it broadcast would help him; it did not. He came across as arrogant and inflexible. She, on the other hand, was receiving a lot of sympathy. She had run a probability program in her implant and with the information she was able to input it stated within the next thirteen years there was a high probability Chris would do something that could destroy peace in the world.

Anna Marie looked at all the information on teleporting. There were no principles other than the zero-gravity principle that needed to be dealt with. She believed Chris lied to her, but why? Was it to intimidate her to stay? And her abilities were coming online beyond her shields. Why did he state she needed six months to a year for him to monitor her? Again, another lie? Then there were his irrational comments; especially when he teased her about marriage, like the time he said to call Mrs. Ryder Mom Edna. That was uncalled for. Anna Marie felt she had found a way to escape. She was thinking about her plan to seek help from other realities when suddenly there he was in front of her.

"Hello, Anna Marie, how is your day going?"

"I am doing okay, how about you? Have you been avoiding me?" she asked.

"No, I am trying to figure you out. You have been too quiet for me to think you are not up to something."

"Why, Mr. Beckett, what could I possibly be up to? I am on your island out in the middle of the Pacific Ocean with a shield keeping me here." Anna Marie had the presence of mind to quickly turn off her personal shield. He reached for her and was surprised he caught her arm and was able to hold on to it. He had just known she had been able to figure out personal shields by now.

Even after he quickly caught her arm and let it go, Chris said, "I'm sorry, I shouldn't have done that, please forgive me."

"You are forgiven, Chris, just don't do it again, please. You promised me no physical contact."

He looked at her with a strange look, not one of anger, but of hurt. He turned and walked away.

CHAPTER 19

"Today is Thanksgiving Day," thought Anna Marie. There would be parades and family gatherings. Aunts, uncles, cousins, and grandparents would be with her parents as all traveled to Virginia to celebrate. She felt alone and sad. She and Chris never ate together anymore. If she ran out of food for her private kitchen she raided the main kitchen and filled up her pantry. One thing she never ran out of was rocky road ice cream. She had made sure he had it on the regular request delivery. She wrote those requests and left them on the kitchen table. They passed one another at the gym on occasion. Other times they even were working out at the same time. Occasionally one would catch the other staring, but nothing was said. Anna Marie left her room to find the television in the living room on showing news shots of the big parade. She also smelled a turkey cooking. While she was glancing at the television, Chris called from the dining room, "I'll have the Thanksgiving dinner ready at twelve. You are invited to sit and eat with me, please."

She turned and looked him in the eye. "Thank you for inviting me, Chris, I'll be there. What's the dress, casual or formal?"

"Jean casual is fine."

"Okay, I'll see you then. Do you want any help with the preparations?"

"No, I've got it, but thank you for asking."

She had continued to pray for Chris as well as the situation regarding his tumor. Nothing else had happened with the US Government except they took him up on his offer and left the submarine. He paid them for it and towed it to a cove on the other side of the island. He went through it from bow to stern, making sure there was nothing that would harm anyone before doing so.

Anna Marie had just about worked out her plan of what to do about leaving Chris. She had even been able to slip out and into one of the realities for about 30 seconds. That feat alone took a lot of concentration and energy, and she knew it would take a lot of work to allow her to be able to stay anywhere for a period of time. The other stopping point of her plan was she had no money. She didn't know where or how to get any. As far as she knew Chris did not have any here either. She had her ID. Her dad had sent her purse by mail to Edna and one of the rocket planes had brought it with the weekly supplies.

Anna Marie also requested novels on the weekly delivery, some romance novels, some just fiction, occasionally a murder mystery. Some she read, some she didn't, just to keep Chris thinking she was doing something to keep herself busy and not planning an escape. She had also made arrangements with him and her school on how to stay in school. She worked hard on that and was just about finished for a December graduation date from her high school. The weekly delivery plane returned to England each week with her completed assignments and any mail she was sending to her parents, brother, other relatives, or friends.

Today she was headed to the gym for a workout and to the pool to swim laps. She was so distracted with Chris's invitation to lunch, that on the elevator, she pushed the button for the fifth floor instead of the first. When the door opened she found herself facing boxes and boxes labeled as coming from the US Mint. She pushed the hold button on the elevator and walked over to an open box that was filled with bundles of $100-dollar bills. "Father, did you just answer my prayer? Thank you!" She had to think, how was she going to get what she needed out of this room? She suddenly had the answer. She could put some in her wrap pocket and head back to the room stating she had forgotten something if confronted. She grabbed several packets, stuffed them in the pocket, hit the down button to the living quarters, and walked efficiently, not too quickly, back to her room. She slid the money under the mattress, picked up a lip balm, and headed back out.

"Forgot something?" Chris asked when she reached the living room again.

"Yes, my lip balm. Don't need chapped lips!"

"I guess not. See you at 12."

Anna Marie waved as she moved toward the elevator.

Once in the pool area she placed her wrap and a couple of towels she picked up on the way in on a chair, slipped off her shoes, and dove in. She swam with a vengeance, forcing herself to tamp down her excitement. Her escape now was more of a positive venture than ever before. She was going to be able to leave and find a way to get help. The only problem left was the problem of staying gone. How was that to work? She put more of her neural implant to work on the problem.

Anna Marie finished her workout and returned to her quarters to prepare for the meal. By 11:50 she was in the living room wearing jeans, boots, and a western shirt. Chris saw her enter, and pulled out a chair for her so she could sit down. She lowered her head to pray and Chris said, "Please pray aloud."

Anna Marie obliged and prayed, "Dear Heavenly Father, thank you for the freedom of the United States of America and for the founding fathers who worked out those freedoms for every citizen. Thank you for providing men and women who through the years have fought for that right, and for families who mourn those who have given their lives for it. Thank you for this bounty of food that is set before us and for the hands that have prepared it. May more men and women, boys and girls bow to the name of Jesus Christ as Savior tonight than last night. In Jesus' name, amen."

"Thank you, Anna Marie."

"Chris, this all looks and smells so good. Is that pumpkin pie or sweet potato pie?"

"Actually, I have each. This is pumpkin and the one still in the kitchen is sweet potato. Are you allergic to either?" he asked.

"No, and I like both. Do you use the same spices?"

"I do. Here, let me cut you some turkey; what do you want?"

"A leg portion, please."

"Certainly. I'll add the dressing and gravy with it."

"If you will pass me your plate I'll put on the cranberry sauce and green beans."

"Sure, here you are. Was your workout productive?"

"Yes, it was. I have found if I keep it up on a regular basis it keeps me strong and lean."

"I'll have to say you do look good. I hope you don't mind my saying so."

Anna Marie blushed and lowered her head. "Chris, I had thought Edna would be here by now. Has something happened?"

"Yes, Sharon in her undercover work had used different names and was not showing any credit worthiness and our bank refused to add her to the checking account on a technicality. Naturally, they couldn't tell them why she had those gaps in her credit record, so Mom is having to switch banks, and with automatic deposits and automatic withdrawals it has become a nightmare. She says she should have it worked out by the first of the year," Chris explained.

"So, Chris, am I going to have another five plus weeks of the silent treatment?"

"I haven't been giving you the silent treatment," he said indignantly.

"Then what would you call it, a cold shoulder? You would think we are a couple feuding. I am so sorry about your tumor. If you need some more of my blood with the nanorobots, why haven't you asked?"

"I don't need anything from you."

"There you go, again pushing me away. You certainly are a strange person."

Suddenly her program on Chris popped up and a clear message came to her. She dropped her fork and placed her hands over her mouth. "Oh, no, it is the tumor that is causing your moods!" she exclaimed. "When was your last scan?"

"I would rather not discuss it, please. Let's change the subject. How are your studies coming along?"

Anna Marie was so shocked he didn't want to discuss the subject, she sat and stared at him for several seconds. Finally, she let herself calm down and said, "If I work hard and don't let something get in the way I should be through by winter break on the 15th of December."

"For the year?" he asked.

"I hope to have everything done to graduate from the 12th grade," she clarified.

"I'm impressed, Anna Marie. That is three years of work?"

"No, that is four. I wasn't supposed to graduate until 1966."

"Do you have plans for further education?"

"You know more than anyone that my work for high school has only been to put on paper that which is required. All knowledge I need is in my head. Hands on experience would be fine if I were to be able to go into a profession that required it, like brain surgery, for instance."

"Why would you mention brain surgery?"

"Obviously you had the training, short as it was, while in college, so my surgery at your hands was aided by that. Should I ever have to do that I do not know if I could be able to do so."

"Anna Marie, please listen carefully to what I am about to say; embed it in your consciousness. You have not been pressed yet to have to do anything. When I had to do your surgery, it was on a first time need. I do not know how, but every move, every cut, every stitch, was guided to correctness. I did not make an unnecessary nor incorrect move. It was as if I were being guided and that I had done it all my life. I believe if and when you may have to do something similar, you will be guided even more so even by Your God, if He is who you say He is."

Anna Marie reached over and touched the top of Chris's hand as she said with emotion in her voice and tears in her eyes, "Chris, you do not know how it thrills my very soul and it sends goose bumps up my arms to hear you say what you just said. You do not recognize Him for who He is, but you do recognize what He has done and I praise Him for that."

"Now, don't get all mushy on me. Would you like more turkey?" The moment was gone as Anna Marie returned her hand to her place.

"No thank you. This is all very delicious and I thank you again for making this special meal for us."

"You are welcome."

"When and how did you meet Edna?" Anna Marie asked.

"I met her this past March whenever I went to England to have my parents buy this island for me. She was a WPPA agent in the negotiations. WPPA stands for Worldwide People Protection Agency. My parents didn't want me to sell my technology to WPPA or Great Britain. Edna called for a break in the discussions. I had met her and her husband only three days prior. She took me into another room and listened to me. She offered concrete suggestions and everything about her showed me she cared for me, not for the technology, but for me. When the subject of emancipation came up, which can be done at sixteen in the UK, she said she could expedite the process and my albatross parents would be gone from my life. She told me I didn't have to have a guardian, but the judge would be more favorable if I did. I made the decision to ask her and her husband to be my guardians. They have been more of a support to me in the few months I have known them than my parents were in seventeen years, and I mean that from the bottom of my heart."

"I am so sorry, Chris."

"I don't need your pity," he said rather harshly.

"I didn't mean it as pity, Chris."

With that, the two finished eating in silence and, except for a few requests for food, did not discuss anything of value the rest of the meal. When finished, Anna Marie tried to assist with the clean up, but Chris refused her help. She then excused herself to her room, saying she had to finish writing lessons. Once in her room, she knelt by the bed in anguished prayer for the soul of Christopher Beckett and after about an hour fell asleep on the floor.

CHAPTER 20

All of her school work was complete, in a packet, and prepared for the afternoon shipment. Work was progressing beyond her wildest thoughts concerning her ability to go to another reality. Her implant had figured out the algorithm to bypass Chris's block on the shield. She was finding she could even teleport herself to different places within her own reality. That would be beneficial whenever she arrived elsewhere, but not so here, because should she show up somewhere else she was unsure of how Chris would react. She did not know what would set him off or when he would lose control, and according to the placement of the tumor and her understanding of the brain that was a likely outcome. Anna Marie's reasoning for all she was hoping to accomplish was for God to receive glory. She had a plan worked out that was very complicated and involved several realities and she continued to pray for God's wisdom throughout it all. It had occurred to her she could try to wrench control from Chris and put him to sleep and do the operation herself, but she felt too many things could go wrong and his anger would cause harm to so many. She didn't want to take the chance. She did know in her heart Chris had lost most all of his special abilities. His ability to make personal shields was being compromised by the tumor. He could not teleport, nor could he place himself in stealth mode. Even though the probability factor was thirteen years, she wasn't sure Chris had that long. He would be thirty years old and she would be twenty-seven by that time. No, she could not wait that long to make the changes necessary.

She must locate, train, and return with her team before thirteen years. She knew the nanorobots in her blood system could build the implant on their own; an operation would not be needed, just an injection. All she would need were some needles, syringes, swabs, and alcohol from the surgical suite.

As Anna Marie had studied realities she had to start almost from scratch. Although Chris had some information, she had to find the mathematical answers on her own. She learned each reality occupies the same space as another, yet in a different dimension. Because each reality had a boundary, a cortex, they were separated and sealed from one another. Anna Marie had her research labeled and filed in her neural implant. She counted her reality as Reality 437269. She didn't know where that number came from, but she was sure she had numbered it correctly. She wasn't sure of the ability of Chris to detect or monitor realities, so she picked 436341, one very far away, as her destination. When she monitored it, she found the Chris and Anna Marie there actually lived on this island they were on and were married. Maybe this would be easier than she thought.

CHAPTER 21

DECEMBER 31, 1962, MONDAY, 2 P.M.
PACIFIC ISLAND

Anna Marie could tell Chris was suspicious of something. They weren't talking much, and when they did it was confrontational. He was asking her if she had learned anything concerning metallurgy or creation of shields or telekinesis using her connection to the planet's gravitational and magnetic fields. She tried to make light of his requests and said she had been too busy on her school assignments to pursue those avenues of interest.

"Besides, what good would they do me? I am stuck here with you for the rest of my life. As powerful as you are what could I hope to accomplish? Would you want a battle of the titans within this shield?"

"Trust me, child, you would not win a battle with me, no matter what you think. I have control of the computer and if I am not available this whole island would be blown up."

Anna Marie didn't know why that statement hurt so much. She knew in her heart he thought more of her than a child. Was it the tumor that caused him to say this? She steeled her emotions and kept herself focused.

Anna Marie had been reading on the veranda of their suite when it happened. She came inside and Chris was in the living room. Chris attempted to put a personal shield around her. She saw it coming and retaliated by blocking the shield and throwing it back at Chris, effectively knocking him off his feet. He was red with anger when he recovered, but Anna Marie gave him no room for error. She hit him with a gravitational burst and then she teleported into her suite. There she picked up the knapsack she had packed and hid, looked around one last time, and was teleporting just as Chris opened the door.

Chris collapsed on the floor, saying, "No, Anna Marie, please don't leave me! I need you!"

She heard what he said but her resolve was not daunted. Seeing no other recourse, she headed for her parents' home. The air crackled as she entered the living room of her parents.

"I do not have any time. Read this letter. Call Edna, Mom, and tell her I am sorry. I love you. Goodbye." Then she was gone.

Her parents were overwhelmed. They sat down to read her letter when the television turned on and there was Chris staring at them. "Where is she?" he demanded.

"We don't know. She just showed up for less than thirty seconds and then disappeared. Chris, how could she do that?"

"Her implant gave her special powers. That was why I needed her to stay on the island so I could help her deal with them emotionally. What's in your hand?"

"A letter she left for us."

"Read it to me."

"Chris, we haven't read it yet, and if she wanted you to know what...."

"I said read it to me and don't skip anything. I will not be responsible for my reaction if you disobey me."

Mr. Koch began reading. "Dear Mom, Dad, and Albert: I have to leave. I do not know for how long. Where I am going is a place you cannot go. Chris is sick. He has a brain tumor. I hope to return to help him in the future. He has asked me to marry him. I told him I could not as long as he was unsaved. I have been praying for his salvation since day one. Please pray my mission will be successful and I will be able to operate and he will be saved. I love you all. I pray he will not harm you because of this. Love, Anna Marie."

"Oh no, she did the unthinkable. She left our reality. You will tell no one of her letter, do you understand?" Chris said.

"Wait, what do you mean she left our reality?" Mr. Koch asked.

"I don't want to discuss that right now. Tell me, you will tell no one of this letter or this incident."

"We won't," they all said.

The screen went blank.

BOOK 2
CONSEQUENCES

CHAPTER 1

Anna Marie, her shoulder length auburn hair flowing in the wind, sat on a large flat grey rock on the beach. With her bright blue eyes, she looked at a native village several hundred yards away at the edge of a tropical jungle. There had been tan-skinned natives on the beach looking for clams and other shell fish when she materialized, but they had dropped their baskets and digging tools as they ran screaming toward the village. Anna Marie, dressed in her western jeans and white cowboy shirt with an onyx boa tie, then walked over to the rock and sat down to wait. She now saw a couple walking toward her. The man was wearing what looked like cutoff jeans and a tee shirt, and the woman was wearing a bright yellow kimono. They were both barefoot. The closer they came the larger their eyes grew.

Anna Marie was suddenly startled. She didn't know she would react this way. He looked exactly like the Chris from her dimension. His dark brown eyes even had the same gold flecks at the center of the iris. His black hair was disheveled and in need of a cut. This Anna Marie, on the other hand, had her auburn hair cut short, just to the top of her shoulders. It was very becoming.

Chris spoke first. "They said the gods had favored us and the goddess looked as if she could be my wife's twin sister. We are sure you are not a goddess, so do you care to explain? My name is...."

"Christopher Lee Beckett, Jr. and she is your wife, Anna Marie Beckett. Her maiden name was Koch. Please sit down."

Both Chris and Anna Marie gaped at her. Speechless, they sank down on the rocks in front of her.

"My name is Anna Marie Koch, and I have a story to tell. I would like for you to listen with open minds and hearts. I pray I have chosen wisely and God has lead me to the couple I need. Anna Marie, I look like you because I am you, only I am from a different reality. There are many different dimensions on our planet. There is only one earth but there are thousands of realities. I am from reality 437269 and you are in reality 436341. I am able to measure reality numbers only because I had a severe brain injury and in the operation that followed, I was given a neural implant that assists me in my logical intelligence ability and in making calculations. This neural implant has given me many abilities I would not have had normally. I will discuss them with you later.

"People and places are similar, yet different in each dimension. The Chris Beckett in mine is a super genius. He actually lives on this same island in our reality which, by the way is unoccupied other than for Chris and his complex. He has a brain tumor. The tumor is growing at a very slow rate, but because of the tumor he has already made many unwise decisions, and within the next few years he is going to make decisions that have the potential to destroy our reality and possibly others if he is not stopped. I have studied a probability chart and from everything I know he has about thirteen years before he makes some really unwise decisions, and yes, his tumor is growing that slow. I need someone to assist me in stopping him. I need to confront and operate on him to remove the tumor.

"I met Chris at a church function only five months ago in my dimension. Two and a half months ago I was in an automobile accident that nearly cost me my life, and I would have died if Chris had not operated on me. As I said, I have what is called a neural implant attached to my brain. Chris invented this implant and he installed it in me because a significant portion of my brain was destroyed by the accident. He duplicated everything he knew and had studied, as well as pretty much all information on all sciences and downloaded all of that information to me in my implant. This implant coupled with what I have left of my natural brain is better than any super computer invented in my reality. It has allowed me to research and to understand much regarding the various sciences, including temporal displacement and cosmic energies, and the spectrum of all light and how they can be used for communication. Chris, through his super intelligence, and I, through the use of my implant, have both learned so much and still have more we can learn. There are many more abilities humans have available if we but used more of our mind's capabilities."

"Chris has also developed tiny biological genetically engineered robots to work inside our blood stream to keep us healed of all types of diseases and sicknesses, and to assist in healing from small accidents. They can also, over a short time, install a neural implant inside someone's head if they do not already have one. I want to inject some of those nanorobots into each of your blood streams and have them do what Chris did for me through his operation. You have not had a trauma, so you do not need brain surgery, you just need the neural implant. When I inject some of my blood into you, it will start the process. You should have type O Positive blood; that takes only a moment to check. The robots will take longer than an operation, but I believe it is better than me operating on you; besides, I did not bring implants with me. Once your brain has been connected with the neural implant and once it comes online with your intellect you will understand everything I am telling you."

"After this is done, I will need you, Chris and Anna Marie, to go to two different realities with me to recruit two more teams. I will need this reinforcement and the combined abilities each of you will develop in order to overcome Chris in my reality. Do I need to tell you more? Do you have questions? Will you help me or must I go somewhere else?"

Chris and Anna Marie #1 looked at each other with bewilderment. They looked back to Anna Marie, and saw the hurt and pain in her eyes. Chris said, "You have a far fetched story here. Your plan will take awhile to absorb and fully understand. We will need several questions answered which will give us some more information. I see your knapsack in hand, and unless you have some place to go, come to the village, spend the night with us, and let us pray until tomorrow about this. By then we should have our questions formulated properly."

"Yes, and I will pray some more also."

"Is your Chris a believer?"

"Sadly, no, he is not, and his arrogance kept me from getting close enough to discuss the possibility of an operation."

"Is that why you are not married?"

"We just met in July, and as long as he is unsaved there could never be even a dating relationship."

They were walking back to the village as they were talking and the villagers were coming toward them with gifts. As they got closer, the villagers began bowing in worship to their visitor. Anna Marie began speaking in the Polynesian dialect.

"No, no, I am not a god; I am the sister of Miss Anna. My name is Marie. I came from a long way and have a different mode of transportation than you have seen before. Please understand, I am a person like you and Mr. Chris and Miss Anna. Jesus the Christ is who you worship. Mr. Chris and Miss Anna have been telling you about Him. You just celebrated his birth at Christmas. Jesus is God, I am but His ambassador, just like Mr. Chris and Miss Anna."

They all finally understood her pleas and Anna Marie was able to carry on different conversations with some of them before they made it back to Chris and Anna Marie's hut. By the time they reached the hut all of the villagers had realized what Anna Marie was saying to them and were going to their huts to allow Mr. Chris and Miss Anna to visit privately with her sister.

Once they were inside the hut, Chris #1 asked, "How are you able to speak the Polynesian language so effortlessly and flawlessly? We have been at it three years now and we struggle. You lost us part of the time while you were speaking; you spoke so fast and fluently. Was this a language you learned in school?"

"No, I barely spoke English correctly before the implant. This is one of the blessings of the neural implant. You can understand, write, and speak all languages on the planet; now I am assuming you do not have any other languages than what I have in my dimension. Another blessing is although Chris is not a believer he had the entire Bible and also all conservative religious studies and commentaries downloaded. As far as the programming, I can start with a word and the entire passage comes up. I can think a reference and the verse follows. It has been a blessing to me in my quiet times and Bible study. I have a file system I put topical studies in and an index to pull them up. Quite frankly, those blessings alone are worth the accident I had. By the way, how long have you been married?"

"We were married on December 29, 1959; three years ago two days back."

Anna Marie's mouth dropped open. "What? Get out of here! Anna Marie, you were only eleven years old!"

"That's right," Anna Marie #1 confirmed with a smile and a gentle look toward her husband. "We met that summer at a Christian Missionaries' Children's camp and our parents, both Chris's and mine, have been on the mission field for around fifteen years each. We sincerely believed we were meant for each other the moment we met and that feeling grew stronger the more we discussed our future plans and where we believed God was leading us. I was saved at age six and Chris was saved at age five. Both our parents had a burden for this particular group of people, this particular island, and Chris and I both strongly believed the Lord called us to this field. Our parents, after a lot of prayer and discussion with each of us and with advice from counselors, consented to recognize our calling and agreed to the marriage, and here we are. There were no laws broken, as both Chris and I are citizens of Sobarus and there is no law here about the age of marriage as long as our ages are close together. In other words, an older person cannot marry a child. There has been only one drawback, but we have been prayerfully strengthened by the Holy Spirit and have not had any difficulty yet; we are both still virgins and we are bound by a promise to our parents and to God not to consummate our marriage until I am sixteen."

"The age of marriage is the same in this culture and on surrounding islands. My prayers go with you to comply with your promise. But what about your school studies?" Anna Marie asked.

"We are both taking school by correspondence," said Anna Marie #1.

Again, changing the subject, Anna Marie asked, "I have another question; you have been on the field now for three years. Are you the only missionaries on this island?"

"Oh, no," said Chris. They had entered the little hut by now and he was offering Anna Marie a seat on a mat on the living room floor. He and his Anna Marie sat on mats opposite her. "This is more informal. Now, where was I? Oh! The island is quite large; it is about 4,000 square miles—a bit smaller than the big island of Hawaii—and there is a missionary compound in the center of the island. I am not sure if you know, but we are between Australia and Easter Island and below both of them. We do not have storms on the island. Yes, it rains and it thunders, but no tropical storms like other areas have. The daily weather is a constant 70 degrees Fahrenheit year-round. There is an airport on the far side from us and there is a thriving tourist business there. There are people who want to really get away from all the hustle and bustle of modern life and come to the island to do that. There are no mobile phones here, but satellite phones do work. That is something new very recently. A businessman came in and set up the system about two months ago. We are told it isn't even available in the US or Europe yet."

Anna Marie asked, "I assume you travel by air, since boat travel would be very hard and longer?"

"You are correct," said Chris #1. "Air travel is the best. Even at that it takes a long time for us to get home, so we were signed up for a three-year rotation so the costs of travel could be budgeted easier into our time of service. We are to leave for home on the 3rd of January, flying to Hawaii and then to California, and then cross country. It's over 9,000 miles and it will take us a week to get to Greenville, South Carolina. Our parents each have a home there and we can rotate between them like they do. They are currently on other islands in the western Pacific and when we go home we will be the only ones in either home."

"How long before anyone else will rotate home and how long do you have off?"

"We do not come back here until next year this time, so we will be gone one year. None of our families are rotating off until after next September."

"So, we have nine months with no one bothering us?"

"Well, friends and other family members will be wanting to drop in and we will be fulfilling some stateside duties, doing deputation, meeting with other missionaries, and also doing some training, so although we will be home, we will not be sitting idle."

"Thank you for letting me know, Chris. I was not aware of all the responsibilities missionaries have. Certainly, missionaries do not have time to themselves when home from the field. Hopefully we will be able to work our way around certain details if you decide to help me."

Anna Marie then changed the subject again. "If the two of you say yes to my plan, I may be in this reality for some time. I do not know how to have an identity without stealing one."

"You do not have to worry. Do you have any money?" Chris #1 asked.

"I have some, I think about $60,000 in $100 bills, and once I have my new identify I can have much more by investing in the stock market."

"I have done research on the laws and rules of the island and it will take about $10,000 and a signed statement and you become a citizen of this island. No questions asked and they do not ask for a record of your past. You change names, promise to pay certain taxes on the island, they give you a new identification, you become a citizen of Sobarus and you get a passport from the island's government. Sobarus' government was founded at the end of WWII and has prospered since. The island population is now only about twelve percent Christian but we are making progress," he replied.

Anna Marie from 437269 was very excited as she rose from her seated position and began excitedly moving her arms and pointing toward the other side of the island, "So, I can go to the immigration department on January 2nd, obtain citizenship papers and a passport, and not be questioned in other countries?"

"That is correct," repeated Chris with a smile on his face.

"I believe God has prospered me in my quest. I can sense this will work. I just need you to let me know tomorrow if you want to help me."

"Anna Marie, we will be praying. You are speaking of doing things that should be God's business and not ours. Please, we are praying even now about what to do, so, we will discuss this tomorrow afternoon," said Chris with some anxiety.

"Anna Marie, would you like to help me with dinner for the two of us? Chris, you have that discipleship dinner meeting to attend. It's now about 5:30 and you will not be back until late. I need to get Anna Marie settled in and you and I still need to talk and pray," Anna Marie #1 said.

"Sure, I'll be glad to help," said Anna Marie.

Chris picked up his Bible and a book, put a pen in his pocket, gave Anna Marie #1 a kiss on the cheek and headed out the door. The two Anna Marie's worked on the dinner and then sat down to a nice chopped salad with grilled fish on top about thirty minutes later after praying for the meal.

"You do know this is New Year's Eve, don't you?" Anna Marie #1 asked.

"You know, I do, but the thought had not occurred to me with all of my planning to escape and then the rush of having it happen. I had no idea people would be celebrating the beginning of a new year."

"We do not celebrate with fireworks because they are not allowed on the island. It has to do with safety. This is a tropical rainforest, and if it caught fire much would be lost. Our church celebrates with a praise and thanksgiving service on the beach at eight tomorrow morning. Sunrise will be at 7:30. You're welcome to attend with us if you wish."

"Thank you, I will be there. I normally am up by five for prayer."

After the meal, they prayed together about Anna Marie's mission and the salvation of Chris from the other reality. Chris and Anna Marie #1 had an extra bedroom with a bed and a chair in the room and their visitor was asleep by 8 p.m. She was not disturbed when Chris #1 came home at 8:30.

CHAPTER 2

JANUARY 1, 1963, TUESDAY, 5 A.M.
PACIFIC OCEAN—SOBARUS ISLAND

Anna Marie was awakened by her internal alarm promptly at 5 a.m. She had her Bible study and prayer, praying especially for Chris. She prayed the Lord would protect him and draw him to Himself; that Chris would not harm anyone, and that her mission would be successful. She walked to the beach at sunrise with Chris and Anna Marie #1. The sky started with black and then deep purple that turned to violet and then all of the gold's, pinks, purples, and oranges of the sunrise were awesome. Chris and Anna Marie # 1 held a wonderful praise and worship service that was well attended by some 200 natives including their children. Anna Marie enjoyed singing in the native language with the natives of the island. Chris and Anna Marie #1 were still amazed at her ability to speak and now sing in the native tongue, and they were awed at her beautiful voice.

When they returned to the hut and were at the entrance, Anna Marie from 437269 sensed someone else was inside. She motioned to Chris and Anna Marie #1 to stay at the door while she walked to her room prepared to place a shield around whoever it was. When she opened the door, she saw Chris standing by the window. Without thinking, she reacted by trying to push him down with a gravitational burst while she also set up a shield. As her hands went up, Chris shouted, "Anna Marie, don't! I am not your Chris!"

She didn't believe him, and tried to shield him anyway. He shielded her instead and placed a restraint on her hands. "Let me go," she shouted. "I am not going back with you, leave me alone!"

Chris and Anna Marie #1 believed interference would not accomplish anything at this time. They held hands, prayed, and waited for the outcome.

"Anna Marie, please look at me. Now, carefully analyze me, I am not the Chris from your reality. I am from 437268, one reality below you. When you left your Chris kidnapped my Anna Marie, thinking she was you. He has also kidnapped four other Anna Marie's. You have opened a colossal dilemma with the realities, damaging all 900 realities you went through, including this one. You are not supposed to go through realities, you are supposed to go directly to your destination dimension. It takes proper calculations. That was why Chris asked you to let him train you. Had you stayed in your own dimension, your own reality, the damage wouldn't have been so great. You had insufficient information and training in temporal displacement, and therefore have opened a rift in the cortexes. Even had Chris been able to complete your training, you would not have been sufficiently prepared to enter another dimension properly.

"It is interesting how Chris was so angry his abilities worked perfectly when he kidnapped the Anna Marie's. You made him so angry he was able to teleport and grab them and return to his own dimension without a hitch. His recognition program wasn't working, but he was able to teleport. When he finally realized what he was doing he was so ashamed, but by then I had blocked him from everyone and unfortunately he couldn't return them. Then he closed off his reality and I can't get in there to release them, including my wife. I admit, I reacted and tried to help, and I am partially to blame for where we are right now. At the time I felt he was going to continue to reach out and take more Anna Marie's from more dimensions, and I should have confronted him first. Confrontation is never pleasant, but sometimes it is the best thing to do. Now we are reaping the consequences.

"Anna Marie, what has happened cannot be undone. We now have some problems that need to be corrected. There are some changes I have made on my way here, but there are other corrections that will take both of us and the couple in the next room who are listening to our dialogue. However, before we can do anything I need to inject some nanorobots from my reality into your blood and they will finish the programming Chris was unable to do because of his brain tumor. Your neural implant has insufficient programming and he did not have some teleporting equations figured properly in your implant. I am glad I caught you before you infected this couple."

Chris and Anna Marie #1 continued to listen to this conversation from the other room and looked at each other with deep concern. In the meantime, Anna Marie finally used her "Reality Location and Matching Program" and found Chris #2 did come from Reality 437268 as he said, but she still wasn't ready to be injected with someone else's blood and artificial intelligence.

"You are holding me prisoner. Do all of you geniuses think you can manhandle us women?"

"Hold on one moment. I have watched you and Chris since you met and he has never laid a hand on you except after you attacked him and he was trying to get you to your room. The other time was when he was trying to determine if you knew how to manipulate gravity and other forces of nature. Tell me now, am I right?"

Anna Marie thought for a minute before she answered, and then with shame in her eyes and a blush on her face she said "Yes, you are right. I just felt I could not stay there with him any longer. He was beginning to frighten me and I knew I could figure a way to help him if I just left and recruited others to assist."

"I understand your reasoning. He is sick, but, if you had stayed and been a Christian witness in spite of the circumstances, perhaps God would have used your witness. It would not have been easy for you. We both know Chris should have allowed you to go home and back to the island for checkups, but now, after what has been done, it will be even more difficult. I believe in my heart he is one of God's children but it will be a long time now before that decision is made. With your lack of knowledge of quantum physics, you have opened up a problem that may cause peoples' deaths if we do not do some cortex repair. Now, please hold still while I inject you and, after my nanorobots reprogram your neural implant and allow you to analyze scientific data correctly, you will be okay. Unfortunately, you will lose consciousness and be out for twenty-four hours, but when you come to it will all be clear. Please, do not jerk from me and allow me to clean your arm and inject these nanorobots into your bloodstream."

Anna Marie did as she was asked, reclining on the bed and extending her arm. Fifteen seconds after the injection she was asleep. Chris #2 pulled out a duffel bag he had in a corner and removed an IV outfit with Ringer's Lactate and attached it to her arm to guard against dehydration. He covered her with a blanket and left the room.

Chris #2 walked into the living room where Chris and Anna Marie #1 were waiting. They shook hands as he introduced himself and then they sat down on the mats as Chris #2 continued to explain. "I know you heard all of that and I hope you understood most of it. My name is Christopher Beckett and I am from Reality 437268. In the layers of realities we have a pattern that follows several realities close together. That pattern follows us for about 250 realities above. In your reality, you are in the middle of about 500 missionary couples. There are CEOs, sports men, policemen, politicians, and investigators; all kinds of careers. Down the layers from my reality there are two realities similar, yet with different patterns. The Chris's born there are not super intelligent. Don't get me wrong; they're smart, just not geniuses. Both will now operate as Worldwide People Protection Agency agents because of Anna Marie's leaving her reality. That was not to be their future. It is a result of her breaking the cortex of her reality, and now their future will be changed drastically. She did not leave her reality at zero gravity and it produced a back flow of energy to their realities. She also went through the realities rather than go directly here. That exacerbated the problem. I was able to shield my reality before it happened because I have been studying her for a long time."

"Regarding these two realities below me, there is going to be an accident between the two realities; a breach of time and space and these two Chris's are going to die if we do not intervene. That accident was created by this little lady in the other room. If she knew more about quantum physics, the pattern of cosmic energies, and temporal displacement she would have thought twice before attempting to leave her reality. We were never meant to leave our realities. With knowledge comes responsibility, accountability, and restraint. I hope she is mature enough to see what she did through the proper lenses and will want to help me to correct the displacement problems she has created."

"Won't the more times you teleport from reality to reality and the more realities you go through cause more problems?" asked Chris #1.

"If we use the proper technique we will not. I have the ability to calculate and teleport perfectly and I have a gift to see potential catastrophic events in the future. Because of that, I have known about the possibility of what she may do for about two months now and prepared for it. I did not know everything, and some decisions have caused other problems. I missed something, but I still believe we can repair the upcoming breech and then get back home. I hope Miss Koch sees the truth and will act properly."

"So, you can see into the future?" asked Anna Marie #1.

"Not really. What I see is when there's a possibility there will be a displacement problem then I am shown that problem. I do know if we do not stop the problem now, much worse can happen."

"What else is the Chris from her reality going to cause?" Anna Marie asked with a frown on her face.

"Well, he has already caused it. In the past twenty-four hours, he has stolen five Anna Marie's, as you heard me say, including mine. When I realized what he was doing, I was able to block him from stealing any more. Unfortunately, he has also blocked anyone from going into his reality, including the Anna Marie from his reality. Because of his tumor and now his anger has subsided he has again lost the ability to teleport, even within his own reality."

"So, what are you proposing?" asked Chris #1.

"We will have the task of saving the two Chris's from the dimensions below mine to begin with, and then we have to endure patiently as we wait for Chris's power to minimize enough for us to go into his reality and confront him and hopefully heal him. I had hoped we would be able to do it in a short period of time, but I fear that is going to be many years away."

CHAPTER 3

Twenty-four hours later Anna Marie #6 woke up. It took her a few minutes to clear her head and be able to focus. Chris #2 gave her that time. He just sat in the chair and continued to read his Bible. Anna Marie closed her eyes. *"Heavenly Father, I was so wrong and I have caused such pain to this man. His wife is gone and it was my fault. Please forgive me for my lack of faith. If I had only stayed it would have been worked out. Please forgive me for walking in my flesh. Please forgive me for the future pain I will cause in the case of the accident that is coming. Please forgive me for the distortions in the universe that are occurring. Please let me be humble and listen to You and obey this Chris as he seeks to right what I have done. May his wife, these other Anna Marie's, and I find our way home. I pray in Jesus' name, Amen."*

Anna Marie opened her eyes and looked at Chris #2. "Please forgive me for the pain I have caused you and your wife and for the work and inconvenience I am still causing you. I walked in the flesh. I had incomplete information and I made a decision on impulse. It felt so right, but it was so wrong. I ask for your forgiveness, please."

Anna Marie felt like the seconds were minutes and the minutes kept adding up. Chris just looked at her and stared into her eyes. After what seemed to Anna Marie like hours, yet was only a couple of minutes, Chris #2 spoke: "I forgive you, Anna Marie. Now, let's get down to work. Let me take this IV off of you and let you have a decent meal. Chris and Anna Marie are holding breakfast for us." Chris #2 removed the

IV and held out his hand and Anna Marie sat up and stood up with his assistance. She was wobbly only for a second before she regained her balance and they walked to the eating area.

"Good morning, Anna Marie and Chris," stated Anna Marie and Chris #1 together. Anna Marie #6 and Chris #2 exchanged greetings as well. As they sat down to eat, Chris #1 returned thanks.

"Our Heavenly Father, we thank You for all of Your provisions for us and pray this day we will be thankful. We do thank You for this food this morning and pray You would bless it to the use of our bodies and our lives to Your service. In the blessed name of Jesus we pray, Amen." Amen was echoed by everyone.

Everyone ate with subdued feelings, especially Anna Marie #6, who was silent the entire meal except when spoken to for a response. She did not offer any conversation until she had a sudden thought.

She looked over to Chris #2 and asked, "Chris, why can't I sense the Chris from my reality? I haven't been able to sense anyone in my reality since I woke up. Did you do something to cause that?"

"No. Chris has blocked off your reality. He had sensed correctly you had gone down in the progression, but he didn't have any idea how far. Since you left him he has kidnapped five different Anna Marie's; He went from my reality down one at a time, thinking you didn't go very far. The cortex problem you caused made him skip two Anna Marie's; the ones whose Chris's we are going to save."

"What is he going to do? Is he going to continue to take them? How can he take care of them? How are they protected from him?" she asked rapidly.

"Please let me handle one question at a time. First, right now he is probably pretty angry; however, that anger has subsided some. I saw that before he cut us off. He cannot take any more Anna Marie's in his search for you because I have blocked all realities from him. He has Edna Ryder, just like we all do, and I will explain that later. She will see to it the women he already has are cared for. As far as their protection, my wife will take care of that with her shield. She will protect all of them from all harm directed to them; not that I would think he would attempt to harm anyone. And trust me, if he thought he had his hands full with you, he has triple that now."

"Oh! I really don't know what to say beyond I am so sorry," said Anna Marie #6.

"Chris, you mentioned Edna Ryder?" asked Chris #1.

"Yes, I did, who is she to you?"

"She is one of our supporters, a precious lady, and always willing to assist us in any way."

"Let her do so, Chris, that is her station in life; to help, and she is fantastic at it."

"Thank you for letting us know that," said Chris #1.

"Alright," Chris #2 said. "Let's get down to business. Anna Marie has to register as a citizen of this island and obtain a passport and other identity papers. We have to return your tickets and get you a refund, and then we...."

"Chris, we have to leave tomorrow. We can't return our tickets," said Chris #1.

"I know that. You will leave this island on my plane."

"On your plane!" Everyone shouted at the same time.

"Yes, do you think I just dropped in like Anna Marie here? I am Joshua Robinson of Robinson Aviation and I came to pick up my chief assistant, Joanne Baxter and her friends. I am flying my experimental aircraft that is now parked at the airport and locked so that no one can enter it. I already have a cover as I am the person who introduced satellite phones to the island which is becoming a very profitable business."

"Excuse me. You tell me I got the universe out of balance and you bring a plane almost 900 realities from your reality? Explain that, please!" exclaimed Anna Marie #6 as she got into Chris's personal space and looked him eye to eye.

"Anna Marie, I told you it was understanding temporal displacement and quantum physics. I know you haven't had a chance to look through the material, but it is all there. You could have done the same thing if only you had handled it correctly."

"How big a plane is this?" she asked.

"It's irrelevant."

"How big a plane, Chris?"

"It's a specially converted 100 passenger jet."

"A what?" she said incredulously. "I don't want to hear any more from you until I have had time to think more of this through. I am going to my bedroom and I do not want to be disturbed!"

Anna Marie #6 stormed from the dining area and into the guest bedroom. She laid down on the bed and closed her eyes, fuming as she began searching through her information on traveling between realities again. She went through the basics, replayed what she did as she left her own reality, and rechecked her information regarding temporal displacement and magnetism as well as temporal and quantum physics. She spent over four hours going through all of the data she had, checking the difference between what she had and what Chris #2 had downloaded to her in the transmittal from the nanorobots. Finally, she saw the answer. She had indeed done harm in her escape and something no human was supposed to ever do by leaving her own reality for another. There were so many physical laws she had broken. Escape was never to be seen as an option. There were so many breaks in the fiber of the universe by her one trip, yet Chris #2 had patiently repaired all but two. The two he did not repair could not be repaired and they alone could destroy everything. How was this man so knowledgeable of all of this? And what could be done now? How could this damage be repaired?

While Anna Marie #6 was handling her crisis, Chris #2 teleported Chris and Anna Marie #1 to his plane and they walked to the airport ticket counter and cashed in their tickets. They arrived back at the hut just before Anna Marie #6 walked into the living room.

Anna Marie #6 walked into the living room and saw Chris #2 on the couch. She sat down on the chair opposite him and looked into his eyes. "Thank you for repairing all of the breeches that you have. I see what I should have done and I see the complexity of the multi-reality universe; at least most of it. I do not know how I could ever understand it all."

"You are welcome, Anna Marie. No, we cannot understand it all, nor were we ever intended to understand. We were never intended to change realities."

"May I speak?" asked Chris #1.

"Sure," said Chris #2.

"Anna Marie, Chris, we did not intend to mislead you. Yes, we are missionaries. Anna Marie is a third-year college student with a major in Biblical Counseling. I am in Seminary and will graduate while home on furlough. As to our intelligence, we are not as simple as you may think. We understand the physics about what you are speaking and the responsibility you have concerning it. And, I believe it is possible for this to be rectified. You two apparently have the knowledge of the sciences and just need to balance that knowledge with not only restraint, but also with great discernment."

Chris #1 looked at his wife and asked, "Are you ready to volunteer for whatever it takes to put our universe back in order?"

Anna Marie #1 replied, "I trust you on this, husband dear."

Chris #1 then asked Chris #2, "When do you want to start the implant process?"

"I think the best way to handle the growth of the implants is to do it while we are on the way to Greenville. I will take the jet at a normal speed refueling in Hawaii and California. We can experiment with true stealth modes later. The inside of the jet has been reconfigured to state rooms and there will be sufficient privacy." He turned to Anna Marie #6. "Anna Marie, I have also already registered you with the necessary island identification. I used my wife two months ago to register you. The accident will occur on June 5, so we have a few months to train."

"So, the date of the accident is already known, as well as the time and place?" asked Anna Marie #6.

"Yes," said Chris #2.

"And there is no way to stop the accident?" asked Anna Marie #1.

"I wish there were," said Chris #2.

"I do not understand all of this, but I have to trust you as you have been correct in everything so far. Tell me what to do, please," said Anna Marie #6.

"Anna Marie, here is your passport and identity card. So, do you want to wear a wig or have your hair dyed?"

"I beg your pardon?" Anna Marie #6 said as she reached for her passport. "This says Joanne Baxter, and that is not me. Also, the age is listed as eighteen."

"Yes, it is. That is my Anna Marie with a blonde wig and glasses. You remember I had two months to plan and you jumped in only a few minutes. Regarding the age, I felt it best we record our ages in this reality as legal ages. I am twenty-one and, as you see, you are eighteen. I already dyed my hair once, now I need Anna Marie #1 to do it for me again."

"But how did you know I would jump here?"

"I just knew. I don't know how else to explain."

"Anna Marie, I cut hair and would be glad to cut yours and dye it for you," said Anna Marie #1.

"Well, okay, I guess. Let's get to it."

Two hours later Joanne Baxter stood in the Beckett's living room along with her employer, Joshua Robinson. His hair was dyed black and he was also wearing glasses. He was dressed in a black suit with a blue tie, and Ms. Baxter with her blonde hair and glasses was in a grey ladies' dress suit with matching pumps. One would not guess they looked anything like Chris and Anna Marie.

"Joshua, I have a couple of questions," said Chris #1. "If you knew ahead of time all that was going to happen, why did you not just prevent it? And if you knew all of this was going to happen, why did you let Chris take your wife?"

"Good questions. First, I did not know it was going to happen. I sensed it could happen; sort of like an imagination in your mind. It was not real until Anna Marie jumped. There was still the chance she wouldn't have jumped. I could not interfere before as that would reveal to her it was true that there were multiple realities. Second, I did not know Chris was going to take my wife or the others. That was somehow hidden from me. I think if I had known I might have acted rashly."

"While I hear what you are saying, I am not sure I understand most of it," Joanne interjected.

"Welcome to the club, Joanne," Said Chris #1.

Joshua knew Chris and Anna Marie had to say goodbye to their friends in the village, so he told them where and when they would meet at the airport in the morning. Joshua picked up his bag, asked Joanne to pick hers up and take his other hand, and said, "Ms. Baxter, this will be different. Just trust me." And they disappeared.

"Whoa," said Joanne as she materialized inside Joshua's plane. "That *was* different."

"Yes, and helpful also. The natives would not have understood your transformation nor my presence."

"Where are we, a hotel?"

"No, we are in your state room of the plane. I shall go to mine and we can discuss things later. Please get settled. This is your home for at least five months."

"What exactly happened just now?"

"That, Ms. Baxter, was proper temporal displacement; the ability to move through time and space using the earth's geomagnetic and gravitational fields, and the solar wind in the same time period without causing a reverse effect. We call it teleporting."

"I did not know we could move through our own reality that easily. It was difficult when I teleported to my room and then to my parents' home."

"Yes, and there were consequences from those two teleports which I have already repaired. We will begin lessons as soon as Chris and Anna Marie from this reality have their implants in place. Each of you as well as the two Chris's we meet on June 5 will have to learn all of these matters, and much more if we expect to save the universe. I'll see you for dinner in the lounge in one hour."

"Yes, sir."

"Anna Marie, a simple 'Yes, Chris' is fine. I didn't detect sarcasm in the tone, so I believe you said it as a formality. 'Yes, Chris' or 'Yes, Joshua,' will be fine at all times. I do not want you to be intimidated or to be bitter, understood?"

"Yes, Joshua, I understand."

"Good, I will see you at dinner."

CHAPTER 4

LESSONS AND WORLD TRAVEL

Chris and Anna Marie #1 had arrived on time the next day as planned and settled in their state room. Joshua and Joanne had a meeting with them the next day at which they were injected and all went well with the transformation. They flew to Greenville as planned and Chris and Anna Marie #1 checked in with their mission board and explained they had met a new friend who was taking them on a trip before settling in for studies.

Joshua now had the plane on auto pilot and it was flying in stealth mode around the world. It was a plane like no other. It had no internal combustion engine, no hydraulics, and all moving parts were controlled by Chris's mind and a computer on board. The flight deck had countless gauges and dials that made the plane look normal should someone of authority enter for inspection. Most were irrelevant to the operation of the plane. Everyone was enjoying breakfast together and conversation was light and friendly.

After a while, Joshua said, "When we finish breakfast we will begin our lessons. It will go very slowly and if some of you get ahead of me I ask you slow down and wait for my detailed instructions.

"Okay, I want each of you to sit in your chairs with your feet on the deck. For reason of a starting point, take both hands, place one on each knee like you see me doing. Now, touch the forefinger and the thumb, leaving the other three fingers on or near the knee. Sit up right. That's it. Now, search for all of the bands of energy from the sun: radio waves, microwaves, infrared light, visible light, ultraviolet light, gamma rays, and X-rays. Seek to bring them into your consciousness, recognizing each band for what it is. Just look at them, do not try to capture them, just be aware of them. They are all around you. When you locate them in your consciousness, check them off, release them and locate them again. Do this for the next hour, focusing on each different wave as an understanding of the fact you are surrounded by each and every particle of light energy."

They all followed Joshua's instruction and over the course of the next hour located all the waves around them. At the end of the hour his voice brought them back from their concentration.

"Okay, focus on us. Take away the focus on the lights and energies."

Chris and Anna Marie #1 both expressed awe at what they had seen. Joanne said, "I didn't take delight in them before. I had a task set before me and I did not see their beauty. The waves and colors are so vivid."

"Thank you for that observation, Joanne. You are right, we can miss the beauty of anything God has created for our enjoyment if we do not focus on its individual characteristics and design. Now, lesson number two. From the sun there is something the scientists call the solar wind. It is the connection between the sun and the earth. It includes all star radiations. I want you to find the wind, watch the wind, and then capture all of the sun's energies while you have it. Practice this for the next hour, please."

Joshua kept instructing the team for the next several hours. He was training them to be able to teleport themselves within their own reality and also to help them work in different realities, which they would have to do on their mission. Once they understood everything with relationship to the earth and quantum and temporal physics they would be able to teleport properly.

After a while, Joshua broke the silence. "Okay, it's time for dinner. How about French cuisine in Paris, France?"

Everyone looked at Joshua with surprised looks, and he just smiled and said, "I have booked reservations at a nice little restaurant at the Eiffel Tower. We will be landing at the Charles de Gaulle Airport in about thirty minutes. I took the liberty of choosing dressy outfits for us all. You will find yours on your beds. A limousine will pick us up at the airport and return us at the end of the evening. Before we go, you need to learn how to communicate with one another through telepathy. Joanne, call me, please."

Joanne tried to locate Joshua in her head and to her surprise, she found him. "Hello, Joshua," she said telepathically.

"Hello, Joanne," Joshua returned.

Chris and Anna Marie #1 had found each other easily, so then Chris tried to communicate with Joshua. "Do you hear me?"

"Yes, I do, Chris."

Anna Marie and Joanne were communicating and then Joshua surprised them all with their being able to hear him and each other all at once as he connected them together.

"Now, you need to understand that should we get separated for any reason you can contact me easily. Please go get ready."

Joshua was ready in record time and went to the flight deck to communicate with the control tower and to land the plane as if it were a normal plane. This included the activation of the sounds of a jetliner coming in for a landing. Once landed, he taxied the airplane to a hanger on the outskirts of the airport at the freight area and taxied into the hanger. A limousine was waiting at the door and the driver opened the door for the ladies. "Before we leave, do each of you have your IDs and passports?" Each nodded affirmative.

The trip to the restaurant was uneventful except for the faces of the passengers in the car who had never been to Europe, much less Paris. They arrived at the base of the Eiffel Tower and Joshua escorted everyone over to the elevator. He instructed the guide in perfect French to take them to the 58 Tour Eiffel Restaurant at the top of the tower. By now everyone was excited beyond measure. When they reached the restaurant, Joshua asked the maître d' for reservations for the party of Joshua Robinson, again in perfect French. They were escorted to a beautiful table at the edge of the tower overlooking the city and given menus which were, of course, in French. Joshua spoke to them in their minds and told them they now had an opportunity to practice French as they were to each give his/her own order. They all did so with perfect ease, the dinner was delicious, and just as they were finishing the skyline lit up with beautiful aerial fireworks which lasted about fifteen minutes. They then ordered desserts and after everyone had their fill Joshua suggested they head for the car. Again, they were escorted royally to the limousine and were dropped off at the Odeon Theatre where a concert was just about to begin. They arrived back at the airport at 1:30 in the morning, completely exhausted but riding on cloud nine.

"I do not know how to thank you for this evening out. My wife and I never had a honeymoon, and this felt like a fairy tale. Thank you, Joshua, very much. It was a lovely evening; one we will treasure in our memories," said Chris #1.

"You are welcome, Chris and Anna Marie. It was a pleasure to serve you in this way. The weeks and months ahead will be stressful so I felt this was a good getaway, one of several I hope to assist with along the way."

They had reached the plane, and Joanne turned and shook Joshua's hand and simply said, "Thank you for a lovely evening."

CHAPTER 5

FEBRUARY 2, 1963, SATURDAY, 8 A.M.
GREENVILLE, SC

The team had been in Greenville since the middle of January. Training had continued. Joshua was residing on his plane at the Donaldson Center Airport. He had rented a large hanger and had a limousine and driver at his disposal. Joanne was staying at the Koch residence in Greenville and Chris and Anna Marie were staying at the Beckett residence. Joshua had asked for everyone to teleport to the lounge of the plane at 9 a.m. for a brunch meeting.

They arrived at precisely the same time to find the room decorated with balloons and streamers and a birthday cake reading, "Happy Birthday Anna Marie and Joanne." The girls were surprised as Chris and Joshua sang "Happy Birthday" to them. A limousine was in the parking area and Chris and Joshua took the girls out to a nice place for breakfast. While there Joanne was returning from the ladies room and a man asked her if she was available for dating. She told him "no" and returned to the table. She was shaking when she sat down and Chris #1 asked her what was wrong.

"That's the third time within two weeks someone has asked me for a date. I am not interested in dating. I don't know what I want, but I don't want to be dating anyone, and certainly not a stranger."

"Why don't you wear your diamond as an engagement ring?" asked Anna Marie #1. "If anyone asks just point to the ring."

"That's a good idea," said Joanne as she changed the ring to her left hand. Once they were back on the plane, Joshua asked everyone to sit down for them to discuss the plans for the rescue of Chris #4 from reality 437266 and Chris #3 from 437267.

"Our next lesson is going to be on stealth management. Basically, we are going to learn how to make ourselves invisible. Now you see me, now you don't." And Joshua disappeared. Chris #1 walked over to where he was and moved his hand around only to find there was nothing there. "Yes, I am here, but you cannot see me nor can you feel me." With that said, Joshua rematerialized exactly from where he had disappeared. "There are computer algorithms, formulas you must learn in order to do this. Because you have an implant you have a computer to compute the formulas quickly. You couple that together with your understanding of the entire spectrum of light, and your ability to manipulate light sequences, and you have the ability to disappear. Now, why is this important? When Chris #3 and #4 have their accident, you will need to assist in allowing both of us, Chris #1 and myself, to appear as Chris #3 and #4 but only to opposite groups. Chris #4's group sees their Chris as injured and not the other Chris who is working over his body to save him. And likewise, to the other group; so as far as the groups, they see only their injured Chris and not us while we save them. You, Joanne, will be maintaining the opening for the plane between both realities just above the accident. The accident will be caused by the cortex rupture of the two realities. We are going to use a program on the plane's computer to keep that rupture from expanding and to close it. We will have approximately five minutes to do everything. You, Joanne, will be in two realities at once and in the stealth mode. You will have to work a little harder but you will be assisted by the plane's computer. Anna Marie, you will be helping your Chris in his stealth project. I will be able to handle my project alone. Does everyone understand the principle of what we are going to have to do?"

No one said anything so he continued. "If not, we will practice, practice, practice until we get it perfect. We have no room for error. We will put nanorobots into each Chris so they will be kept alive until their operations and then they will be able to help us in the future. Now, before that project, we need to go to each reality in the stealth mode and find and prepare a Dr. Jeff McNealy, one from each reality, so they will be available to operate on Chris #3 and Chris #4 repairing their skulls and inserting the implants. Each doctor will need to be injected and introduced to

WPPA. Yes, we are going to need to manipulate the timeline in these two realities in order for the mission to be accomplished."

"Wow," said Joanne. "Is this the only way to deal with what is going to happen?"

"I don't know," said Joshua. "I only know I have run many different scenarios through my mind and that of my super computer. I have not come up with any other solution that will keep the two Chris's alive and, at the same time, give us someone with enough power to overcome Chris from your reality. Your neural implant design is the best one in existence. It is perfect, and with the programming from my nanorobots it will operate most efficiently. With three more implants like that we should be able to repair all the damage caused by you and Chris."

"Wait, you said three more implants. I know about the two Chris's we are going to save on June 5th."

"That is correct, Joanne, along with one of their two Anna Marie's as well."

"I don't understand, Joshua."

"One Anna Marie is going to almost die and need brain surgery. The other Anna Marie will receive nanorobots in an attempt to give blood to her Chris who will be at the point of death in 1972."

Joanne was stunned. She staggered with the weight of what she had just heard and sat down on a couch quickly. Anna Marie was by her side in an instant and took her hand to comfort her.

"Joshua, you are speaking ten years from now. I thought we were recruiting to take care of this at least late this year."

"I did not mean to deceive you; I just never found the right time to tell you that Chris's power will not wane enough for us to take control until early 1973. Please believe me when I say this is as painful, if not more so for me, since my Anna Marie is already my wife."

Joanne did not respond, she just sat there allowing Anna Marie to comfort her with her presence. Finally, she said "I must go back to the Koch's house. Please excuse me."

CHAPTER 6

Two weeks had passed since Joanne left the meeting with the other members of the team. They had respected her privacy and not pushed her. They had knocked on the door, but no one had teleported in on her or tried to contact her through the link they all had. The team was assembled in the plane for further training when she materialized in their presence.

"Good morning, everyone. Joshua, I want to ask for your forgiveness again. I have tried to think of another way out of this mess and cannot come up with any other plan. I know I am responsible for the damage you are trying to repair. Chris and Anna Marie I am so sorry you have been dragged into this. Joshua, please fill me in on what I have missed and give me a schedule for the next meetings. I am committed to following your orders and I am resigned to my outcast status from my reality. I will attempt to do all of my duties to the best of my ability and pledge myself to not fail you as much as it relies upon me."

"We forgive you," said Chris and Anna Marie together as they gave Joanne a hug.

"I forgive you also," said Joshua, as he rose from his chair and shook Joanne's hand. "Now let's get back to training."

"Joshua, before we do, I need a private time with Joanne, please," asked Anna Marie.

"Can't it wait?" asked Joshua.

"No, it's urgent," said Anna Marie as she took Joanne's hand and they disappeared.

Joshua looked at Chris and asked, "What was that about?"

"Joshua, when Anna Marie and I hugged Joanne we could feel her ribs. I believe she hasn't eaten for two weeks. Whether it has been fasting or grief, I don't know. Anna Marie told me through telepathy she was going to see if we need to get Joanne to a hospital or not."

Anna Marie and Joanne were at the Koch residence. "Please forgive me for intruding, but, Joanne, have you been fasting?"

With a blush, Joanne replied, "Yes, a food fast, but not a liquid fast."

"So, you are not dehydrated?"

"No, and I did have a piece of toast and some apple juice this morning as I broke the fast. Why are you so concerned?"

"Joanne, we are not overweight, and when I hugged you I could feel your ribs."

"Yes, I know. I did loose ten pounds and I know I need to put some of it back on," Joanne said with a blush and a giggle.

"So, you do feel alright and ready for training?"

"Yes, I do, and thank you for your concern." Joanne said as she hugged Anna Marie.

They reached for each other's hands and teleported to the plane where they found Joshua and Chris just finishing prayer.

CHAPTER 7

Joshua was flying the plane in stealth mode and was monitoring every known measurement he could. He was able to see the thinness of the cortex through the computer image over the road. He turned to the assembled team and explained what was going to happen.

"When the two cars being driven by the two Chris men of realities 437266 and 437267 hit the exact spot at the exact same moment with the cortex being so thin a rupture will occur. Both Chris's will be severely injured. Our goal is to assist these two men while help is on the way so they will be healed and not die. We are also here to prevent the cortex rupture from expanding and destroying these two realities, and quite possibly the universe. Here is the plan:

"Joanne, you will be holding the cortex edges with the plane's computer on full power which will help you keep the rift small so it can repair itself. We will have about five minutes before the repair will be made. You'll need to sense when to transport your passengers on board and move the plane to one reality or the other before anyone gets left behind or trapped with their covers blown. You have the most important responsibility, carrying with it the largest consequence should you fail by making an error of any type.

"I will be helping Chris #3 in reality 437267. My goal is to inject the nanorobots without being seen and to stop the bleeding from the head wound so the loss of blood will be as little as possible. I will be using my stealth mode so reality 437266 sees their Chris as injured, while at the same time the passengers from 437267 will only see their injured Chris while Chris and Anna Marie #1, also using stealth mode, help him. We actually will be hiding each injured Chris from the opposite reality and cloaking ourselves in such a way that only one reality sees us. It will be tricky."

CHAPTER 8

The accident happened right on time as Joshua had predicted. As time progressed in the incident, Joanne was holding the rift as tight as she could with the plane's computer and her own abilities that Joshua had taught her to use properly over the past few months. They had practiced and practiced some more and she had become very proficient in controlling the gravitational and other metaphysical energy forces. Currently she was doing a good job and the rest of the team was performing their duties perfectly. Both best friends of each Chris, Kenneth Knight, were hovering over their friends, causing the ability to inject the nanorobots by both team members to be rather risky of being discovered. Joanne, seeing what was going on, signaled mentally to both teams to be ready as she was about to do something not practiced. Both realities suddenly saw a bright light above them and their attention was diverted to the light while the two teams made the injections. Just as the rift closed the teams made it back on board and they were in reality 437266. They watched as the ambulance carried Chris to the hospital. Joshua turned to Joanne.

"That was a brilliant move. It gave us the perfect timing to inject. You did well, Joanne. I am proud of you. And you, Chris and Anna Marie, you performed your jobs perfectly. Now, Joanne, I am going to trust you to take us to 436341. Do you believe you are up to the challenge?"

"You know what, I do. Let's go." With that being said, she quickly teleported them and the plane to the correct reality without causing any disturbance in the universe.

CHAPTER 9

Over the next ten years the team monitored the lives of the members of 437266 and 437267 realities. They made a couple of visits, but mostly left them alone. Joshua continued to monitor Anna Marie's home looking for the time they could enter there. He had earlier been blocked from even viewing that reality, but he had found a way to do so and Chris #6 was not aware of the observance. The team trained for the time they would confront Chris #6, but they also took the time to work with Chris and Anna Marie #1 as they served in the church they had built on the island. Joshua and Joanne became a vital part of the church family and each had their own huts in the village. They kept their singleness, and even though well-meaning natives tried to get them together, they resisted gently and with devout remembrance of who they were and their goals of being reunited with their own friends and families in their own realities. Joshua and Joanne also invested in businesses worldwide, each amassing a significant amount of money. They found time to go to college and medical school where Joanne was trained and certified in brain surgery and Joshua trained in general surgery. Joshua and Joanne also decided to go to law school, and each received a law degree with the ability to practice corporate and criminal law.

"I believe I am going to give my money to Chris and Anna Marie for their ministry," Joanne said one fall night late in 1972.

"I think that is a good idea. I believe I will do the same. I know it will help the cause of Christianity worldwide in this reality if they continue to invest and then give it away properly. How can we do it without it causing them to pay lot of taxes?"

"Maybe they have a suggestion for an accountant; we could set up a trust fund, or leave them full control? Maybe we should ask them?" suggested Joanne.

"That is a great idea. And thank you for dinner tonight; it was delicious. I hope we don't get the natives talking and plotting again."

"Well, having dinner on the porch and not going inside should have helped them understand we are not in a private, personal relationship. Also, we have each told them time and again you are married; they can see the ring, and I have worn my engagement ring on the left hand to let them know not to find anyone else for me."

"That should be true, Joanne, but people will be people."

"Joshua, I remember every day what Chris said when I left. I cannot get over the pain of what he said."

"What did he say, Joanne?"

"He said, 'No, Anna Marie! Please don't leave me, I need you!'" Joanne suddenly broke down in tears. Joshua attempted to comfort her, but nothing he said seemed to help. Quickly and quietly he started to pray and ask God to give her the strength she needed, in spite of all the circumstances, to carry through with the plan to return to Chris and rectify the situation. After awhile, she calmed down and thanked him for his prayers and comfort. She then said goodnight and went inside. He stayed for a few moments, praying for the mission in general and then went to his hut.

CHAPTER 10

Joshua, Joanne, Chris, and Anna Marie were in Chris's hut when Joshua made an announcement.

"I had found a way to monitor Joanne's home reality and have been watching it for some time. There is a battle about to happen and we need to pick up our other team members and be ready. I believe the time will be very soon and we will be able to finish this task and get back to our lives. Not that Joanne and I have not enjoyed our time here, it is just that we miss being in our home realities and I have missed my wife very much. We will leave here in the plane on February 24 at noon. We will go to Realities 437266 and 437267 to pick up the rest of the team and then we will wait near the cortex for the right moment to enter 437269."

"Joshua, is Chris in any danger?" asked Joanne.

"I won't lie to you, Joanne. Yes, he is. Our timing has to be perfect or he may die."

Joanne's hands went to her mouth as Anna Marie came to her.

"Consequences" is concluded in "In The Nick of Time" book 5. You need to read "The Trap" book 3 and "The Unexpected Storm" book 4 in order to understand the complete story.

BOOK 3
THE TRAP

CHAPTER 1

JUNE 5, 1963
REALITY: 437267

Chris Beckett had just graduated from Aiken High School and was on a double date with his best friend, Kenneth Knight. They were traveling on Vaucluse Road from Aiken to LBC (Langley, Bath, Clearwater) to return Chris's date home when the car was hit by another vehicle traveling at terrific speeds. Kenneth and the two girls escaped injury, but Chris had several severe injuries. He came to momentarily in the operating room at Aiken County Hospital to hear someone telling the surgeons, "I do not care what hospital protocol says, he will be provided better care at The Worldwide People Protection Agency Medical Facility in England. The helicopter is waiting to take him to the airport; tell these doctors to make him stable for the trip."

Chris's last thought was confusion about what he had to do with the WPPA before he lost consciousness.

AUGUST 6, 1963: AT AN UNDISCLOSED LOCATION IN EUROPE.

When Chris awoke this morning, Commander George Whitfield, the director of the WPPA, was in his room. When Commander Whitfield saw Chris was awake he began to speak.

"Chris, I know you are not sufficiently recovered yet, and you still have many questions. I hope to answer most of them now. You are doing well with the physical rehabilitation as well as the operation/function of the implants. I would like to brief you on the circumstances that brought you here. Kenneth Knight had been recruited for our agency and was instrumental in your receiving the medical attention you needed after the horrific accident and in your recruitment to our agency. The accident has been covered up and no one knows of it except for the passengers in the vehicle and a small number of police and emergency personnel who were sworn to secrecy. As far as they are concerned you and Kenneth were not even in the vehicles. All occupants in the offending vehicle were dead on arrival. That took a lot of manipulation and much paper work. Your parents were notified that you and Kenneth decided to take a world tour together and afterward you would enroll in business school in England this winter. Your father was overwhelmed with the news of the scholarships, and your education here keeps you away from prying eyes and ears in the United States for now.

We will give you the full education you need; you will receive a Master's degree in Business Management and a PhD in Global Business Operations if you study hard and listen to what we tell you. Your implants will continue to be upgraded and your cover story will be firmly in place by the time you return to the United States. You are to be fully trained in all forms of martial arts and you will be disciplined in all areas of your occupation as a private investigator, as well as proficient in the use and care of all weapons. You will be able to fly the most modern air machines offered, and in my estimation you will be remarkable!

You are agent number 44 in our staff, and, because of your accident, the best equipped human being in neural-electronics. You are going to be fully trained as an agent for the WPPA and you will act on our behalf when necessary. There is, however, a matter of your spiritual status and we need to discuss that now."

"Why does my spiritual status make a difference?"

"A WPPA agent is very involved with people's lives. We all take our work very seriously. Our agents on the front lines have to make quick decisions that could mean life or death for them or another person. It would not be in your best interest for us to place your life on the line and not have given you the opportunity to have placed your trust in Jesus Christ. Since you are unsaved we…."

"Wait, unsaved? I made a decision at age twelve and was baptized in…."

"Yes, we have that record of your decision, but it was not a heart decision. You mouthed the words, but you did not have true repentance, nor did you really accept the gift of salvation from God. A look at your choices, your words, your entire life since that day—I do not think I have to mention what I am talking about—shows your heart. For now, your first class will be with Dr. Grey, our resident Elder."

AUGUST 25, 1963: STILL AT WPPA HEADQUARTERS

"Now, Chris, you understand why we had you go through this religious study and the need for you to have made the heart change?"

"Yes, Commander Whitfield, I understand, and I thank you for giving me the opportunity to see my sin, repent, and accept Jesus Christ as my Lord and Savior."

"Now, Chris, you are ready for training."

CHAPTER 2

June 30, 1969
At An Undisclosed Airfield in England

"Where are Agents Beckett and Knight?" asked Mr. Whitfield.

"They are in the air, Sir," said his personal assistant, Agent Morton Richfield.

"Doing what?"

"They are engaging in a dog fight like they have been doing since they learned to fly the F16s."

"Who is winning?"

"Neither, Sir, they are equally matched as long as Agent Beckett doesn't cheat by using his implant. Wait, I am receiving a report on my radio…my goodness, Agent Beckett scored a kill on Agent Knight and they are coming in to the airstrip now."

The two walked from the airstrip into the building, talking about the exercise they had just completed. Chris had stopped his F16 at 32,000 feet. Kenneth's F16 rushed by him, He set the missile, aimed, and fired immediately before powering up the engine again. Kenneth was toast as far as the computer was concerned.

"Chris, that was a stupid move. You could have gotten us both killed! What made you do that?"

"Hey, I saw you were above me and I calculated you would not hit me, so I did it. It worked, Kenny. I am sure you would do it if we ever sparred again."

Before Kenneth could retort, an announcement came over the PA.

"Agents Knight and Beckett, report to the director immediately."

They walked into Commander Whitfield's large blue carpeted office and stood at attention. Agent Beckett could see the snow-covered mountains in the distance and the forest outside the agency grounds.

"At ease, men. Agent Beckett, good show; never heard of that move before."

"Thank you, Sir."

"Are you Okay Agent Knight?"

"Yes, Sir, just a little embarrassed. After all, I was taken by a 'Cyborg.'"

"Agent Knight—that was uncalled for," Commander Whitfield chastised.

"Yes, Sir. I am sorry, Chris, will you forgive me?"

"Sure, Kenny, no harm done. And, by the way, I did not use my enhancements," Chris replied.

"Men, I have called you here for your first mission. The man you see on the screen is Mr. James Abernathy, an Englishman who has involved himself in international smuggling of jewels, money laundering for illegal gambling, and human trafficking. As you know, our concern is with the human trafficking most of all. He needs to be taken down, he and his organization; we need an ironclad case. I am asking the two of you to take this case together due to the complexity of the operation and Agent Knight, you are to head up the operation. Agent Beckett, you are to keep your eye camera on at all times since this is your first mission and we want to see its effectiveness in law enforcement."

SEPTEMBER 24, 1969: BIRMINGHAM, ENGLAND

Agent Beckett and Agent Knight were in the office of James Abernathy at his home. Agent Knight was speaking. "Mr. Abernathy, you have heard the charges against you, you have listened as we have spoken to you of your spiritual condition, what do you have to say?"

"I reject what you are trying to offer me. No, I reject what you say your God offers me. In my studies of world religions and so-called gods it is my conclusion that when I die life is over; there is no afterlife and there is no reincarnation, and there is no heaven or hell. When I die that is it. As for your charges, I'll take my chances with the jury."

"There is no jury; you will be tried and sentenced by a WPPA judge according to international law."

"That's not fair, what about my rights?"

"You have no rights as far as the WPPA is concerned; our jurisdiction is above any local laws and the case against you is solid and complete."

Kenneth spoke into his satellite phone and then listened as Director Whitfield had determined the judge would hear the charges the following week. In the meantime, Mr. Abernathy was to be transported to the top-secret maximum-security prison in South Africa.

Agent Knight then said, "You are bound over for trial next week. May God have mercy on your soul." Mr. Abernathy was then transported to the facility by jet with other agents of WPPA.

CHAPTER 3

JANUARY 10, 1972
COLUMBIA, SC

Agents Beckett and Knight had just finished a case in South Carolina and were taking a couple of days' break in Columbia, South Carolina. They were at a diner on Taylor Street enjoying some great home-cooked BBQ.

"Tell me, Kenny, who is this Carmen Coolidge?"

"She is a wonderful, sweet lady."

"Okay, that doesn't tell me who she is. Should I look her up or are you going to tell me?"

"She is a graduate of The University of South Carolina and she is CEO of a non-profit agency that assists those who have been rescued from human-trafficking. I met her when we inquired about placing some individuals we helped in our last case in Alabama. It was love at first sight for both of us."

"Sure, love at first sight! You were just taken by her beauty."

"Yes, I was. Here, look at this picture. Please notice the long auburn hair and the cute button nose. Also, you can't see in the picture, but her eyes are the brightest blue I have ever seen. However, you can see in the picture she is almost as tall as I am. She is 5'11"."

"Yes, Kenny, she is a beautiful girl. Does she know anything about us?"

"No, she does not. She thinks I am just a lawyer with a sympathetic ear—which I am—but no more than that. I do plan on full disclosure way before the wedding. Carmen is visiting this weekend. Why don't we go to dinner Friday and make it a double date. You can bring Rhonda."

"Kenny, how many times do I have to tell you, that woman is not a part of my life."

"Well, you need to tell her that because she is entering the restaurant now, heading straight for you."

Chris stood and turned around quickly. His eyes found those of Rhonda's and he speared her with his look. "Rhonda, how did you know I was here?"

Rhonda took Chris's shoulder and placed a kiss on his cheek. He wiped it away with his napkin. "Your mother told me. Oh! Hello, Kenneth. I heard about the lucky girl who has cornered you. Are wedding plans all set? Maybe we could have a double wedding."

"Rhonda, must I tell you again…."Through his neural implant Chris received a call from central office and politely excused himself from the conversation and left the restaurant. Commander Whitfield met him at a diner on Gervais Street. "Good to see you, Sir. What is this emergency? And what is so important that it takes you from England?"

"There is an organization, The Elect. They call themselves such because they deal in human trafficking while operating as a so-called church, the worse kind of deception. They are a plague to girls as young as age twelve. The leader is Lucifer Jones. He is scheduled to be in Atlanta, Columbia, and Charlotte the two weeks prior to Agent Knight's wedding. Because of Agent Knight's upcoming nuptials in July, I need you to head this case. I have downloaded all information on Mr. Jones to your server and you can access it at your will. I know you will be Agent Knight's best man, but I do not see this as interfering with your part in the wedding plans."

"Are you planning on attending, Sir?"

"Yes, I am."

"Well, it's good to see you, Sir. I'll send you a report as soon as I study all the details," said Chris as he stood and left the restaurant.

CHAPTER 4

JUNE 21, 1972
CHARLOTTE, NC

Agent Beckett had just finished speaking with the District Attorney for the state of North Carolina and was wrapping up the investigation regarding Lucifer Jones. He had already spoken with the Georgia district attorney and would be speaking with the district attorney of South Carolina while he would be in Columbia the week before Agent Knight's wedding. He was returning to his hotel in Charlotte and was in the hotel lobby when he received a signal letting him know his suite had been compromised. He quickly entered the elevator banks and pushed for the top floor where his Presidential Suite was. He noticed from his signal it was one person and that person was in the front bedroom, so he silently entered the second entrance at the dining room. Upon entering his bedroom, he noticed there was a woman going through his chest of drawers. He pulled his revolver and before pointing it at her told her to stop and turn around. She did so and as she turned a very surprised look appeared on her face. Agent Beckett was taken aback by her beauty and the outfit she was wearing; clearly marked for undercover work in black pants, shirt, and an Eisenhower jacket.

"Well, who do we have here?" Agent Beckett had already activated his camera with one blink of his left eye and was waiting for an ID from corporate headquarters.

"You'll get no answer from me," the woman responded.

"And why not?"

"I have a search warrant from the district attorney and I am searching for my company's merchandise."

"May I see the warrant?" Agent Beckett asked.

"I do not have it with me."

"So, you *are* a thief?"

"I am not a thief!" she replied indignantly.

"You obviously think I am. Let me guess, you are room service searching my clothing for stolen bars of soap?"

"That's absurd!"

Agent Beckett received identification from her facial features from headquarters. "Well, Ms. Koch, do what…."

"How do you know my name?" she interjected.

"I know a lot more…."

"How do you know, have you been following me?"

"Ms. Koch, you are in my suite; how do you figure I am following you?"

Miss Anna Marie Koch became quite frustrated and tongue tied; she had been caught checking on a possible lead on some stolen diamonds and now found herself in the room of a person who for all intents and purposes should be dead. She had no idea of the connection between Chris Beckett and the corporation who rented this room. She knew the suite was registered to The Ryder Corporation, but her understanding of that corporation was they took advantage of businesses in financial trouble, so she felt they may also be involved in the diamond smuggling business.

June 6, 1963, Aiken, SC
(Flashback)

Anna Marie arrived at work at 6 a.m. She worked taking care of projects from the day before and set up the office for the day. While sorting papers, she noticed on the Sergeant's desk an accident report from the night before. She listened to the police scanner at night and last night heard a call for ambulances and a coroner, but then a call came back to state it was a hoax; there was no accident. She looked at the report and saw the names and recognized three of them. All three were from her school and had graduated, and of these, two had attended her church. One, in fact was the pastor's daughter. Only one person was injured and he was not expected to live according to the report. She had never met him in person, but she had seen him on campus. She was puzzled by the report and the fact there was no need for ambulances. At 7:30 she headed to the rest room to freshen up for the day. Soon, she heard two men come into the office and they were discussing the accident from the night before. One was saying, "Remember, this accident never happened. The call was a hoax. I am sorry we did not get this copy last night. Who is in here this morning?"

"Anna Marie Koch is our license and tag manager. She sometimes comes in early to get started on the day. That was her car outside," said Sergeant Moore.

"Where is she now?" asked the unnamed agent.

"Probably in the ladies' room."

"Do we need to talk to her?"

"No, she never bothers anything in this office."

"Let's pray she did not this morning!"

Anna Marie had remembered that conversation and what she saw on the accident report until this day. In fact, she had made some inquiries at the hospital, and, after reaching a dead end, felt it was in her best interest to stop asking.

℮   ℮   ℮

Here she was in the same room with the man who supposedly was injured so badly he should have died. Then his death or disappearance was covered up. She sat down on the couch to steel herself.

"Ms. Koch, I understand you are an insurance recovery detective; that is, you recover stolen property for insurance companies."

"That is right, Mr. Beckett."

"Well, you do know who I am," Chris said in a somewhat curious and startled manner.

"You bet I do; everything from your accident in 1963, to your disappearance, and now all of a sudden your reappearance some nine years later."

"Just what accident are you speaking of?" he asked.

"June 5, 1963, Vaucluse Road...."

"Stop. Hold it. Say no more... Edna, did you get that? Speak with Director Whitfield and get back to me."

"Are you on a mobile phone?" Anna Marie asked.

"Ms. Koch, you have no idea."

"Well, I am not going to stick around; I'll be leaving now...." Anna Marie stood and quickly walked toward Agent Beckett. She suddenly grabbed his weapon and turned it on him. He smiled.

"Are you going to shoot me now?"

"I may. Just move so I can leave."

"I do not think so," Agent Beckett said as he grabbed his weapon back, threw it on the bed, slipped Anna Marie's hands behind her, and tied her up with a rope. "How's that for calf roping?"

"I am not a calf, Mr. Beckett."

"Didn't say you were; just speaking of my tying talents. Now, you sit here on the couch while I retrieve my weapon. And for your information, you could not have fired it. It is useable only by my DNA," Chris said with a tinge of pride.

"Your what?"

"It has a failsafe mechanism that recognizes I am holding it and can then be fired."

"Well, that's new technology."

"Yes, it is, now to the point of your being in my room, no weapon, and dressed in burglar clothes, yet non-threatening...."

"You do not find me threatening?" she interrupted.

"No, ma'am, I do not. Attractive, maybe, but not threatening." Anna Marie tried to hold back a blush unsuccessfully. "Ms. Koch, you apparently think I am someone I am not, yet you do wonder about where I have been since my accident and what have I been doing? In the few minutes since I have met you I have learned much about you and am very pleased with what I have learned, so, I am going to tell you an interesting story. A lot will be hard to understand and much will be highly classified, so I will expect your honor of not repeating this information to anyone, please. Do you agree?"

Anna Marie crossed her fingers and said, "I will not disclose the information you share with me."

"Thank you. Yes, you see me using a communication device; it is linked directly to my brain. I have a camera in my left eye. That is how I was able to identify you so quickly with my home office in Liverpool, England. I have been in discussion with the office all the while we have been speaking. I can communicate through brain waves connected to the magnetic field of the planet. I have made a proposal to them about our encounter and am waiting for the director to approve my plan. I can only ascertain you did look at that document on the Sergeant's desk on June 6, 1963. That, coupled with your photographic memory and naturally curious instincts gave you the information you needed to determine in your mind I was linked up with something foul."

"Secretive," she corrected.

"Okay, secretive. Why you slated my suite for search is a mystery."

"I did not know the suite was yours. I only knew it was in a foreign company's registration."

"You mean 'The Ryder Corporation' from England?"

"Yes, a multinational corporation that buys other corporations when they are in trouble."

"That is correct, but it is all legitimate work. It is not secretive in a bad way," he paused. "Anna Marie, I have now received approval to proceed and here comes the rest of the story you may not want to hear. The company you are working for, Liberty National Insurance, asked you to recover jewels from a robbery that occurred this year in Denver, Colorado. The jewels were insured for $4.5 million dollars. Do you know the chairman of the board for the company for whom you are working?"

"No, it never crossed my mind to need to know."

"I am the chairman of the board for Liberty National Insurance."

"No way."

"If I take off the rope and ask you to stay and talk with me and have a couple of phone conversations to understand who I am, will you remain calm and not try to run or beat me up?" Chris asked.

"Why should I want to listen to you?"

"Because it is in your best interest to do so. I have a proposition I believe you will not want to refuse."

"Okay, I am curious Mr. Beckett. Untie me and tell me who to call," Anna Marie said.

"Make a call to the person you report to at the insurance company and just ask him who is the Chairman of the Board." Chris waited after he untied her while she called and found out he was correct.

"Now, in about fifteen seconds your phone is going to ring and it is going to be your dad. He works for the Savannah River Plant in Aiken and has a fairly high security clearance."

Anna Marie's phone began ringing. "Hello, Anna Marie, this is your dad calling. Are you in some kind of trouble?"

"Hi, Dad. You could say I am in a difficult situation."

"Honey, I was called by a high-ranking official in my line of work and he told me you are in a hotel room in Charlotte with Chris Beckett, Jr."

"Yes, that is correct," she said.

"Are you being held against your will? If I have to get the local police involved, I will."

"No, that is not necessary. I believe I have it under control."

"As long as you are sure you are okay."

"I am. Why did you call?"

"I was told to tell you Christopher has the highest security clearance next to the President of the United States. He works for the WPPA. Whatever it is he is telling you or has told you, if he says it is the truth then it is the truth. I was told you needed to hear this from someone you trust; I guess that is me. But, if there is something wrong, I need to know."

"Thank you, Dad, and no, there is nothing wrong." After a short conversation with her dad, Anna Marie ended the call and turned to Chris.

"Okay, Mr. Beckett, what do you have to tell me?"

"As an agent for WPPA I am here on an assignment concerning a Mr. Lucifer Jones. I know through my investigation that his organization stole the jewels in question. My investigation, however, goes beyond stolen jewels. Our organization hopes to eradicate human trafficking. Mr. Jones is very heavily involved in that vice in the United States with connections in Europe and Asia as well. I am going to travel to South Carolina soon to deliver my report to the District Attorney of South Carolina. I had a visit earlier today with the DA here in North Carolina. The purpose of the reporting is to allow the DA to bring charges against many people involved in Jones' organization and to free several hundred unfortunate souls trapped in their grip through 'The Elect,' a cultic church."

"I had Mr. Jones in my list of suspects as well. I have notes in my car that may help you."

"Thank you, I would appreciate your continued assistance in this investigation."

"Now, Mr. Beckett, I have heard people who come under the surveillance of WPPA are never brought to trial; they either are found dead or they disappear. No one can prove this, but there is this awe and fear among many people. Why would you be working with the DAs?"

"Ms. Koch, I do not give you enough credit; my apology. What you state is the normal way things happen. They are brought to trial through international jurisdiction at an undisclosed location and incarcerated in a secure secret prison. Those who are found dead are those who resist and our agents are very good marksmen. We hope to resolve that in the near future as we have a new weapon that does not kill but incapacitates and allows for easy transfer to the prison. As for this particular case, we have a cultist church involved. We have to be careful how we handle this and that is why the DAs are involved. Mr. Jones might wind up dead and he might disappear. That is a decision he will make. It will be his choice, I assure you."

"Thank you for letting me know who you are and for the information regarding Mr. Jones; I will leave the package at the front desk. I pray I do not see you in the future. Now, may I leave?" Anna Marie asked.

"Ms. Koch, I have divulged some top-secret information to you and you are in possession of some level of knowledge that could jeopardize my life. So, no, you may not leave. We have some further business to discuss."

"Mr. Beckett!"

"Please, hear me out. You have a job to finish. Your assignment is technically involved with mine. You have information that is highly classified therefore I need you to finish hearing me out."

"Okay, talk, but I am getting hungry."

"Fine, I'll call room service," he acquiesced.

"I am not eating in a stranger's hotel room."

"Well, you were going through this stranger's unmentionables an hour ago!"

Ms. Koch blushed again as she lowered her head hoping Mr. Beckett would not see.

"Ms. Koch, before you or I go anywhere, I need to finish my conversation with you. In order to go anywhere you must submit to a vow of silence and allow me to place a tracker in you should you be kidnapped."

"What? That is bizarre!"

Chris rubbed his temple. "This is becoming more difficult than I thought. Please let me explain. In my entire plan I have worked out with headquarters as we have been speaking...."

"And that is another thing, how are you speaking with headquarters when you have not left my presence and I have not heard any other conversation going on? And where is your mobile phone?"

Chris rubbed his head again and muttered under his breath, "What was I thinking; this isn't going to work."

He heard his assistant chuckle and he mentally asked her, *What is so funny?*"

"You really want me to tell you, or are you in denial?"

"No, I know you have seen my accelerated heart rate and you know I am attracted to this woman. You know she frustrates me; I even have trouble enunciating clearly."

Anna Marie waved her hand in front of Chris's face; "Mr. Beckett, are you in there?"

Chris gave her a hard look and asked her to sit back down.

"You blanked out, so tell me really what is going on. I will forgo my hunger for now, but only because I am an extremely curious person."

"You need to know, Ms. Koch, Anna Marie, if I may be so bold… from the moment I saw you a little over an hour ago I have been attracted to you. I want to get to know you. Oh, I have your profile and life history, but I want to get to know *you.*"

"Mr. Beckett, I am flattered, but men do not fit into my life. I also found you to be somewhat attractive when I turned around; even though I have seen pictures of you, I have never been in your presence, so I am affected. How, and why, I do not know. But I will not give you the privilege of finding out if this meeting needs to turn into a relationship. I have decided God has left me single and I am going to remain single for my entire life. I have no interest in saddling myself with a man; especially one as arrogant as you."

"So, you plan to be a spinster. Are you a cat lady? No, you are a dog lady; Old English Sheepdogs, to be exact."

She gave Chris a small smile, her first since they met, and he melted.

"Please follow me," said Chris.

The suite was a large suite, and they left the master bedroom to go toward the other bedroom. There was a door to the left which entered the dining room. It was through the outside door to this room Chris entered when he found her in his bedroom.

"Oh, there are two entrances," Anna Marie said to herself.

As they entered the room, Anna Marie noticed the smell of fresh cooked food. There on the table were two settings and covered food plates. Chris pulled out a chair and offered the place to her. She sat down and placed her hands in her lap, totally confused.

"I took the liberty of ordering your favorite food."

"And what might that be?"

"Grilled shrimp with no seasoning, broccoli, spinach salad with raspberry vinaigrette dressing, and sweet potato French fries on the side. Iced tea is in the pitcher. Ketchup is in the container to the left."

Anna Marie was now in total shock and decided to listen to whatever this man had to say.

As he sat, he asked if he could pray for the food and the meeting. Again, she was shocked, so all she did was nod her head yes. After the prayer Mr. Beckett began talking.

"There is nothing in your background, in your vital signs, or in your way of life that gives me any qualms about sharing what I am about to share with you. You will need to sign some documents when we are finished to become an official agent in training for WPPA and to vow not to disclose this information upon severe penalty. Regardless of your noninterest in men you are a highly-qualified individual and your country, no, WPPA needs your expertise and experience." He paused, and when he saw Anna Marie listening attentively he continued.

"On June 5, 1963, I was the driver in a car that was involved in a very horrific accident. Our vehicle was struck from the left side at the driver's door by another car of the same make, color, and year model. In fact, when the state patrolman arrived he noticed he was looking at twins of the drivers and passengers of the cars."

"That was Officer Atkinson."

"Yes, it was. The rest of this happened while I was unconscious, but I was told before the ambulances arrived, some five minutes after the accident the other car and all of the people from it disappeared. Not before Kenny and the two girls…."

"Your dates and your friend," Anna Marie interrupted.

"…could speak to them for a short while. What we have determined is they were from a different time and space reality."

"You are speaking science fiction now."

"No, this is true. There have been enough substantiated reports and interviews to ascertain that indeed there are many different realities.

However, this is the only record where there has been an actual breech in physical dimension. All of the rest of the reports have been those in which one has crossed over mentally and then returned. In those encounters the people in the other reality do not even know they are being observed."

"And you expect me to believe this?" she asked.

"No, you do not have to, but you just need to know I was in a severe accident and who and what I am now is a result of that accident," he replied.

"Please proceed. By the way, thank you, this shrimp is delicious."

"You are welcome."

"Kenneth Knight was a graduate of Aiken High and friend of yours. He was the other male in the car," Anna Marie said.

"Yes, Kenny had been recruited by WPPA and had already been inducted. He had a mobile phone…."

"No mental hook up to communicate?" she asked sarcastically.

"No, I will explain that as I go along. Anyway, Kenny saw I was in pretty bad shape, made a call to WPPA headquarters, and explained what was going on."

"No one else was injured?"

"No, no one else was injured. In fact, the driver of the other car, who apparently looked just like me, came over and gave me medical attention. I attribute him with saving my life. Kenneth and the girls, other than being shook up by the encounter with their alternate beings, were okay. Back to the story: I was transported by ambulance to the local hospital in Aiken. There it was determined that not only did I have severe head injuries, but there was also body trauma, and both my arms and legs were broken multiple times. There was a tremendous loss of blood, and they gave me several units of blood to keep me alive. I was then transported to a military hospital in Alabama where some temporary surgeries took place and then taken to Liverpool, England, the headquarters for WPPA and their top-secret medical research facility. I won't tell you everything right now because it will all seem to come from a science fiction movie, however, suffice it to say I am more of a Cyborg than a human being."

"You say that rather flippantly. Is that how you feel about yourself?"

"No, not really, but let me begin by saying my left eye has a camera that can be turned on at the blink of an eye. Like I said earlier, that was how I identified you by sending an image to headquarters. It is fully operational to send visuals that cannot be seen by the naked eye; something up to the distance of four miles as if you were next door. I can type a word document, communicate with my personal assistant, dial a phone number, drive a car, and handle a conversation like you and I are handling without so much as breaking a sweat."

"So, what are you doing right now?"

"Anna Marie—you never did say it was okay to call you by your given name—I am speaking with you and you only."

"It is permissible to call me Anna or Anna Marie if you prefer."

"I prefer Anna Marie, and thank you. Concerning my reconstruction: the bones in my upper and lower arms were replaced with a very strong metal alloy. My shoulders and hips were reinforced. I have full use of my hands and feet and the ability to feel as a normal person. My brain is another matter. About forty-two percent of my brain is bionic; that is about as close as I can get to the detail of what it is. The neural implant is such that some is electronic, some is biological, and it's power is from something top-secret. To our knowledge no one else has ever been built like I have been and, hopefully, no one will ever have to be. I am worth over $4 billion in medical bills, not to mention the hardware."

"Wow, when you said 'Cyborg,' you meant it!"

"Does my admission of what I am make you think any less of me?"

"No, why do you ask that?"

"I ask because, as I said earlier, I am attracted to you and I have never been attracted to anyone else before," Chris admitted.

Anna Marie blushed again and again lowered her head.

"To continue, there are sensors that let me know the degree of embarrassment or aggressiveness of those around me. Like in a ballroom or a conference room I can pretty much access everyone there, up to 400 people. I can measure heart rate, blood pressure, number of breaths per minute, access weapons carried, and monitor mobile phone conversations. That pretty much about sums it up with a few minor details that are classified higher than you need to know right now."

"So, you know that you have embarrassed me?"

"Yes, three times now…whoops four times," he corrected as Anna Marie again turned red. "Okay, enough of that. Since you are through with your dinner, how about raising the lid on that silver platter in front of you."

"Chocolate pudding, my...."

"Favorite, I know."

"Mr. Beckett, are you sincerely trying to woo me?"

"Yes, and that is five now. Now, back to business. Since I am the Chairman of the Board of the Insurance Company that hired you I am technically your boss. Because of your qualifications and because of your photographic mind, my director wants you as an agent. Since I have just opened my life to you and declared to you my affections as well as my current assignment I wish to pursue a relationship with you. In the interest of logistics and protocol and our being able to work on this assignment together, I propose to you the following plan: First, I ask you to be my girlfriend; that will make it easier for us to be together in this operation."

Anna Marie started to object but Chris held up his hand.

"Let me finish, and then you can object or agree. If at the end of this assignment you have not felt anything good about a relationship then it will be easy to end it right there. Second, I always stay in Presidential Suites. They have two separate bedrooms and baths. I will need you to check in with me at each and every hotel until this is over as a 'live-in relationship.' You will, however, have one of our field agents staying with you. I am certain you will like her. Her name is Donna Smith. Yes, we have several female field agents, so you will not be the first. We will hold hands in public, perhaps even share a kiss on the cheek, but I will not touch you once the doors close. You cannot go anywhere without Donna or me with you. That as well as this last thing are nonnegotiable. I have a serum I will inject into your blood. It has an agent in it that makes you traceable by satellite down to exactly where you are. I do not want you to be kidnapped. But, if you are I can find and track you immediately without losing you. This way throwing away a mobile phone won't change the ability to track you."

Anna Marie's head was spinning. She couldn't deny her attraction to him, but his arrogance and the fact he had been rebuilt prevented her from agreeing immediately. Watching her silence, Chris continued.

"I can see you are in deep thought. Let me add one more thing. Before returning to the United States I had one date with a woman named Rhonda Fleming. Please hear me out; I had only one date with her and I told her I was not interested in her. She has made my return to the States miserable as she has come here, told my parents we were an item in England and they, especially my mother, are on her side. No, I have never been intimate with this woman nor any other woman and I am especially not interested in her. You being my 'girlfriend' will also make it easier for me to avoid her."

"Well, I knew there had to be a catch somewhere!"

"What do you mean by that?"

"You want to use me in a fake relationship to get rid of a stalker."

"You are right, it does look like that, but that's not the whole case. I do want to get rid of her as a stalker, but… Just a minute, I am being interrupted by my PA. *Which channel? Okay.* Anna Marie, let's watch this together. It will shed some further light on the subject of Rhonda Fleming. What has she done now?"

Anna Marie followed Chris to the sitting room connected as part of the dining room where he turned on the television to the channel for Augusta, Georgia. The announcer was just finishing her report. "Well folks, that is the news for tonight. But before we close for the evening, as we told you earlier, for you who are people watchers and want to know which celebrity is available and who is attached; there are two very rich men who have been taken off the market. Mr. Kenneth Knight, a top rated corporate lawyer, has been recently taken off the eligibility list as he is getting married in Birmingham, Alabama on July 9th to Carmen Coolidge. The other young man is Christopher Beckett, a mysterious business leader in the corporate world, and the lady who has taken him off the market is here in our news room. Meet Rhonda Fleming. So, you followed Mr. Beckett home from England?"

"Yes, he is such a gentleman and so shy. I had to follow him if I expected him to propose, and he did so this afternoon at his family estate in Clearwater, South Carolina. I needed to share this news as soon as possible. Yes, this is his grandmother's ring…."

Several noises could be heard from the hotel room while the news was continuing. Chris was gasping for air and turning redder by the moment. Anna Marie had only given a surprised "Oh," and then Chris grabbed the remote and turned off the TV.

After several minutes she asked, "Did your twin propose while you were here with me? And, that person on the TV in the studio; she has changed her name and looks, but that is Jessica Fisher. She was in high school with me in 1963 and then moved away suddenly with no forwarding address."

Chris had recovered his composure by this time and was looking at Anna Marie as if she had two heads. In his mind he heard his PA gasp, *"We never checked her background!"*

"Please do it, right now," Chris signaled to her.

After several more minutes of silence, Anna Marie stood up from her chair and moved to the couch where Chris was seated. She sat down beside him, took his hand, looked into his face, and said, "You, my young fellow, are in a lot of hot water. I do not know much about your life before or after 1963. However, I would like to get to know you better. Besides, I would be lying if I told you I was not attracted to you in some measure."

Chris squeezed her hand and said, "Thank you."

Edna chose that time to report on Ms. Fleming/Fisher. "Just a moment, both of you," said Chris.

Chris pulled what looked like a small mobile phone from his pocket, pushed a couple of buttons, and said, "Edna Ryder, meet Anna Marie Koch; Anna Marie, meet Edna Ryder, my Personal Assistant."

"It's nice to meet the lady in Mr. Beckett's head."

"That's not funny," he said, and Anna Marie smiled for the second time that afternoon.

Chris, couldn't stand it; there was something about her smile that disengaged him. He melted and just flopped back down on the couch.

"It's nice to meet you also, Ms. Koch. Let's get down to business before Agent Beckett passes out."

"Why, is he sick?"

"I am not sure about all of his feelings right now, but he is indeed very upset over the TV announcement and the hand squeezing didn't help his emotions any."

"Oh!"

"I am right here, you know," Chris said with a pink glow on his face.

Edna coughed into the phone connection as she began. "Rhonda Fleming is indeed Jessica Fisher. She moved to England in 1963, and finished her schooling here in Oxford. In 1964, she petitioned the courts that she was being harassed from the US and as an emancipated minor requested for an identity change. She graduated in 1965. When she graduated, she went to Oxford and studied Criminal Justice. She is an accomplished martial arts master. She graduated with honors early as she took her courses twelve months out of the year. She met Chris at a charity fundraiser while he was still in school in 1969. She asked him for a date, they had one date in January of 1969, and…"

"Is that date recorded?"

"Why do you ask?" Edna and Chris stated at the same time.

Then Edna replied, "Why, yes, it is."

"Thank you," Anna Marie answered.

"You didn't answer my question," Chris said.

"Nor do I intend to!" Anna Marie responded coolly.

At that moment, another voice came over the speaker. "Chris, I decided to interrupt now and hope I can help you through this situation."

"Director Whitfield, meet Anna Marie Koch," Chris said.

"It is nice to meet you, Sir," said Anna Marie.

"It is nice to meet you also, although under rather unusual circumstances, I must say. Ms. Koch, I believe you and Chris have handled this encounter very well this afternoon, and as it is getting late in the day, we need to contact the media and put other things in motion. I propose Chris announce his engagement to you tonight."

There were two gasps in the room. Chris and Anna Marie held their hands to their mouths.

"Our team has found several venues where you are photographed at dog shows, etc. Since Chris is not out much in the public we can picture him in at those shows standing on the sidelines without duplicating where he was on a particular date. We can go back a couple of months. We can place the two of you at different anonymous restaurants and have these pictures available to the media within an hour. It can make the 9 p.m. news. Agent Smith is already packed and on her way to your location. Tiffany's of Charlotte has several rings to show the two of you and will be calling from the main desk soon. Ms. Koch, your clothing and bags from your hotel are also being delivered as I speak."

"With all respect, Mr. Director Whitfield, Sir… I haven't agreed to anything," Anna Marie said.

"No, you did not, however, in the interest of my agent's well-being and the needs of your country regarding the case he is on, not only, but most importantly, the souls that are trapped by this cult, I am recruiting you and asking, no pleading, for your help."

There was a silence for several minutes, interrupted by the hotel suite's phone ringing.

"Okay, okay, I'll do this, but there will be parameters and I am not promising anything; this is ridiculous!"

There was a knock on the suite door at the dining room and Anna Marie went to answer it as Chris reached to answer the phone. "This is Chris, how may I help you? Okay, send them up."

Anna Marie looked through the door peep hole, and told Chris, "It is a tall, red-headed woman."

"That's Agent Smith; you can let her in."

Anna Marie opened the door. "Hello, Agent Smith," she said.

"Call me Donna. We are going to be roomies, none of this formal stuff." Donna came in with her own luggage and Chris pointed to the second bedroom.

"Hello, Agent Smith."

"Hello to you too, Agent Beckett."

Director Whitfield also chimed in and said, "I'll be leaving you; you have this under control, I am sure."

There was another knock at the door and Chris checked the peep hole before opening it. Luggage was wheeled in and Chris directed them to the other bedroom as well. One more knock followed, and Chris let in a very nervous jeweler who was flanked by two of WPPA's agents.

"Mr. Beckett?" the man asked.

"Yes, and you are John Snider of Tiffany's of Charlotte." Mr. Snider weakly nodded his head. "Okay, John let me see your engagement rings. Anna Marie, come over here, please. Sit down and look at these, please. I like this pink diamond cluster; how about you?"

Anna Marie was so flustered she could not speak. Yes, the ring was beautiful, but no, she did not want to be engaged; not like this. All of this was moving too fast. She felt trapped. She nodded her head yes. Chris got down on one knee and actually proposed to her. She nodded again and did manage to smile. The jeweler was paid by Chris's personal credit card and then he and the two agents left. During this time Agent Smith had a camera and had been filming the entire exchange.

Edna interrupted the moment as Chris and Anna Marie had been quietly looking into each other's eyes, each one with a world of different thoughts. Edna chose that moment to announce, *"Chris, WJBF is on the line and holding."*

Chris turned on the TV, placed his communication device on speaker again and the interview began. "This is Joan Childress of WJBF news. In an earlier news report we were given wrong information. We have Mr. Chris Beckett on the line and he denies giving a ring to Rhonda Fleming earlier today. In fact, we are about to show you some pictures and then a short footage of an event that occurred just a few minutes ago in Charlotte, NC. Mr. Beckett, please begin."

"I cannot stress to you how much I appreciate your going out of the way to clear up this matter tonight. I have actually been pursuing a young lady for a short period of time and tonight she has agreed to marry me. Anna Marie Koch is an independent business woman as well as a breeder of Old English Sheep Dogs. I am sure your people will look her up, but we have forwarded to you several photographs and a video from tonight's private moment. I will ask that the media refrain from bombarding us with questions. The trauma from the previous erroneous newscast has already taken a toll on our short relationship. We will be glad to answer questions through WJBF and will grant an interview in the near future. Neither my real fiancée nor I have anything further to say tonight. Again, thank you for allowing this to be cleared so quickly. Goodnight."

Anna Marie looked at Chris with awe in her eyes. "That was well said and done with a minimal amount of lying. I am impressed."

"Thank you."

"Chris!" Edna exclaimed.

"Yes, Edna? What is it?" Chris still had his communication device on speaker mode.

"Chris, your father is on hold waiting to talk to you, as is Rhonda."

Chris turned to Donna. "Agent Smith, why don't you and Anna Marie get settled while I take these calls."

"I already have it taken care of Sir," she responded.

"And I want to listen to what you have to say to my future father-in-law and your other fiancée," Anna Marie added. She raised her left eyebrow and smiled at Chris as he tried to look fierce, but he melted again while Anna Marie held up two fingers, then three as he collapsed on the couch. He closed his eyes a few moments and then just looked at Anna Marie resignedly and took the first call. "Yes, Dad, how may I help you?"

"Son, you know I work at the Savannah River Plant with Mr. Albert Koch, do you not?"

"Yes, I do."

"I had an interesting conversation with him this evening. He came to my house. He wasn't too happy. We were discussing your relationship with his daughter when the news interrupted us. Son, can you tell your old man what is going on? Mr. Koch wants to speak with you also, but he is too angry just now."

"No, Dad, I can't at this time. I can tell you what currently is happening is very complicated and involves many people other than Anna Marie and me. I cannot tell you anymore at this time. However, please reassure Mr. Koch that as much as is in my ability I will not allow his daughter to come to harm by others, nor will I hurt her."

"Thank you, son. I will be praying for you; and as far as this Rhonda situation, I'll speak to your mom."

"Thank you, Dad. Goodnight."

"Goodnight, son."

Anna Marie walked to the couch and sat down near Chris as he took the call from Rhonda. "Good evening, Rhonda. Has your day gone well?"

"You know perfectly well how my day has gone, Christopher Beckett! How could you humiliate me this way? Your mother and I had an agreement; she was going to talk to you and persuade you to marry me. I am in love with you. I have told you that since our first date."

"Our only date, Rhonda, and I am not in love with you."

"What am I going to do now? My visa to England has expired and they will not renew it! And not only do you reject me, you announce an engagement with that mouse from school!"

"Watch what you say, Rhonda," Chris said warningly.

"She never was part of the 'in crowd.' She always had her nose in a book. She…."

"Rhonda, I believe this conversation is over; or should I call you Jessica?"

"So, you finally found out," Rhonda said bitterly.

"Well, your rant revealed it if nothing else."

"Please do not call me out in public."

"I am certain the paparazzi will do that without my help." The connection went dead.

"She hung up, Mr. Beckett," Edna said.

"Thank you, Edna. Goodnight."

"Goodnight to you too, Sir. I will be praying."

"Thank you."

Chris disconnected from Edna and turned to Anna Marie. "Anna Marie, do I need to call your dad now?"

"No, Mr. Beckett. I have several missed calls from him. I will call him later and explain as well as I can."

"Anna Marie, my name is Chris or Christopher to my fiancée. Is that going to be too difficult?"

"No, Mr. Bec... No, Chris, it won't."

"Thank you. When you call your father, let him know that WPPA agents will be guarding him and your family until this case is closed. Also, please let him know I apologize for not asking him for your hand in marriage at this time."

"Will the protection be necessary, Chris? Also, I will not bring up the engagement unless he does if he is that angry at you."

"I would rather be overzealous in protection rather than sorry."

"Okay. Goodnight."

"Wait, please. Agent Smith."

"Yes, Sir?"

"Come over here, please, and sit down. Ladies, it has been a long, confusing yet prosperous afternoon. We will need our sleep to be refreshed for what tomorrow will bring to us. Let us pray: Heavenly Father, You are Sovereign. You knew about the events of this day before they happened. You are our creator and in Jesus Christ You are our Savior. May we each listen to the Holy Spirit and desire to walk in Your will. Please protect us through the night and work in Anna Marie's heart and mine to make right decisions for the future. I pray these things in the name of Your Son, Jesus Christ, our Lord and Savior, Amen. Goodnight, Anna Marie, goodnight Donna."

Anna Marie and Donna echoed a goodnight to Chris as well.

"Wait, the tracker injection," questioned Chris.

"We'll take care of it, Sir," answered Donna.

"Thank you."

"I don't think...." interjected Anna Marie.

"Just come with me, Anna Marie. We'll talk about it first," Donna said.

～e ～e ～e

Later that night Anna Marie returned a call to her dad.

"I am sorry I did not answer the calls you were making; everything around here has been so intense."

"He hasn't harmed you has he?" her dad asked.

"No, Dad, it is not like that. I can tell you Chris and I are involved in a top-secret mission that involves many people and I cannot say anything more."

"This requires you to be engaged to him?"

"Yes, it is rather complicated. Please don't tell anyone the engagement is a farce!"

"So, you are not planning on marrying him?"

"No, but this information is top-secret. Do you understand?"

"No, but I trust your judgment; you are a grown woman. My supervisor also called me and said there was a possible threat to my life and WPPA agents were guarding your mom and me and Lily. Is that part of what you are telling me?"

"Yes, it is, and I am sorry you are in danger, but the WPPA agents are the best there is at what they do."

"Really? And just what do you know about WPPA?"

"Enough to have been recruited as an agent trainee."

"So, is that what this is about, you are a WPPA agent in training? How did that happen, and how does this affect your detective work?"

"Since Mr. Beckett is an agent he recommended me and the Director spoke with me this afternoon."

"So you are on a case with WPPA, not your normal detective work, *and* with Mr. Beckett?"

"Yes, I am, but my detective work is also involved. It's complicated."

"Please be careful, Anna Marie. Your mother and I will be praying for you, and for young Chris also."

"Thank you, Dad. Goodnight."

"Goodnight, Anna Marie. Your mother sends her love also."

Anna Marie hit the disconnect button and laid her phone on the table. As she snuggled into the soft covers she said a prayer for protection for her and her family. She included Chris in that prayer. After a few minutes, she was asleep.

CHAPTER 5

Anna Marie awakened slowly. She looked around the room and saw unfamiliar surroundings. She sat up in bed suddenly and noticed the beautiful ring on her finger. She smiled a satisfying smile of happiness and snuggled back into the bed just as she noticed the light in the sitting room and some noise of paper rustling. She checked the other bed and noticed Donna was not there. She got out of bed, put on her robe, and went to the sitting room door and opened it. There she saw Donna reading what appeared to be a Bible. Donna looked up from her reading as Anna Marie entered the room.

"Good morning, Anna Marie. I hope I didn't wake you."

"No, you didn't. Donna, I need to ask you a question. The business you and Agent Beckett, Chris, are in; how does that not conflict with your faith?"

"That is a good question, Anna Marie. Please sit in this chair across from me. One of the requirements for working at WPPA is that we be committed Christians. We uphold the law of the land and the loving Spirit of our Lord with discipline. We do not indiscriminately kill people. In fact, the first part of our mission is to try to lead people to Christ. Changed people change society. We do not see much of that going on around us in today's world, but in some communities, the Gospel of Jesus Christ is spreading. As part of our Spiritual discipline our director has challenged all of us to read five Psalms and a Proverb a day. We are also encouraged to listen to Scripture on our phone ear buds. We attempt to witness every day to those we meet. We attend church regularly; we may not get there on mid-week services, however, we do attempt to attend both services on Sundays."

"Are you members of the same church?"

"Yes, we are all members of a local church in Oxford, but in the states and other countries we try to attend Bible believing, Bible teaching churches where God is exalted and Jesus Christ is glorified in preaching, in music, and in people's lives. I haven't had the opportunity to check your profile and history, but I know Agent Beckett, and he would not have fallen in love... let me rephrase that, he would not have proposed to nor become involved in such a situation as this with a non-Christian."

"What you just said, is that true?" Anna Marie asked.

"I was out of line; I cannot repeat what I just said about Agent Beckett, please forgive me for trying to place my thoughts in actions I have observed. Please forgive me for speaking out of place."

"I forgive you, but I need to talk to someone."

"Maybe after we get to know each other better, okay?"

"Okay. Are you almost through with your morning devotions, or just starting?"

"I am just starting."

"May I join you?"

"Yes."

"Let me get my Bible."

Two hours later the women heard a muffled, "Breakfast is on." They had finished their devotions, prayed separately and together, and were dressed for the day. Anna Marie was in a blue dress suit and Agent Smith was in the typical black business suit. She was armed and ready. They opened the door to the hall leading to the dining room and upon entering, found Agent Beckett standing behind a chair he was intending to pull out for Ms. Koch. He was startled again by her beauty. "I was told blue was your favorite color; it stands to reason with the beautiful blue eyes you have, and now I see it is a perfect color for you. Please, have a seat here."

Anna Marie watched the man as he pulled out her chair and motioned for her to sit. She noticed a tall stack of blueberry pancakes at her place and more on the table. As she sat, Chris commented, "I made the pancakes myself in the attached kitchen; I was told blueberry was your favorite."

"They are."

"Did you sleep well, Anna Marie?"

"I did, and you?"

"Not as well as I should have, I do not sleep well while on a case. Let's pray: Our Heavenly Father, we thank you for this new day and the opportunities to be Your witnesses before others. We thank You for this food and pray for its nourishment to our bodies. I thank you for the opportunity this day brings to learn more about Anna Marie; may this day not be as intimidating to her as yesterday. Please calm her heart from all fears. I pray in Jesus' name. Amen. Agent Smith, did you inject the tracking agent last night?"

"Yes, Sir, and I have already checked with headquarters and she is online."

"Anna Marie, I understand there is a dog show here in Charlotte. Is your handler going to be there? Were you planning on showing today?" Chris asked.

"Old English Sheepdogs are in the working class and they will not be shown until tomorrow. I was not planning to meet Mary until then," Anna Marie answered.

"Will you be showing?"

"No, she does a very good job and Christopher does not like just anyone handling him."

"Christopher? He is your champion, is he not?"

"Yes, Mr. Bec…Yes, Chris, he is. He is my first dog, my favorite, and the only house dog I have."

"Yet, he still shows well?"

"Yes, he is up for Grand Champion status, and with just a few more points he will be."

"Did you know that the Old English Sheepdog was first bred in the west of England? Mostly in Devon, Somerset, and Cornwall."

"Did you find that information on the internet?" Anna Marie asked dryly.

Chris turned pink, lowered his head, and began to eat his pancakes. They ate in relative silence for several minutes before he spoke. "I am sorry, I was hoping to show you I was interested in your life and in your dogs. I do like dogs and Golden retrievers are my favorite. I have never seen an Old English Sheepdog in person."

"Are you planning to accompany me to the show?"

"I am. We are to make ourselves available for the press as well."

"I hope they will not make a scene at the show; the organizers of these shows are rather protective of the dogs and do not like distractions of any type. Besides, many of the breeds are skittish and owners and handlers are discouraged from bringing in visitors to the staging area."

"But you are allowed to take visitors to the staging area?"

"I am allowed to, but only for short periods of time. Besides, Jumbo does not like many people, especially men."

"Jumbo, that is your pet name for Christopher?"

"Yes, it is."

"Anna Marie, do you have plans for today?"

"I did, but they involved my searching for the diamonds and you have handled that for me. Will I be able to recover them?"

"I hope so; Mr. Jones has not concluded his arrangement with the purchasers yet. We are monitoring that transaction and hope to add the international sale of stolen goods to the list of charges we have against him." Chris paused and then changed the subject. "Your home is in Virginia; why did you move from Columbia and not go back to Aiken?"

"I was hired as a recovery detective for a couple of insurance companies right out of college. Their retainers helped me to purchase a little pecan farm outside of Charles City, Virginia."

"I believe you call it Sheep Dog Haven?

"Yes. The temperate climate is good for the sheep dogs. It also had a separate house I was able to rent to my dog trainer and handler, Mary Wright. I have worked out an arrangement where she farms the pecans and it gives her a good supplemental income. She has a van equipped to transport the dogs and their equipment. I have made good money in the short career I have had and I have been able to restore the farm house. I am pleased and thankful with how God has provided for me. If I continue to work for WPPA will I be required to kill people?"

"My first assignment was in 1969. Kenny handled the trial—"

"The trial?"

"I'll explain it all later. Anyway, in the assignments I have had I have not been required to judge anybody...."

"Judge?"

"...yet. Can we change the subject, please? I will have to explain this to you sometime, but I would rather not just now."

"Okay, I'll wait."

Agent Smith's phone rang and she listened for a bit and then looked at Chris with a question on her face as if to get his attention.

"Yes, Agent Smith?"

"It appears your suspicions were true. Mr. Jones has been very busy since you went to the DA yesterday. He must have someone undercover in the DAs office. Mr. Jones has been inquiring and has identified you and has several 'hitmen' on retainer as we speak. We have been able to detain all of them but two; one called John-John and another called Baker. They have somehow slipped through the net and our agents have lost them."

"Okay, what are their specialties?"

"John-John uses sniper tactics and Baker is a munitions expert, specializing in C4 explosives."

"Anything else I need to know?"

"Not at this time. Pictures of the two are being downloaded to your server."

"Thank you, Agent Smith."

"Anna Marie?"

"Yes, Sir... um... Chris?"

"I need you to allow Agent Smith to fit you for your new attire for today. You will be wearing a larger suit because you will have body armor under it."

"They are after you, not me...."

"Yes, they are after me and anyone who is part of my life. Agent Smith, are Mom and Dad protected? And do you have agents on the Koch family yet?"

"Yes to all the above, Sir."

"Proficient as always."

"Thank you, Sir. Will you be using the shield?"

"You are right, I should be, shouldn't I? This is becoming too complicated and dangerous for there not to be sufficient protection for all of us."

"What is the shield?" Anna Marie asked.

"It is something I have invented that places a protective field around us that cannot be penetrated."

"Have I entered another dimension? All this is so unbelievable."

"Anna Marie, it will all make sense in time."

CHAPTER 6
June 23, 1972
Charlotte Stadium, Dog Arena

"Thank you, Chris, for allowing me to rely only on the shield and not have to wear that heavy suit of armor you were describing."

"You are welcome, Anna Marie. Are we on the way to see Jumbo?"

"His name is Christopher when we are in the arena."

"Well, that is awkward."

Anna Marie laughed. "I guess it is."

"Wow, there certainly are a lot of sheep dogs," Chris commented.

"This is a big show and a large number of points can be made on winning. Oh, here he is. Chris meet Mary Wright. Mary this is Chris Beckett, my fiancé."

Chris and Mary each exchanged greetings as Christopher sat up, moved over to be in front of Chris, and sat down again, raising his paw in greeting.

"How do you do, Christopher," Chris said as he put out his hand to shake with Christopher. "What a beautiful dog you are."

"Well, would you look at that. This dog has never liked any man and look at his manner around you," said Mary. "I need to start for the arena. Come on Christopher," said Mary as she tugged at Christopher's leash. "Heel," said Mary as she tugged again.

Anna Marie took the leash and said "Heel, Christopher, heel." She tugged on the leash and Christopher just sat there.

"Chris, maybe you should leave the area and Christopher will obey us." said Anna Marie.

"Sure," said Chris as he started to move away. Christopher followed him and stood at his right side as if he were in the show.

"Mary, I need these points, what are we going to do? I don't want to withdraw him as it will be six months before a show this big will come our way."

"Christopher, heel" said Chris as he took the leash from Anna Marie and led Christopher to the arena. Anna Marie and Mary followed with shocked looks on their faces. During this time Chris was accessing videos and information on showing dogs in competition. As he looked at everything he said to himself, "I can do this."

When they arrived at the competition area Chris asked Anna Marie, "Do you need to tell anyone if I am going to show Christopher?"

"Chris, I need these points, I just don't know...."

"Let me show him this first round, and if he doesn't show well I'll leave the arena area."

"Chris, if I list you as the handler you have to handle him the complete show."

"Well, what other choice do you have at this time? Anna Marie, let me try, please," said Chris as he reached and held her hand.

Anna Marie went to the registration desk and made the changes and brought to Chris his ID tag. She and Mary then went and sat in the owner's spectator area.

Christopher happened to be the first Old English Sheep Dog to show and went through the program with Chris perfectly. At the close of the first judging Christopher took first place. Later in the day was the judging for the Best of Breed, Best of Opposite Sex, and Best of Winners. During the whole day Christopher would only allow Chris to handle his leash and at each show they came through with flying colors, literally. He won all judging categories and he was named Best of Show and had more than enough points to be named Grand Champion. The only problem throughout the day was the photographers. They would not relent with their shots of Chris and Christopher and also of Anna Marie when she was near them.

"I am amazed; and you've never shown a dog before?" asked Mary.

"No, I have not, and that was a lot of work. My congratulations to you for a job well done in grooming Christopher and for the training you have given him. Your work is to be commended; I only wish you had been named as handler in the awards."

"That is alright, I was named as trainer and that means a lot to me. So, tell me about you and Anna Marie. I have never seen you before, and I am a very observant person, so I don't think I have missed you."

"Our relationship has been very secretive, but after Ms. Fleming's announcement last night we felt we had to come forward."

"Like I said, Mr. Beckett, not very much gets by me and I have not seen you around before today."

"Well, whatever your suspicions and misunderstandings, I hope you will keep them to yourself, at least until you and Anna Marie have had a chance to talk."

"Oh, I intend to speak with Anna Marie at length, thank you," Mary said as she turned and walked away with Christopher in tow.

Anna Marie came in from speaking with the awards committee and collecting her documents and noticed how Mary and Chris parted. "Is Mary upset Christopher showed so well with you?"

"No, Mary is concerned for you and our relationship and the fact she has never seen me near or around you. Frankly, she is unhappy about that. I cautioned her about saying anything to anybody before she talks to you."

"Do you want to be present when she and I do talk?"

"If possible, but it is not necessary. I believe you can handle it with discretion. I just don't want to see your relationship with your handler harmed."

"Thank you, Chris, that is very thoughtful of you."

"You're welcome. I am starved. That dog show took a lot of energy. Christopher is a big dog and a terrific sheep dog, which may be my favorite breed now. May I have your arm and let's go to dinner?"

"Yes, you may."

As Chris and Anna Marie stepped from the arena he felt his chest tighten as a shot that was fired hit his individual shield. His training instantly took over. He quickly found the target, set his eye laser, and fired back, hitting the assassin in the head, knocking him down but not hurting him. Agents were at the target quickly and he was taken into custody. Other agents surrounded Chris and Anna Marie and rushed them to the limo.

Once in the car Anna Marie turned to Chris and with a frightened voice asked, "What was that?"

"I was hit by a rifle shot. It did not penetrate the shield. I was able to shoot back and disable the assassin immediately."

"That is what I was talking about. What was that blue light?" Asked Anna Marie.

"That's classified."

"Chris, think carefully; the paparazzi were all around us. Do you think they have a picture of that?"

"I hope not."

"Agent Beckett?"

"Yes, Agent Smith?"

"Damage control is complete. Two pictures were identified by Ms. Ryder and the cameras have been wiped."

"Thank you, efficient as always."

"Especially since you were not thinking clearly," said Edna in Chris's mind.

He sat back in his seat and frowned. Anna Marie did not understand the movement, but he was clearly upset about something.

Chris's light-hearted demeanor had returned once they arrived at the restaurant. What Anna Marie didn't know was Edna had a long talk with him on the way there. She pretty much told him he had to be more careful with his implants concerning public display and he need not be moody in his relationship with Anna Marie or sharp in his answers to her. If he truly loved her, it needed to show!

When they arrived at the restaurant the place was swarming with reporters. Chris took Anna Marie's arm and kept her walking straight for the entrance. Suddenly halfway to the door he turned with her hand in his and said, "Okay, ladies and gentlemen; two questions for each of us; and be gentle, please, this is a fairly new relationship. Yes, George from the Chronicle."

"Have you and Anna Marie talked about a date for your wedding?"

"George, you can tell your readers we are being respectful of Kenneth's and Carmen's wedding on July 9th and will be making an announcement later that month."

"Follow up?" asked George.

"Yes, George?"

"We have heard the two of you are calling yourselves committed Christians, yet you are staying in the same suite. Do you care to explain?"

"Honest question, George. The suite has two bedrooms and Anna Marie has a chaperone. The chaperone, Donna Smith, is always present. We are not living together in that sense, we are just making it convenient to see one another without nosey people being involved."

Chris pointed to another reporter and then said, "Yes, June from The Standard."

"Anna Marie, you have never dated any men we can find. What made you go from never dating to being engaged in such a short order?"

"June, I find your question interesting. It is not refreshing to know our lives are completely open to the public eye for anyone with a computer. As far as my personal dating record; I am now in a relationship that is very public and I am not wanting to let everyone know the what's and why's of my relationship with people. In other words, no comment."

She pointed to another reporter. "Yes, Alton from WHKK news."

"Anna Marie, we noticed you have a dog named Duke of Christopher and now a boyfriend by the name of Christopher. Any comment on that?"

"No, and that concludes our interview. I am hungry."

With that statement she swirled around, took Chris's hand, and entered the restaurant. Once they were seated at the table she looked at him and he could tell she was boiling. "Don't people have anything else to do than conjecture and propose vain things?"

"Chris, there is a bomb under the third table close to you. Please activate individual shields around each table," Edna said to Chris through their mental connection.

"Thank you, Edna. Do we know where the perpetrator is?"

"Yes, he is behind the stage. Agents are attempting to apprehend him before the bomb goes off."

"Are we safe?"

"Yes, the explosives are not large."

Suddenly, a table approximately ten feet away exploded and because of the shield the debris was kept inside the table area. Many people scrambled for the exits.

"Anna Marie, stay here with me. We are safe inside the protective shield I have around us."

"Did you just get a warning from Edna?"

"Yes."

"I remember your saying there were two assassins not captured. Does this mean no more attempts? Did your men capture this one?"

"Did you hear that, Edna?"

"Yes, and yes. Unless he hires more, that's it."

"That should be all the attempts, Anna Marie."

"I certainly hope so."

The rest of the dinner was uneventful. The police had come and gone; the kitchen had stayed open and the patrons who remained were served. The floor show was great, and Anna Marie and Chris had even danced. Agent Smith and the others were keeping their eyes and ears open and the paparazzi were confused about the events surrounding tonight's interview and the bombing at the restaurant. They were especially confused there was no debris scattered around the restaurant; so were the police.

After dinner, the limousine took the group back to the hotel. There, Chris prayed with Donna and Anna Marie and said goodnight. The women sat up in their bedroom for a time talking about the events of the day and about how Chris was fairly subdued this afternoon and evening. Agent Smith mentioned Agent Beckett had a lot of responsibility within WPPA and he was very concerned with everyone's safety today. In Anna Marie's mind, that did not answer all of her questions. He would certainly be the object of her prayers tonight. Before she laid down to sleep, she decided to call Mary.

"Hi, Mary. Was the trip home uneventful? I want to thank you again for your training of my dogs. Your talent was really shown today in Christopher's obedience."

"Hello, Anna. The trip home was uneventful. I appreciate your compliments. As to which Christopher showed more talent today I am not sure. Tell me, is this play acting, or what is going on here?"

"Mary, I am engaged. We do not know what the future will hold. I need to discuss some things with you. I will check with Mr. Beckett, Chris, in the morning and see about making a trip home to have a much-needed conversation with you."

"There, you see what I mean. What woman calls her fiancé Mr.?"

"I am glad you made it home safely. I will call in the morning about my trip there. Goodnight, Mary."

"Goodnight, Anna. Please take care of my friend!"

Anna Marie hung up and bowed her head.

"Heavenly Father, what am I in the middle of? Please give me wisdom and discernment. Please give me your strength to do the right thing. Please give me a restful sleep tonight. I pray in Jesus' name. Amen."

‎‎‎ ‎‎ ‎‎ ‎‎

Back in his own room Chris was also fervently praying. "Heavenly Father, Your word says for 'everyone to whom much is given, from him much will be required; and to whom much has been committed, of him they will ask the more'. Your word also says, 'Moreover it is required in stewards that one be found faithful.' Through circumstances I have been given many abilities; much beyond what the normal human being has. These abilities can be used for good or evil; for man's glory or Your glory. Please let me be ever mindful of my responsibilities to You first and my fellow beings next. May I understand the talents I have are not to be flaunted nor are they to be publicly shown in many cases. I cannot fail these particular people currently caught in human trafficking, nor can I fail those friends around me who could be hurt if I do something wrong. I pray for Your wisdom, Your strength, Your guidance, and Your mercy in all things. Please protect those whom this cult would like to ensnare, and please stop this organization. For all of our agents in the field I pray for Your protection. Father turn hearts to You and heal souls tonight. I pray in Jesus' Name. Amen."

CHAPTER 7

Chris, Anna Marie, and Donna had been through their morning routines and convened for breakfast. This morning it was omelets, grits, and sausage accompanied by orange juice and milk. Chris and Anna Marie were dressed in jeans and colorful tops with matching bolo ties and Agent Smith was wearing her typical working outfit.

"Chris, what are the chances I could catch a ride to Charles City or book a flight to Richmond? I need to see Mary and take a look at Sheep Dog Haven as well."

"How about I take you? I have nothing scheduled today and I would enjoy seeing your farm and kennel."

"What do you mean take me? As in a car or a private jet?"

"No, in a WPPA Helicopter. Just a moment." Chris asked one of his guards to come in.

There was a knock at the door. Chris opened it and in walked one of the WPPA guards. Agent Smith immediately said, "Good morning, Agent Hydrick."

"Anna Marie, this is Agent Joe Hydrick, my pilot. Joe, this is Anna Marie Koch, my fiancée."

"Yes, Sir. It's good to meet you ma'am."

"It is good to meet you also."

"You wanted me, sir?"

"Yes. How long would it take us to get to Charles City, Virginia?"

"In the jet or the helicopter, Sir?"

"The helicopter."

"Can I land on the property or will we need to go through Richmond?"

"Anna Marie, do you have a clear field?"

"Yes, about an acre between the house and the river. There are no trees or power lines."

"Okay, let's land on the property. Anna Marie, do you have facilities enough for us to spend the night?"

"I have five bedrooms, would that be enough?"

"Do you mind if we do?"

"That would be fine."

"Agent Beckett, the flight time would be two to three hours depending on the weather and air traffic," said Agent Hydrick.

"Alright, let's all get our gear and meet at the Charlotte Airport at, let's see, 11AM? Is that time okay with you, Anna Marie?"

"Yes, Sir, uh Chris."

Agent Hydrick raised his eyebrows and directed a quick look at Agent Smith whose hard look told him to keep his mouth shut.

"Can you have a flight time by then, Joe?"

"Yes, Sir."

"Okay, then it's settled."

At the airport they were directed to a special hanger away from the normal passenger area and behind a military fence marked "Special Clearance Only."

"Can you tell me what is going on, Chris?"

"Sure, Anna Marie. You will be flying in a WPPA helicopter. An HN1, actually. It is different than other helicopters and also is considered to be a military aircraft."

"Military as in US or WPPA?"

"Actually, WPPA, but due to treaties we use US Military facilities whenever we can. Well, here we are."

Anna Marie had never seen a helicopter like this one. It was sleek and beautiful and colored purple. "Wow," was all she could say.

The helicopter could hold ten passengers including the pilots, and there were already six men on board. Chris and Anna Marie sat in the middle and Agent Smith sat beside Agent Hydrick as co-pilot.

"Is Donna a pilot also?"

"Yes, she is, as well as everyone on board except you."

"Oh!"

When the engine was started there was only a low hum. There was not a lot of noise at all, and during the flight Anna Marie found they could talk at normal volumes.

"Is this a new style engine?" she asked.

"Yes, it is. What we are riding in is technology developed by The Ryder Corporation for WPPA. We have not decided to make it available to other governments as yet. Everything is patented and copyrighted. The inventors have made it clear they do not want the technology to be used wrongly."

"And do I get three guesses as to who the inventors are?"

"Why, is it necessary to know?"

"I guess not," Anna Marie said rather dejectedly as she lowered her head. *"Chris, you hurt her feelings,"* Edna interjected to Chris silently.

Chris reached for Anna Marie's hand and found it rather stiff as he squeezed it and told her he was sorry and he did not mean to cut her off. He found it rather embarrassing at times to mention his accomplishments. "You see, Anna Marie, I am the inventor, but it is only because of the abilities that have come with the neural implant and nanorobots."

She squeezed his hand back but did not say anything.

The helicopter landed at Sheep Dog Haven without a hitch exactly two hours after taking off from Charlotte International Airport. Chris had ordered a catered lunch from a Williamsburg deli and everyone ate when they could. Everyone was settled in by 3 p.m. The six body guards were staying in a large tent next to the helicopter. Agent Smith and Anna Marie were settled in her master bedroom. Chris was in an adjoining room that had its own bathroom, and Agent Hydrick was in a bedroom downstairs. The bathroom of another bedroom downstairs was to be used for the agents guarding the estate. Anna Marie and Agent Smith went to the kennel about 300 yards from the main house and Anna Marie was speaking with Mary while Agent Smith was monitoring the area, but keeping just out of hearing range of the conversation between Mary and Anna Marie. The property was protected by a shield. Chris was in his room changing and getting ready to go to town to purchase what was needed for dinner when there was a sudden crackling sound and his shields went down. As he attempted to contact Edna he saw himself looking at himself. "Hello, Chris, is it you again or are you from another reality?"

"It is me, and I have only sixty seconds, so please listen carefully and comply. I need to inject some more updated nanorobots into your blood stream. You need these to complete your assignment. In their programming is also information that you may read for further directions."

"I did not know I had an assignment."

"Listen," Joshua said as he prepared the syringe and wiped Chris #3's arm with antiseptic, "You will see the answers to questions you are having once these have settled in your system. Keep yourself pure and keep trusting in Jesus. Do you understand?"

"Yes, but...." And then Joshua was gone immediately after he injected the nanorobots.

"Chris?"

"Yes, Edna?"

"What happened?"

"I can't tell you just yet, but everything is okay. Are the shields back in place?"

"Everything is back to normal."

At that moment Agents Smith and Hydrick rushed into the room with weapons drawn.

"Stand down, everything is okay."

"What happened?" they chorused at the same time.

"Nothing. Agent Smith is Anna Marie covered?"

"She will be when I get there," Agent Smith said as she dashed back out the door and down the stairs. She didn't get very far because standing just inside the front door was a woman holding Anna Marie and Mary with a gun pointed at them.

"Drop your weapon!" the woman shouted.

Agent Smith laid her weapon on the foyer table and backed away with her hands in the air. Chris and Agent Hydrick came down the stairs. Agent Hydrick walked to the table and laid his weapon there as well. Chris activated a shield around Anna Marie and Mary to protect them and said "Rita Hayes, what brings you here? Why are you threatening my fiancée?"

"I am not interested in hurting her, I just need to get your attention and to take care of you since the CIA has rejected my information request and involuntarily retired me."

Agent Beckett moved to the living room and waved Rita, Anna Marie, and Mary inside as well. "Come, let's talk about what is troubling you."

"You know what is troubling me; you killed my husband. You murdered him."

"I did not kill your husband, his friend Jody Harrell with the CIA killed him and I saw to it that Jody was punished. Did you ever see the film?"

"What film? I have seen nothing and received nothing except heartache. No one will talk to me about the entire fire fight."

"Rita, would you put the gun down and let me show you the film? Please."

"No. I can only be appeased by your death."

"Anna Marie, you are in no danger. She cannot harm you. Sit down."

Anna Marie sat down and Rita found she could not touch her.

"What have you done? I cannot move."

"Rita, I did not kill your husband. I need you to watch something so you will have the answers you need to have peace."

Chris walked over to the television and picked up the remote. He pulled what appeared to be a small mobile phone from his pocket, and pushed some buttons on the remote and on the mobile phone. Images came on the television of people arguing and then pulling weapons and firing at one another. From the vantage point of the camera it appeared someone was firing a taser. "What you see, Rita, is the fire fight in question. I am taking the pictures with a special camera. I am firing a taser. I was not shooting to kill anyone. Now, soon you will see…."

"…my husband, there, in your line of fire; who is that who rushed in? He shot my husband. I see you shot the man with your taser. Oh, I have been lied to and I have been so mistaken. Mr. Beckett, Sir, please forgive me."

"I forgive you, Rita, but you must come to trial for tonight's display. Agent Hydrick, will you preside?"

"Yes, Sir. Rita Hayes you are charged with kidnapping and attempted murder. How do you plead?"

"Guilty, your honor, and I ask for mercy; I never would have done this if I had only known the truth. Believe me, please."

"Rita Hayes, do you know Jesus Christ as your Saviour and Lord?"

"Yes, I do, He has been by my side for many years. I let hate take hold of me on this situation and I need to ask Him for forgiveness as well."

"Anna Marie Koch, please state your understanding of this matter?"

"I can only say Ms. Hayes told me she was not going to hurt me, but to please follow her instructions," Anna Marie said.

"Agent Beckett, do you have any words to say?" Agent Hydrick asked.

"Yes, I do. I do not attempt to kill people in my job. I use a taser. For someone to threaten my fiancée and her friend leaves me upset and angry. I would appreciate justice to be taken."

"Agent Beckett, may I see the weapon used by Ms. Hayes?"

Chris walked over to Ms. Hayes and retrieved the weapon from her grip, because she couldn't move until Chris allowed her to do so. He checked the chamber, walked over to Agent Hydrick, and handed him the weapon.

"It is unloaded," both of them said in unison.

"I really did not want to hurt anyone and I was willing to die. I miss my husband so much," Rita explained.

Agent Hydrick was still for a long time. Agent Beckett was looking at him face to face as well. Finally, Agent Beckett turned, looked at Ms. Hayes and sat down.

"Ms. Hayes, please stand up and face the judge. By the International Powers invested in me through WPPA and US authorization by Protocol 1345, I pronounce you not guilty. You are free to go," Agent Hydrick said.

"I have nowhere to go," Rita said.

Anna Marie and Mary walked over to her, took her hands, and walked outside together. They were whispering, but didn't know Chris could still hear. "I could use some help on the farm. It's just me when Anna Marie isn't around, why don't you come and live on the farm with me in the farmhouse and help me? I will pay well and have the extra room."

"Are you sure it is alright with you Ms. Koch? And, again, I am so sorry."

"Rita, it is okay, and yes, I would like it if you worked here. I will make sure it is alright with Chris too," Anna Marie replied.

"Thank you."

Chris just smiled to himself and said, "Thank You, Lord."

One of the guards was at the main entrance to the farm. A catering van stopped at the gate. Agent Henry Smart called Agent Beckett. "Williamsburg Fine Foods is here and the driver says they have dinner for us?"

"That is correct, Agent Smart. The van has already been scanned, let them through. I'll see to it you are also relieved for dinner."

Chris walked out on the front porch and let Anna Marie, Agent Smith, Mary, and Rita know dinner would be ready in about an hour. The van pulled around to the kitchen entrance and started unloading.

"Anna Marie, is there time for us to talk?" Chris asked.

"Yes, Chris, I'll be right there."

"Agent Smith, please see everyone knows about dinner and let them also relieve Agent Smart at the front gate," Chris directed.

"Yes. Sir. You have responsibility for Ms. Koch?" Donna replied.

"Yes, I do as there is an extra shield activated. We will be walking to the river and then to the kennel. I want to see Jumbo." He turned to address Anna Marie. "May I have your arm?"

"Yes, Chris. What is it you wanted to discuss?"

"I wanted to discuss us."

"There isn't any 'us.' We hardly know one another and people are trying to kill us; you anyway. I am about at my nerve's end. This isn't my idea of life. I have always been extremely careful and no one has ever had a contract out on my life. You act as if it is an everyday occurrence that your life is in danger. I cannot live like that. When Agent Knight's wedding is over I am leaving as well. I have not, I cannot fall for you and be worried everyday if you are coming home safely. I just cannot."

"Well, you have about fifteen days for me to change your mind."

Anna Marie stopped, turned, and looked into Chris's eyes as she replied, "Chris, I just do not believe my decision will change."

They walked in silence for some forty-five minutes, each in their own thoughts. When they reached the kennel, Jumbo fell in step with them and walked back to the house next to Chris.

"Anna Marie, which church do you attend and may we attend with you tomorrow?"

"We attend Sandy Point Baptist about two miles away. Mary won't be attending tomorrow as she is watching Beulah who is about to have pups."

"May I stay and watch Beulah for her so she can attend?"

"No, it would take someone who knows how to birth puppies, and I do not believe you fit the bill."

"Okay. We'll have a van here for everyone and your car will be back, so may I take you in your car?"

"That would be okay. How did you move my car? I didn't give you a key."

"I had one made." Anna Marie just shook her head.

After everyone had dinner and the catering van had left, the guards set the watch for the night. The shield was in place as well as individual security for Chris and Anna Marie. Chris dropped Anna Marie off at her door after checking to see that Agent Smith was inside the room. Jumbo didn't want to go in with Anna Marie and went to Chris's room with him. Once in his room, Chris called Edna.

"Edna, this is Chris."

"I was hoping you would get back to me tonight."

"It was him; the Chris from the accident. He calls himself Joshua and that is the code name for an assignment he has for me. He injected me with some more nanorobots. When the shield was down Rita Hayes got in and I guess you heard all the rest."

"I even heard what Anna Marie had to say."

"I know you did."

"We will keep all on alert. Goodnight, Chris. I will be praying."

"Goodnight, Edna, and thank you."

Jumbo nuzzled against Chris's hands as he petted him and he dozed some five minutes later.

CHAPTER 8

JUNE 25, 1972, SUNDAY, 5 A.M.
SHEEP DOG HAVEN, CHARLES CITY, VA

Chris, Anna Marie, and Donna were up at 5 a.m., each in their respective rooms and having their individual quiet times. At 5:30, Chris left his room with Jumbo for a walk along the river bank. Sunrise was at 5:49, and he just wanted to be outside. Jumbo followed and nuzzled Chris's hand occasionally. Chris was quiet. He was thinking and praying, mostly for the safety of Anna Marie. Jumbo went down to the kennel and Chris went back to his room at 7. He showered and changed, but he did not dress for church. He was back in the kitchen at 8 preparing breakfast for everyone. Agent Hydrick joined him shortly after, and by 9:30 breakfast was fully prepared. Chris had contacted the agents, including Agent Smith, and each one came in at that time.

When all were seated Chris returned thanks: "Thank you, heavenly Father, for this food and for this day of worship. May we worship You in truth and spirit today. We continue to pray for those in bondage, especially the bondage of sin. Use us today for Your glory. Bless this food to the nourishment of our bodies and our lives to Your service. In Jesus' Name, Amen. Dig in, folks. The van and car will leave at 10:30 for Sandy Point Baptist."

At 10:45 Anna Marie and Chris were pulling into the church's parking lot, Chris was driving her 1972 Oldsmobile 98. It was a beautiful white car with leather interior.

"Thank you for cooking breakfast this morning. That was very nice of you and Agent Hydrick."

"You are welcome. Here we are."

As they approached the church an older gentleman greeted them.

"Good morning, Anna Marie."

"Good morning, Pastor Bennett."

"Are you going to introduce me to this young man?" he asked.

"I'm sorry, Pastor Bennett, where are my manners? This is Mr., this is Chris Beckett, my fiancé. Chris, this is my pastor, Reverend John Bennett."

"It's good to meet you, Sir," Chris said.

"And you also. I had heard of your engagement. Have you chosen who will do your premarital counseling? I would like to be available if you haven't."

"No, Sir, we have not. We haven't set a date yet, so we will keep your offer in mind."

"Thank you. Anna Marie's a fine young lady. We would hate to see her taken away from us."

"Yes, she is a very fine young lady, and I understand you would not like to lose her. Neither would I, Sir."

Anna Marie was startled by Chris's statement, but said nothing. Chris and Anna Marie moved off and found seats. The service began and other than an occasional glance in each other's direction, there was no hand holding or conversation between them. They left the service with a few hellos to the congregants and started for Anna Marie's home.

"I need to go into Richmond tomorrow for some personal business. Does Agent Smith have to go with me?"

"Yes, she does, but she can stay away from the conversation you may be having if you so desire."

"No, that isn't the issue. I just wanted to be alone and having a body guard just keeps me tense."

"I'm sorry, we'll be out of your way soon," Chris said as he got out of the car and walked away.

❧ ❧ ❧

It was about 3:30 in the afternoon when Jumbo came running up to Chris who was on the front porch of the main house working on a problem with the programming for the shield system Joshua had left him in the nanorobots. Jumbo was barking frantically.

"Hey, Jumbo, what's wrong? Want me to follow you? Okay, let's go."
Jumbo ran to the kennel and Chris opened the door and they went inside.
He could hear some noises and was beginning to be concerned when he
saw the newborn puppy on the floor not cleaned up and not breathing.
Chris reached for the gloves, the rags, and began massaging the little
guy's chest while talking gently to him and breathing into his nostrils
before looking for Beulah. She was in her nest and two more puppies
had been born and needed cleaning, but they were breathing okay.

"Come on, little guy, we don't want to lose you. Come on, breathe."

About that time the doors burst open and in rushed Anna Marie,
Mary, Donna, and Rita.

"Why didn't you call me?" exclaimed Anna Marie.

"I just got here myself. This little guy wasn't breathing, but I think
he is okay now," Chris said as he laid him next to Beulah and picked
up another one to clean. Beulah was dropping the fourth, and Anna
Marie and Mary each had one in hand. Rita was getting herself ready as
number five came forth. About an hour and a half later seven puppies
were nursing and the birthing team was getting cleaned up and chatting
about what beautiful puppies they were. Proud Poppa Jumbo was
watching protectively, taking it all in.

"We were all at Mary's and I glanced at the camera monitor and saw you
had a puppy in your hand so we all dashed down here," said Anna Marie.

"Jumbo came to the front porch and was barking up a storm for me to
follow him. I found the first puppy in the front hall and he wasn't breathing."

"How did you know to breathe into his face like that?" asked Anna Marie.

"God helping me when I prayed for wisdom?"

"Well, it was the right thing to do. Thank you."

"Thank God, he answered my prayer. However, you are welcome,
goodnight."

"Chris, do you want to walk me to the house?"

"I would be glad to, Anna Marie."

Anna Marie reached for Chris's hand and they walked in silence to
her home. Jumbo walked beside them most of the way, but then turned
back and went to the kennel for the night. Agent Smith was about
twenty-five yards behind.

"Thank you for helping with the puppies. Beulah never was one to
handle the process like a good mother should. This was her third litter

and she has needed help each time. I have never lost a puppy, and I don't know what I would have done if we had lost one today. Thank you, Chris, really, for being there."

"You are welcome, Anna Marie. Goodnight. Agent Smith, please take over."

Anna Marie just watched as Chris walked away toward the helicopter.

"He has a lot on his mind, Anna Marie, things we can't discuss. Just know he really cares about people trapped in human trafficking. I should not tell you this, but you need to know; he is deeply in love with you."

"Let's pray for him when we get to the room."

CHAPTER 9

Chris had checked with Agent Hydrick the night before to have the helicopter ready for a trip to Columbia, South Carolina for him to speak with the District Attorney there. He had decided not to wait to talk with the DA. He had his quiet time, showered, and dressed after preparing breakfast for everyone. He didn't eat with them, but had Agent Hydrick bring him a plate to the helicopter as they prepared to take off at 8:15 a.m. Anna Marie was watching from her bedroom and a tear fell from her eye as the helicopter took off.

"Care to share?" Asked Agent Smith.

"I guess not, he's only doing what I told him I wanted. I just didn't know what I really wanted."

"Love hurts, Anna Marie. I know."

"Yes, I guess it does. You just about ready for breakfast?"

"Sure am; let's go," said Agent Smith as she hugged Anna Marie.

After breakfast Anna Marie asked, "Did Chris tell you I was going into Richmond for some personal business?"

"He did, he also told me you wanted to be alone. I will attempt to be as unobtrusive as possible, but I do need to remind you of one caution. You have misspoken several times while introducing either Chris or me to your friends. Chris told me about the introduction to the pastor yesterday. Just think, today, and say 'My friend, Donna'. And remember, I am your friend, not just your body guard."

"Thank you, Donna, I will try. Oh, and will we have shields around us?"

"Always. We cannot be too cautious. I do not want you hurt or missing on my watch."

"Do you really think I am in danger?"

"Do you really have to ask that after Rita?"

"No, I guess not."

Anna Marie drove to the Kennel Club office on Main Street in Richmond and parked in the city parking garage. She went inside with Donna in tow, made the introductions properly, and registered Beulah's litter. She had pictures and everyone cooed over the precious puppies. She also made sure Christopher's awards were applied properly.

They left the AKC office and walked to the library only a block away. Anna Marie went through the stacks and found the book she wanted to read and sat in an overstuffed chair at the edge of the reading room. They were there about an hour when she was approached by a man. Agent Smith stiffened but Anna Marie apparently knew him and they engaged in a congenial low volume discussion. When he rose to leave about a half hour later he pulled Anna Marie into a hug. It appeared innocent enough, so Agent Smith calmed down as he released her quickly and left. Anna Marie sat back down and read for another hour before signaling to Agent Smith she was ready to leave. They walked toward the garage and found a deli, walked in, ordered, and sat down to eat together.

"Thank you for allowing me that time. It was refreshing," Anna Marie said.

"You are welcome. May I ask who the visitor was?"

"You may. His name is Peter Croft. He is sort of a patron of the arts. He is rather affluent and has been a friend since I moved here and attended one of the galas two years ago. He is a phenomenal dancer, a good conversationalist, and a good friend."

"Do you have a romantic interest in him?"

"No, why do you ask?"

"Just noticed the hug, and the smile on your face during the conversation."

"No, I am not interested in him. Like I said, he is a good conversationalist. It may be of interest to you to know I have never had a boyfriend. I have never kissed a man. I have had no need for a man in my life, not even now, but my heart is really giving me difficulty and I am going to cry if we keep this conversation going."

Donna reached for her hand and squeezed it. "That's alright. I told you this morning love hurts. I'll say it this way, falling in love and not knowing the other party's thoughts on the matter is very hard. Are you ready to head for home?"

"Yes, let's go before I break down."

CHAPTER 10

JUNE 27, 1972, TUESDAY, 5 A.M.
SHEEP DOG HAVEN, CHARLES CITY, VA

Agent Hydrick had brought the helicopter back late the night before, along with Anna Marie's and Agent Smith's luggage from the Charlotte hotel. Tagging along with everything came Agent Stephanie Riggs.

"Good morning, Ms. Koch," Stephanie said from Chris's room when Anna Marie knocked on the door. "Agent Beckett is not here. I didn't know where to go last night, so I parked myself here on the couch. Agent Beckett did not come back with us but he sent your things from Charlotte along with Agent Smith's belongings. He gave me this letter to give to you."

"I wanted to talk to him about this headline, is there any way I can contact him?" Anna Marie was holding the Richmond Times paper in her hand with the headline 'Is One Man Not Enough, Anna Marie Koch?' The picture under the headline was that of Peter Croft's hug in the library the day before.

"I'll give you our contact information. It goes through his PA, Edna Ryder."

"Thank you."

Anna Marie's hand was shaking as she dialed the number: "Good Morning, Ms. Ryder, this is Anna Marie Koch. I need to reach Chris, Agent Beckett, please."

"Anna Marie, I wish I could connect you, but he is on a case and is unable to be contacted for the next thirty-six hours. I will take your message and ask him to call you."

"Yes, please tell him pictures and words don't always tell the truth; it is not what it looks like. And please ask him to call me."

"I certainly will, Anna Marie. Also, please know he already has a report from Agent Smith on this matter."

"Thank you, Ms. Ryder."

"It's Edna, Anna Marie."

"Yes, thank you, Edna."

After hanging up the phone Anna Marie went to the chair in her bedroom. Agent Smith was sitting on the couch on the opposite side having her quiet time. Anna Marie opened the letter and sobbed the minute she saw the greeting.

"Dear Miss Koch:

My heart jumped the moment I saw you for the first time and my heart beat hasn't slowed down since that day. I cannot, however, hold you to something that is meaningless to you. Please continue with this facade through Agent Knight's wedding and we will continue to protect you for a time after the wedding. Your life is in danger and it is mostly because of your connection with me.

I cannot expect life to be only a bed of roses, for there will be trials. Included in those trials is heartbreak. I will live through this, but I will never forget you. I will try to keep my distance as much as possible and attempt not to have you do anything you do not want to do.

Please forgive me for messing with your life and trapping you into this engagement.

Please do know, however, I do love you. Again, I am so sorry.

Forever yours,
Chris"

Anna Marie was bawling by this time and shaking all over. Donna came over and attempted to console her to no avail. They stayed like that for over two hours; Donna attempting to console, and Anna Marie filling the room with her heartbroken, anguished sobs. Finally, she fell asleep.

Donna pulled a quilt over her and left the room. She asked Stephanie to sit on the couch and be with her when she woke up. She had a mission.

After making sure the door was shut solidly behind her, Donna called Edna.

"Edna, do you know what Chris wrote in that letter?"

"No, I do not, Agent Smith, and neither should you."

"She didn't show it to me and it was crunched in her hands the whole time she was sobbing. I have never seen a woman in her state."

"Agent Smith, I cannot do anything about it. Chris did confide in me she didn't care for him and he had hardened his heart about her. I don't know what he was thinking, nor do I know what he said, but apparently it was pretty final."

"Apparently so. Now what? She was just starting to like him."

"Well, all of you are still assigned to her compound and Stephanie has been added to give you some time other than 24/7. Chris will not be available for another thirty-four hours now, so I cannot help."

"I was only hoping you could."

CHAPTER 11

JUNE 30, 1972, FRIDAY, 5 A.M.
SHEEP DOG HAVEN, CHARLES CITY, VA

Chris was twenty-four hours overdue from reporting. Anna Marie had not left her room since reading the letter on Tuesday. It was still in her hands and she was still in the chair. She had not eaten nor drank any water. Mary, Rita, Donna, and Stephanie had all pleaded with her to leave her room and eat, but all they had received was blank stares. Another helicopter landed in the yard and Agent Knight was shown to Anna Marie's room. "Anna Marie, I am Agent Kenneth Knight, I am Agent Beckett's best friend. Everyone has told me what is going on with you and I do not know the answers, but I am here because of Agent Beckett. He has been shot and is in a hospital in Atlanta, Georgia. Our own medical staff is with him, but we also know he needs you. He is in a coma and has been calling your name since he was brought in."

Anna Marie sat up when she heard Chris had been shot. And he was calling for her. She must go to him! "Will you take me to him?"

"I will, but first you must clean yourself up. Agent Smith take care of her, please," said Agent Knight.

About an hour passed before Anna Marie was ready for the flight. Her bags, Agent Smith's bags, and Agent Riggs' bags were on the helicopter. Food and water were packed for Anna Marie to have on the flight. This was a different helicopter. It was black, sleek, and smaller, and only held six passengers. Agent Riggs sat in the co-pilot seat and Agent Smith sat with Anna Marie. Anna Marie had been praying for Chris from the moment Agent Knight told her about his injuries. She was asking God to heal him and to make their relationship work. As they were strapping themselves in Agent Knight told Anna Marie on the intercom that the flight would be a fast hour flight. They would land on the hospital roof in Atlanta. Agent Beckett was on the top floor and she would be in his room in a short while.

Anna Marie ate some food, drank some water, prayed, and found herself really nervous.

"This is Kilo, Henry, Niner One Four calling Echo Four Seven, do you read?" said Agent Knight.

"We read you loud and clear, Scorpion. All air traffic has been cleared from the area and radar shows you on the correct flight path," returned the Control Tower in Atlanta.

"I should be landing in ten. Please have the team ready," he announced into the separate radio at his side.

"Roger that!" Returned the flight control operator at the control tower.

"Scorpion, out."

Agent Knight landed the helicopter smoothly and it was quickly surrounded by a dozen agents with assault rifles pointed around the perimeter. Another twelve agents lined a path to a door that opened and Anna Marie was rushed through that door by Agents Smith and Riggs. They came to a desk with scanners and Anna Marie was scanned. The agents were not. Double doors were opened and Anna Marie was asked to dress in a white coat over her jeans. Another set of doors opened and there he was, lying on a hospital bed with tubes and machines hooked up to him. Anna Marie almost lost it, but went to him and eagerly touched his hand. His hand moved slightly, but that was all.

"Anna Marie," a lady said, "I am Edna Ryder."

Anna Marie collapsed into her arms, hugging her with all she was worth. Determined not to break down, she asked Edna about his condition.

"Anna Marie, the other day when you met Rita Hayes, the shield had gone down. Do you remember that?"

"Yes. I do."

"Well, what happened was the Chris from the dimension that helped our Chris when he was in that car crash in 1963 came back here to inject some more nanorobots into Chris's blood stream. Their purpose was to help our Chris with the shields and other things that are classified right now. Chris had been working on the information those robots gave him when he was called to a special stake out here in Atlanta. What he didn't know was those nanorobots made his personal protection shield unstable. When he confronted the traffickers, they fired upon him and his shield failed. When his shield failed so did his contact with us. Fortunately, he had a tracker in him and it was only a matter of minutes before we found him, but he had still lost a lot of blood. He has five bullets in him and we cannot operate until he gains some strength, but that will not happen until we get more blood into him."

"How long has he been here?" Anna Marie asked.

"He was brought here yesterday at 5 p.m. and wasn't stable until 3 a.m. today. He has received four units of blood and still needs two more. There was a shortage of blood due to several vehicle accidents in the area."

"What type blood is he?"

"Type O Positive," Edna replied.

"So am I. Please ask the technicians to set up a transfer of the necessary blood from me directly to him now."

"Are you sure, Anna Marie?" asked Edna, surprised.

"As sure as I will ever be."

Edna Ryder barked a few orders and after only a few minutes another bed was in the room, Anna Marie was prepped, and the transfusion was being made. The transfusion would take about two hours. She was also given an infusion of liquids to ward off any dehydration since she was giving two units of blood to Chris. Anna Marie suddenly felt tired and went off to sleep as the transfusion was being made.

CHAPTER 12

Chris was stirring. He saw all the tubes and was wondering what was going on. He could see Edna on a chair next to his bed and turned toward her. He felt the presence of another bed but could not turn in that direction. "Edna, will you tell me what has happened and what is going on?"

"I shall try. You were shot several times because your shield failed. Something happened and we believe it was because the nanorobots you were injected with had not stabilized yet, so when you were shot the trauma caused the failure. You've been here about twenty-six hours in a coma and you've been calling for Anna Marie during most of that time. You needed six units of blood and the hospital only had four. The person on the bed next to you gave the other two units. You began stabilizing and improving after about an hour into the transfusion of these final units."

"Who is he, so I can thank him?"

"He is a she and it is Anna Marie."

"What? How could that be?"

"Agent Knight picked her up and when she arrived and found out you needed blood she insisted she be hooked up. She is asleep right now, but she is fine. Oh, and I have a message from her to you from this past Tuesday: 'Please tell him that pictures and words don't always tell the truth; it is not what it looks like. And please ask him to call me.'"

About that time, Anna Marie opened her eyes and saw Chris sitting up. "Hello, Chris, how do you feel?"

"Much better, and I am told I owe it all to you."

"No, you don't owe me anything. I am just grateful you are going to be okay. I would hate for my fiancé to back out of our engagement just because he needed a little blood when I had some to spare."

Anna Marie's eyes began to flutter and she was back to sleep. Chris also lay back down and was asleep in a few minutes as well.

CHAPTER 13

July 1, 1972, Saturday, 10 a.m.
Emory University Hospital, Atlanta, Georgia

Because Anna Marie had not eaten hardly anything in three days before the transfusion she was still receiving liquids through an IV to combat dehydration. In the meantime, Agent Beckett was having an argument with his physicians from WPPA.

"I tell you I have done six system checks this morning. My systems are the best they have ever been. I have even reconfigured the entire shield system and all of the satellites. I have never felt better. Either those bullets you tell me I took passed through me or the nanorobots dissolved them. Regardless, your scans cannot find anything wrong with my body. I am free to leave this hospital as far as I am concerned, and as soon as my fiancée is able we are going to go find us a place to have a good meal and talk until the cows come home. Agent Smith, does Anna Marie have a nice outfit in her luggage?"

"I think so, Sir."

"My physicians and I are leaving this room. Please get her dressed and ready to leave as well. I will be right outside the door."

"Yes, Sir, Agent Beckett, Sir!"

"Are you sassing me, Agent Smith?"

"Oh, no, Sir," Agent Smith said with a smile on her face.

"Good. Let's go, men. Out, out, out!" he said, shooing them from the room.

Thirty minutes later the door opened and Anna Marie stepped out wearing a blue chiffon dress with long sleeves and a lace collar.

"Anna Marie, you look absolutely lovely. Are you ready to go out with me?"

"Yes, Chris, I am. Please lead the way and I will follow."

Chris took her arm and they walked down the hall past several doors. Just before reaching the elevator Chris turned and opened the door to a chapel. Anna Marie followed him in. There were several people in this chapel, including her mom and dad, Chris's parents, Edna Ryder, several agents, and Anna Marie's friends. Agent Smith walked in behind them. Chris still had Anna Marie's arm as they walked down the aisle to the front. He turned to her. "While you were still out I called your father and I have asked and received his approval, now all I need is for you to agree. Anna Marie, you are wearing my engagement ring. It was given to you a whole world of time ago and for reasons that weren't honorable for a good start to a good marriage." Chris got down on one knee. "May I take that ring off and put it back on while I ask you, Anna Marie, will you really marry me?"

Anna Marie gasped and put her hands over her mouth. She slowly removed the ring while looking in Chris's eyes and said, "Yes!"

Chris took the ring, put it back on her finger and said, "Anna Marie Koch, will you do me the honor of being my wife?"

"Yes, Christopher Beckett, I will."

The room exploded with clapping and shouts of "Wonderful," "Finally," and "Hallelujah!"

Chris rose to his feet, looked Anna Marie in the eye and said "May I kiss you?"

"Yes, Chris, you may."

And he did! It was the very first kiss either of them had ever had.

Agent Knight walked forward, asked for everyone's attention and bowed his head for prayer: "Our gracious Heavenly Father, you have spared my friend, Chris. For this I am extremely thankful. We praise You for his miraculous recovery and for Anna Marie's part in that. Your ways are not our ways, and we are finding day after day there are mysteries too marvelous for us to understand. Heavenly Father, for us in this time and place, may we glorify Your name and may we honor our Lord and Savior Jesus Christ. Our lives are not our own; You are Sovereign and You allow what You will and deny what You will deny. Please give us guidance, wisdom, and discernment in all things. Please protect us as we seek to protect those around us. Please watch over our agents in the field who are combating human trafficking and other sins of mankind. May You guide us to rescue many in the days that lie ahead. Thank You for this moment in Anna Marie's and Chris's lives as we see them begin a new journey, a journey where You are truly at the center of their relationship. May each learn to know Your will for the rest of their lives and walk in it. I pray for those in this room, Lord, that You would comfort, strengthen, and fill each one with Your Spirit. In Jesus' name, Amen."

At the completion of his prayer, Agent Knight addressed the crowd. "Everyone, listen up. There is a conference and convention center on the third floor of the hospital. Chris and Anna Marie are having an engagement brunch there in fifteen minutes. Please make your way there. When you get off the elevators people will direct you to the area you need to go. We will all meet you there shortly."

Agent Beckett gasped and whispered to Agent Knight, "Kenneth, what have you done?"

"Nothing you would not have wanted done, I assure you."

Anna Marie reached an arm around Chris, hugged him and whispered in his ear, "It sounds like fun and when we finish this celebration with our friends and family we have each other the rest of the day."

"Now that sounds like a plan," Chris said with a big smile on his face.

Anna Marie's parents walked up and she turned as her mom grabbed her in a huge embrace. Her father hugged them both.

"Anna Marie, we love you and pray God's best for you."

"I believe I have God's best, Mother, and I am very thankful."

During the engagement brunch, just one hour later, Anna Marie looked into Chris's face with sudden fright. She turned white and passed out. Chris, with obvious concern, quickly called Edna, asked her to locate the medical team and have them meet him in the emergency room of the hospital. *"Edna, wait, I am getting a message, do you hear this?"*

Another voice interrupted their mental conversation. *"Take me upstairs and hook me up to Ringer's Lactate. Do not attempt anything else."*

"Edna, what is going on?"

"Chris, the message you just received came from Anna Marie, I am sure of it."

"But how?"

The room was in pandemonium now, with some rushing toward Chris and others clearing a path to the elevators. They were pushing the down button when Chris told them to push the up button. WPPA agents were banking Chris on either side and Agent Smith was right there. Chris thought the elevator would never open on the special top floor surgical suite, but when it did a gurney was there as well as people to hook her up as requested. She was wheeled into the suite that Chris just left a few hours ago and he was still holding her hand. The nurse started to take her pulse when he ordered all of them out of the room. Agent Smith was by his side as he monitored her vitals and Edna walked into the room.

"All of her vitals are okay. They're slightly elevated, but within normal range. There is no fever. How was she talking to us, Edna?"

Agent Smith looked at Chris with a question on her face. Chris noticed, and explained what happened to her.

"Donna, just as she passed out she gave instructions to me in the similar mode with which I talk to Edna and the rest of you through my communication device. Wait, I know...."

Chris activated his magnetic imaging device and started to utilize it when he received another message. *"Chris, this is Joshua. This is a recorded message. Do not image her. Anna Marie asked you to do nothing else, that was in the programming. When Anna Marie was hooked to you for the transfusion nanorobots swam through the connection to Anna Marie's body. When you kissed her the transformation began. They are currently reconstructing her brain and healing her body. This is necessary for your dimension to combat the coming threat. Their instructions and guidance are perfectly controlled and this has been done before. It will take twenty-four more hours to complete. All she needs is the liquids attached and your touch. Do not leave her side for a moment. Continue to hold her hand. Twenty-four hours, Chris, and she will wake up. I pray for your reality. Goodbye."*

Chris was stunned. Agent Smith went to the lavatory and wet a rag and brought it over to him. She placed it on his forehead and he wiped his face with it. Edna came over to his side. "What is it, Chris?"

"Edna, Agent Smith, what I am about to tell you is top-secret, never to be repeated and never written down in a report. Understood?" They both said they would comply and Chris proceeded to tell them what he had just heard. All three were asking themselves where the nanorobots would get the material for the power source for the neural implant.

"Chris, just what type of technology is this? This is like some science fiction movie I am watching, or some horror movie. I do not understand at all," Donna said.

"Agent Smith, you knew I was different, but you were not given the clearance to know the whole story. Because you are where you are, I want Edna to bring you up to date and give you the clearance to know, since you will be Anna Marie's guard as long as you work for WPPA. Edna, please explain to her at the other side of the room while I sit and pray for Anna Marie."

Donna and Edna removed themselves to chairs at the other end of the room. A coded knock came from the door.

"Okay, Kenny, you may come in," said Chris.

Kenneth and Carmen entered and walked over to the bed. Carmen went to reach for Anna Marie's other hand and Chris stopped her. "No, don't touch her." She looked at Chris with a shocked look on her face. "I'm sorry, but she cannot be touched right now except by me. Kenny, I don't know when you were going to tell Carmen, but since you brought her into the room, right now is probably the best time. You can either go back to the hotel and tell her privately, or take a corner and explain to her as Edna is doing with Agent Smith."

"Agent Smith, Donna is who, what…." Carmen was trying to ask.

Chris raised his hand and put his finger over his lips and gently said, "Just a minute, Carmen. Kenny come here." He leaned over and whispered into Kenny's ear, "Anna Marie is having her brain reconstructed by nanorobots to match mine."

As the rest were, Agent Knight was also stunned. He took Carmen's hand and walked her over to another corner and began the story. Agent Beckett, still holding his fiancée's hand began praying silently.

CHAPTER 14

It was exactly twenty-four hours after Anna Marie passed out that Chris and Edna got a code three emergency call from Headquarters. They each answered immediately.

"Commander Whitfield, Agent Beckett, Agent Ryder, the computer has been compromised. Someone has accessed it and it is downloading all of the data." Exclaimed Agent Andrew Murphy from WPPA headquarters.

Chris was the first to respond. "Can you get a location on where the data is going?"

"Negative, Sir, it is being channeled through one of our satellites." Said Agent Murphy stationed at headquarters.

Chris received a call on his magnetic line.

"This is Joshua, stand down. All data is being uploaded to Anna Marie. This is a recording, I am not actually there. It is timed to coincide with the upload. Do not worry, everything will be okay."

"Stand down, Agent Murphy. Data is being downloaded to a new member of the team."

"But Sir, not even you have taken data at this speed."

"It's okay. Stand down. Code 1344457."

"Yes, Sir," Agent Murphy replied.

"Agent Beckett, is everything okay?" asked Edna.

"Yes, it is, Edna. Anna Marie is downloading. Did you copy that, Commander?"

"Yes, Chris, I am totally out of my league here. Was there no warning to you from Joshua this was going to happen?" Commander Whitfield responded.

"No, Sir, there wasn't. I am not happy about this and I can only imagine how Anna Marie is going to react when she wakes up in about thirty minutes."

"Can you handle the situation should there be a problem?"

"Yes, Sir, I can."

Thirty minutes later Anna Marie opened her eyes. She looked directly at Chris. "Agent Beckett, clear the room now; everyone except you and me."

"Are you sure you mean everyone, including Edna and Donna?"

"I mean everyone, Agent Beckett, including Agents Ryder and Smith. You have thirty seconds."

"Yes, Anna Marie, I...."

"It's Miss Koch to you. You are wasting time."

"Okay, everyone, you heard her. Leave us alone, please."

Everyone exited the room quickly and efficiently and closed the door.

"I know you know how to take this thing off of me. Please do so, now."

"Yes, ma'am," Chris stated as he removed the IV and cleaned the area with a swab and then put on a bandage.

"Now, sit down."

"Yes, ma'am."

"Agent Beckett, did you know these mechanical robots were going to hijack me and rebuild my brain and other areas I would rather not talk about right now?"

"Anna Marie, Miss Koch, I did not know anything about what has happened to you these past twenty-four hours. I am just as surprised as you and I am not happy about not knowing either."

Anna Marie hesitated a few seconds while looking Chris in the eye, then took his hand and said, "I believe you, Chris, but you can understand why I am so upset."

"I do, Anna Marie, and I am so sorry this has been done."

"Chris, during the last three hours I have been programmed by constant teaching about an upcoming war. Apparently, I have information you do not have. I need to give it to you now."

"How are you going to do that?"

"Kiss me, please."

"I am not going to argue with that request, but how can that...."

Before Chris could finish speaking, Anna Marie grabbed him and kissed him.

"Wow, Anna Marie... whoa... I am in your mind...." And Chris stopped talking and began downloading all the updates Joshua had for him through Anna Marie. They also chatted in a most unusual way during the downloads as long as they held each other's hands. It took about fifteen minutes and the people outside the door were beginning to get upset, frightened, and curious. When the downloads were completed Chris let go of Anna Marie's hands and walked over to the door. He opened it and called out, "Agent Knight, Agent Smith, Agent Ryder, Carmen, please come in. For everyone else, please know Anna Marie is okay. We will update you some time soon. I would suggest those who need to go home do so. Thank you for your concern. She is okay, I assure you. Mr. and Mrs. Koch, you may come in also.

"Mr. Koch, I knew it would be best to let you see your daughter, to know she is okay and to see her bright smile. In the midst of all that is going on we have decided to ask Kenny and Carmen if they would like a double wedding next week or if they would like to keep it as it is."

Carmen looked at Kenny, then over to Anna Marie and asked, "Are you sure?"

"Yes, I am, Carmen. We would elope tonight, but I would miss the formal wedding," Anna Marie replied.

"Kenny?" Carmen asked.

Kenny looked at Carmen and nodded with a smile on his face.

"Okay, then - a double wedding on July 9th," confirmed Chris.

"Mr. and Mrs. Koch, we have some WPPA business we need to discuss, so if you will excuse us."

"We will, Chris. It is good to see our daughter is okay. Can you tell us what happened?" Mr. Koch asked.

"No, Sir, it has to do with WPPA business. However, as you can see she is okay."

"Call us when you can, Anna Marie," Mr. Koch said.

"Yes, Dad, I will." Anna Marie hugged her parents and they left.

"Edna, do we have an eight-passenger helicopter here?" Chris asked.

"We have one, yes."

"I have the Presidential Suite at the Hilton downtown reserved. The hotel has a helipad. Let's go there where we can talk. This is going to take some time."

"Chris, it is already 9 p.m. and by the time we get settled and sorted it will be rather late. Can we handle this conversation in the morning?"

"Okay, Anna Marie, I'll go ahead and order a light dinner for the room and we can eat separately as we get settled. Agent Smith, see to it that sufficient agents are engaged. Is Agent Clarke outside, Kenneth?"

"Yes, she is. I'll see to it she is with us as well."

Thirty minutes later they were ready to go to the helipad. Anna Marie had told Chris she wanted to fly the helicopter. He wasn't too sure, but he agreed anyway. He was the copilot. They made it to the Hilton in fifteen minutes and with a perfect landing.

"Very good, Anna Marie."

"Why, thank you."

CHAPTER 15

They had the entire top floor and several other agents, Kenny and Carmen, and Edna were in a sort of newsroom area with separate bedrooms. Chris's and Anna Marie's were adjoining rooms with a common sitting area. Their doors were open and Agent Smith was sitting in the room as Chris and Anna Marie were talking in the sitting room. They were holding hands, looking into each other's eyes, discussing details related to the day before.

"Chris, in several dimensions both Chris and Anna Marie have had head traumas and have had the operation. Chris tells me in his notes I am not the only one who was reconstructed using my entire brain and the neural implant. In other words, I and others who have been reconstructed have more capacity and faster reaction time than anyone, including you. I don't say that except to say they felt I needed this done because of the reality that someone has to stop; the one who is preparing to destroy dimensions."

"I now understand more as well. My accident was caused by an Anna Marie who left her reality to go to another. She left because her Chris was unsaved. They were not married at the time. She had been given the neural implant only two and a half months earlier and it had problems in its programming because her Chris had a brain tumor. She, because of insufficient understanding, caused riffs in the fabric of time and space. I may have died in my accident, but the Chris, who goes by Joshua, engineered things for my operation and now your reconfiguration. At some point in time, you and I are going to go with him and others to confront the Chris with the tumor and hopefully to operate on him. All of the riffs in the fabric of our universe have been corrected, but the damage to be caused by the premature death of the Chris who has the tumor would be catastrophic. We are being given specific instructions to train for this upcoming time when Chris will be confronted, operated on, and hopefully healed with a desire to be saved and love his Anna Marie. I pray all of us involved will do our jobs to the letter and everyone will be safe with all goals being achieved."

CHAPTER 16

The week leading up to the wedding was filled with several eventful moments. Chris and Anna Marie had to find groomsmen, bridesmaids, and a maid of honor. Anna Marie chose her twin sister, Lily, to be her maid of honor. They shared the wedding expenses with Kenneth and Carmen.

The day of the wedding arrived and all of the members of the wedding party were at the church getting ready. As the guests were arriving and Kenny and Chris, along with their best men, were in the ante room, Chris received a call from Edna.

"Agent Beckett, we have three agents on coverage whose radio signals we have lost, one of which is Agent Smith."

"What, how can that be? What about the backup signals, as well as the signal on Anna Marie?"

"They are still being tracked and according to satellite they are all at the church."

"Okay, can you pinpoint the signals clearly?"

"Yes, they all have moved from the Bridal Chamber to the rear of the building in the office area."

"Thank you."

"Kenny, let me bring you up to date. Something is happening now and our agents and Anna Marie are in trouble. We need to go help them."

"Agent Beckett, Agent Clarke is with Carmen and her signal just went down."

"Kenny, they have Anna Marie and Carmen. Let's go."

Agents Beckett and Knight headed toward the office area and called for more agents to surround the building. Agent Beckett activated his electronic hearing and his x-ray vision and searched the offices as they traversed the halls with weapons drawn. They were at the library in the rear of the building when Agent Beckett picked up sounds and saw movement with his x-ray vision. *"Edna, library."*

"Understood. Protocol is being followed. There is a shipping and receiving dock there and satellite shows a large truck backed up to the dock."

"Get the truck deactivated immediately, and get men to the loading area now."

"Yes, Sir!"

Agents Beckett and Knight went to the library doors and Agent Beckett activated a fire fight security shield around the two of them. This particular shield allowed bullets to be fired through it but not into it. They opened the doors to find four men armed with AR17's aimed at them and firing. Agents Beckett and Knight were not harmed and they were able to disable all four men immediately using taser technology. A man came around the book stacks with Anna Marie. He had a hold around her neck and a gun in his hand. Another man came from another stack and he had Carmen in the same hold. He too was armed. Both women apparently had put up a fight, for it could be seen that they were disheveled.

"Hello, Lucifer," Agent Beckett said. "It would be good for you to let the women go."

"Not a chance, Beckett. Drop your weapons." Agents Beckett and Knight looked at one another and slowly laid their weapons on the nearby tables. "I believe the best thing for me to do now is to dispatch you two men here and for me to leave with these lovely ladies."

"Before you do; Anna Marie, I am glad I have met you and want you to know I love you. Please do me a favor just now and shut your eyes so you do not have to see this."

"Carmen, you know I love you also. As Chris asked Anna Marie I am asking you, please shut your eyes." As the two ladies shut their eyes, two blue laser beams struck the two men holding them one right after the other. They were immediately paralyzed and dropped to the floor effectively freeing the ladies who rushed to their men with tears in their eyes.

"Agent Beckett, all is clear and the area is secured."

"Thank you, Edna. Have agents come to the library and secure the men here. Transport everyone ASAP."

"Yes, Sir."

"Ladies, we will explain much to you later, for now we have a wedding to finish."

"Are you okay, Carmen? Do you still want to get married?" Kenny asked.

"Yes, I do, Pump-ken."

"Pump-ken?" Chris asked snickering. Anna Marie elbowed him in the side as they went down the hall. "Anna Marie, do you still want to get married? I would understand if you said no."

Anna Marie answered in Chris's mind. "If you still want me, I want you, forever."

"Then this is a double wedding. Let's go!"

It was a wonderful, well-attended wedding. The bridesmaids were all lovely, the maids of honor were beautiful, and the brides were stunning in their lovely white gowns with trains and veils. The vows were God-honoring and the men were totally enthralled with their brides. There were many tears, and not only by the women. The reception was a delicious meal and the toasts were enthusiastic. It was after midnight before Agents Beckett and Knight were able to escape to the presidential suite with their brides. Also in attendance were the women's agents, Edna, and Director Whitfield.

Once in the rooms, Director Whitfield addressed the group. "I know you four want to head for your honeymoons, however, I felt it necessary to give an explanation to the two ladies who have just learned new things about their husbands. Mrs. Knight, you met Agent Knight as he was taking care of business regarding our care of people hurt by human trafficking. By our care, I mean the organization we are members of, WPPA. Agent Knight was injured in training and lost his right eye. In its place is an eye capable of many things, one of which is using a laser beam as happened earlier today. Because of an accident that actually ended with his being in the agency, Mr. Beckett has a similar eye. Thank you, ladies, for closing your eyes quickly, as that saved your sight from injury since you were so close to the apex of the beam. It was a wonderful wedding. You men have done yourselves proud. You have lovely brides. Ms. Ryder and myself and several agents are taking an overnight flight back to London. Good evening to you all. I do not expect to see you men before the end of your month's honeymoon."

Carmen and Anna Marie looked at each other and smiled; both were wondering where their husbands would be taking them. During the wedding the hotel staff had redecorated the suite into double honeymoon suites. The men asked their brides and the agents to have a seat. Chris was speaking.

"We will spend the night here and tomorrow we will fly to Hawaii and after a week there it's on to Japan, Italy, Germany, and Spain for some touring. We will actually be gone for six weeks and will be spending a week at each spot and then a week at home preparing our living quarters. Our plane is a WPPA plane with separate Honeymoon Suites and separate housing for the agents. There will be ten agents on board other than Agents Smith and Clarke. We will be on separate ground tours, however, we will have agents watching us. Agents Clarke and Smith you will be with us, but watchfully aware and not within hearing distance. Should the ladies need to be excused, you will be with them every step of the way. We will have shields, however, we will be extremely cautious. Kenneth and I have discussed this at length. The bottom line is we each just found our wives and do not want to lose them. Let's make the best of it. Kenneth, you and Carmen are in Suite A and Anna Marie and I are in Suite B. Let us pray before retiring."

After the prayer, Kenneth picked up Carmen and carried her over the threshold of their suite as they each said goodnight to all. Christopher picked up Anna Marie and they said goodnight to all as they entered their suite. Both men put "Do Not Disturb" signs on the doors as they closed them.

CHAPTER 17
Christmas Day 1972, Monday
Sheep Dog Haven, Charles City, Virginia

Chris and Anna Marie had decided to stay at the farm for a quiet holiday. The acreage was protected by a shield and all of the agents were given time off with their families. They had also given Rita and Mary time off and Chris and Anna Marie were taking care of the dogs by themselves. They had opted not to start a family just now, knowing they would be needed for the assignment Joshua had for them at anytime. Kenneth and Carmen had announced at Thanksgiving they were expecting twins. The babies were due on June 1, 1973.

Chris and Anna Marie were practicing teleporting, both tandem and single teleports. They had not tried any long-distance teleports because they were told that would not be needed. They were also practicing communication skills and telekinesis. All in all, life was going well. Pastor Bennett had done marriage counseling classes with them and they each learned much about how married life should be; communication, selfless love, cherishing, and nurturing, and praying for one another.

Since his marriage, Chris had worked out a different system for Edna to contact him. There would be a cell phone beep before she could connect. Strangely the connection was for him and Anna Marie at the same time. The phone beeped.

Edna was on the line. "Chris, sorry to disturb you but you are about to be attacked by a ship off the shore of the James River. It is a small battle cruiser and it will be firing several large rockets. You need to be sure you and Anna Marie have strengthened the shield to maximum using the power from both of you."

"Did you hear that, sweetheart?" Chris said to Anna Marie.

"I did."

Chris and Anna Marie held hands and willed the elements to strengthen the shield to maximum.

"Edna, are they nuclear?"

"No, for that we are thankful."

"Yes, we are. How many men on board?"

"There are twelve on board and I have already alerted the Coast Guard. They are about ten minutes away."

"Anna Marie, do you think we can take this ship and tie up the men with our shields on?"

"Why not? Let's do this," she replied.

"Chris," called Edna.

"Yes, Edna?"

"I think you should let the Coast Guard do everything."

Suddenly some of the rockets slammed into the shield and both Chris and Anna Marie felt the impact. The shield held, and they heard Edna say more were being prepared. As they were launched Chris and Anna Marie placed a shield around each one and stopped them in mid-air. They just hung in space.

Chris and Anna Marie held hands and teleported to the rocket launcher area on the cruiser. There they encountered three people who were quickly encased in individual shields and encapsulated so they would not be able to move. Anna Marie noticed two more coming in the door behind Chris and she quickly incapacitated them.

"Five down and seven to go," said Chris as they teleported to the bridge. There they found four more and Chris encapsulated two while Anna Marie encapsulated her two. Suddenly someone grabbed her, but she slipped from his hands and encapsulated him.

"Two more," said Chris as they teleported to the main cabin. There sat a man and a woman with their hands in the air.

"We surrender," the man said. "We would like to exchange information for our freedom."

"What information do you have and what makes you think you can exchange it as a bribe?" asked Chris.

"I have in my hand a button, and when I press it, your friends, the Knights, will die."

"Okay, where might my friends be?"

"Where you cannot find them."

"Maybe so, maybe not," Chris said as he encapsulated the two quickly before the button could be pressed. Chris was linked with Edna who found Carmen and Kenneth and sent the location to Chris. Chris told Edna what she would find on the cruiser and Edna dispatched agents immediately. The Coast Guard was also on the way. Chris and Anna Marie joined hands and teleported with the man to the location Edna had told him. They took the button from the man and froze it through encapsulation and Chris put it in his pocket. The man was horrified as they then teleported him and themselves inside a warehouse where they saw Carmen and Kenneth safe, but tied up with four men guarding them. These men were soon encapsulated in shields by Anna Marie.

"Now, tell me who hired you to do this?" Chris demanded.

"I'd rather face your wrath than his," the first man replied.

"He'll never get to you where you are going."

"What do you mean? I'll go to trial and our lawyers will get me off with a light sentence."

"Mister, I work for WPPA. You attacked our agents. We have jurisdiction. You are going to our facility in South Africa."

The man looked at Chris with a horrified look. "Okay, I was hired by Anthony P. Dickson. He lives in India. His agency is very large and there is no way you can reach him."

"That is a good challenge. Thank you."

After hugs were exchanged by friends, Anna Marie and Chris dropped Carmen and Kenneth off at Sheep Dog Haven on their way to the WPPA prison in South Africa with five people in tow.

"Edna, what have you found out?"

"I know where he is, but, Chris, I believe it really is too dangerous."

"How so? In our shields we are invincible."

"And if your shields failed again?"

"I would hate to see some of our men and women killed but this monster has got to pay for all the women and young girls whose lives he has ruined."

"Okay, Chris, use stealth mode and see what information you can find and then follow up later."

"Okay, send me the location."

"Anna Marie, you want to do this?" Chris asked.

"Chris, I am appalled about this type of crime just as much as you are. Let's get this organization."

They took a break at the London Facility and ate dinner and then headed for Bangalore which is the capital of India's southern Karnataka state, and also the center of India's high-tech industry. Here they found the address they needed and since they were already in stealth mode, teleported into Anthony Dickson's office. No one was in the offices. They did find he kept good records. There were several file boxes full of records. Chris and Anna Marie made a decision. They teleported the records and the desk to WPPA Headquarters in London.

"Commander Whitfield, we felt with these records we have a chance of breaking one of the largest human trafficking organizations in the world. There are names and addresses and amounts of money paid and the names of those who were enslaved. What do you think?"

"You have pulled off the biggest robbery of the century. Thank you. Now, go home and enjoy the rest of Christmas, which is almost over. We will send agents into India and capture Dickson and his henchmen."

CHAPTER 18
FEBRUARY 23, 1973, FRIDAY, LONDON, ENGLAND

Chris and Anna Marie were helping with some of the files that were taken from Anthony Dickson in December when Chris was contacted by Joshua. Anna Marie heard the call also.

"It is time, we must go now. The event is about forty-eight hours away," Chris and Anna Marie went to the Director's office and Chris said one word.

"Joshua."

With that, Chris and Anna Marie disappeared.

BOOK 4

THE UNEXPECTED STORM

Reality 437266

Chris #4

The circumstances and future of Chris and Anna Marie of this reality were supposed to be similar to the circumstances of reality 437267. Because of what Anna Marie from 437269 did, their future was also changed. This story begins at the meeting of Chris and Anna Marie from this reality.

CHAPTER 1
MEETING

Christopher Beckett flew in from New York on Friday afternoon February 9, 1973. He landed his WPPA KLN10 at the Columbia, SC airport at 1:30 p.m. He taxied to the hanger and left it with the maintenance personnel. There was a call for snow and this was a large storm that reached from Mississippi to lower North Carolina. His radar had shown the large extent of the storm, but the direction and speed of the storm were still changing. Christopher thought this would be like most of the calls for snow in South Carolina - a false alarm. The storm would probably pass them by. His thoughts, however, that it would be an easy trip home to Aiken for a quiet weekend to ease his grief would turn out wrong, for this would be a life-changing event. He rented a four-wheel-drive Jeep Cherokee at the car rental agency, and that was his saving grace.

He had some personal business to attend to in Irmo, South Carolina, and it was around 2:30 before he was able to get on the interstate to Aiken because of the snow. As he neared the half-way part of his trip the snow was really coming down and the roads were pretty covered. There appeared to have been a snow plow in operation, but it certainly was not going to be able to keep up. By the time he reached the turn off for Aiken at mile marker twenty-two of Interstate 20 they were closing the interstate to further traffic. As he started up Highway 1 he saw a car, a little Oldsmobile Cutlass, stranded on the side of the road and a young lady stomping through the snow on foot toward Aiken. He slowed down and lowered the passenger window.

"May I help you?" he asked the startled girl who was not wrapped up enough for the bitter cold.

She shivered as she said, "I got it, thank you, though."

"If you will pardon my statement, ma'am, but it is nearing twenty-five degrees out here and you are not dressed for it."

"I live in Aiken. This snow will stop any minute, and it is only another eight miles. I'll be okay."

"Miss, please get in the car where it's warm and let me drive you."

She measured him with a glance, looked up at the sky to see the snow cascading down, and turned, opened the passenger door, placed her purse on the floor, and sat down.

"Okay, cowboy, let's move it," she said as she put her seatbelt on.

Christopher was distracted by her beautiful sparkling blue eyes and the shiny color of her auburn hair. She appeared to be about 5'9" and had on a light jacket over a blue dress. When he came to his senses he said, "Cowboy? The name's Christopher. And you are?"

She stuck out her hand, and he shook it feeling how unusually warm it was. He started to say something when she said, "Anna Marie Koch. Let's move this steer, I have a date tonight."

As they drove they saw a barricade and a detour sign to Reynolds Pond Road. Christopher slowed and asked the policeman on duty there what happened.

"There has been a very bad accident up ahead and the road is completely blocked. We have no way of clearing it in this weather."

"Was anyone hurt?" Christopher asked.

"No, just shook up."

"Thank you," Christopher replied. Noticing a snow plow had cleared the secondary road, Christopher turned and headed on.

"I am not sure you are going to be able to go anywhere for a date tonight, Anna Marie. If this snow keeps coming down, traffic is going to be paralyzed and nothing will be open."

She reached for her mobile phone and attempted a call. "Well, I have no signal to call home, or anyone for that matter."

"This road connects with Highway 19 and it also goes into Aiken, so sit and relax while I negotiate getting you home."

"Sure," Anna Marie said, as she removed her shoes and curled her feet into the seat with her. "Actually, home is Columbia and my parents live in South Aiken."

"What do you do in Columbia?"

"I am a surgeon at Richland Memorial Hospital. I specialize in heart surgery for children."

"You are a cardiologist?"

"Actually, I am a cardiothoracic surgeon. I am the chief surgeon in the children's ward."

"You look very young to have such an important position."

She muttered, "I'm glad you weren't the one to make that decision," and then faced front with nothing else to say.

The snow began coming down furiously and Christopher was having a difficult time seeing clearly. "Anna Marie, my parents live on this road and have a land line, and I do not see myself trying to attempt a drive into Aiken. Do you mind our stopping there, checking the news, and making a call to your home?"

"That would be fine," she replied as she studied the snow falling.

Christopher turned into a subdivision and negotiated the snow-packed road carefully. He stopped at a nice sized ranch style home that appeared to be a duplex.

"Let me check to see if they are home. No, come on let's get you inside as quickly as possible."

The snow was over a foot deep. Christopher rang the doorbell with no answer. He used his house key from his wallet and opened the door.

"Mom, Dad, are you home?" Anna Marie followed him in, they shut the front door, and Christopher moved through the house looking for his parents. He came back to the kitchen and noticed a note on the counter.

"Christopher, make yourself at home if you happen to visit. Your Mother and I are in Hawaii until March 1. We'll touch base when we return. Love, Mom and Dad."

"That's just great!" exclaimed Christopher.

"No one home?" she asked.

"No, they are in Hawaii."

"I wouldn't mind that," replied Anna Marie.

"Neither would I," he admitted.

"The phone is over there," he said as he pointed to the phone on the counter.

"Okay, I'll make the call," replied Anna Marie as she walked toward that end of the kitchen.

While Anna Marie called home, Christopher moved to the den, searched for the remote and turned on the television.

"…and no one, I repeat, no one needs to be traveling in this weather. We are to receive around two feet of snow before this is over early tomorrow afternoon. I hope you folks have plenty of food on hand, but be prepared for local blackouts. The roads will be impassable for a few days. Get out the checker boards, folks. Well that's the weather for today…."

Anna Marie was watching from the kitchen as Christopher turned off the television.

"What now, cowboy?"

Christopher turned and noticed she had taken off the light coat she was wearing. She was dressed in a light blue chiffon dress with a collar to the neck and sleeves to the wrist. "You must have already been dressed for your date?"

"I came straight from surgery and this is my surgical attire," she said, dryly.

"Are you ever serious about anything?" retorted Christopher.

"Cowboy, if you ever get to know me you would find that I am. Well what's for dinner, Chris?"

"Did you reach your parents or your date?"

"I called dad and asked him to call George since I do not have his phone number. By the way, our dads work together at the Savannah River Plant."

"Really?" Christopher replied, already knowing the answer to be true, yet not letting on that he knew. He never knew much about Mr. Koch's family.

"Yes. Dad told me they are both engineers for DuPont. He also told me I am in safe hands, Mr. Beckett. So, what do you do and where do you work?"

"It's a long story, Anna Marie."

"Well, we have plenty of time, so let's talk while we prepare supper."

Christopher found pasta and meatballs and ingredients for his special spaghetti sauce as Anna Marie located chocolate pudding and began to prepare it. He didn't find the time to talk much with any content and gave her short answers as he appeared to work hard at his cooking. They worked well together in the kitchen, not discussing much of anything as Anna Marie backed off with her questions. After an hour, they were able to sit down in the dining room to a delicious meal. During this time, Christopher had also retrieved his luggage from the Cherokee and taken it to his old rooms. He found candles and they had a candlelit dinner. Christopher even pulled out the chair for Anna Marie and as she sat she thanked him.

"Do you object if I pray for the meal?" Chris asked.

"No, I would object if you didn't pray," Anna Marie replied.

"Our heavenly Father, You knew about this storm. I pray for safety for all who are out in it. I pray especially for the emergency personnel and their families. Please strengthen, comfort, and protect all who have to work tonight. May everyone trapped in vehicles be located and find a haven of rest in this cold. Thank you for allowing me to find Anna Marie and being able to get her to safety. Thank you for this food, bless it to the nourishment of our bodies. I pray these things in Jesus' name. Amen."

"Amen," Anna Marie echoed.

"Anna Marie, I am an attorney and a business advisor and manager. I travel all over the world to assist businesses who are in trouble financially, and if they will accept my help, I do so."

"You seem very young to have such a position."

"Okay, touché. Please forgive me for my earlier comment concerning your age. I am actually twenty-seven and will be twenty-eight in April. How old are you?"

"Mr. Beckett, how forward you are. I was twenty-five on February 2."

"Happy late birthday. I hope you had a big party for such a momentous occasion; quarter of a century birthday."

"No, I just ate rocky road ice cream with my friend, Candi."

"So, where did you do your residency?" he asked.

"Boston Medical. Say, this sauce is delicious. I really like it," Anna Marie commented.

"Thank you. Have you and George dated very much?"

"Actually, George is a date my mother found because she doesn't want me to be a spinster and she wants grandchildren. I have never met him. How about you?"

Christopher lowered his head and let out a heavy sigh.

"I'm sorry, I am a good listener, though," said Anna Marie.

"I dated a girl while in high school. She was two years older than me. She studied in Atlanta and we kept in touch and dated for several years and I asked her twice to marry me. She said 'No' both times. Her wedding is in Maryland this weekend to a Navy midshipman. I came home to weep over the loss."

"You don't really mean that. You need to be happy for her that she found true love."

"I'm sorry, this conversation is over," Chris said angrily.

"Hey, don't be upset with me. I am sure in God's Word you can find comfort over this. Be happy for the couple, and move on with your life. Listen, I have counseled many parents over the loss of a child who didn't make it through surgery or who died later, so, Mr. Christopher Beckett, this isn't the end of the world and you should recognize God is sovereign. If you and this girl—"

"Mary," Chris interjected.

"Okay, Mary. If you were meant to be together then it would have been you at the altar and not some Navy guy."

They sat in silence for several minutes as Christopher thought over what she had said. He had been selfish and moody for some time now, even though he knew in his heart Mary was not for him. He had not trusted God in the matter as he should have done. Anna Marie had put him in his place very quickly, and he was not angry with her about it. In fact, he rather appreciated what she had to say. After awhile he looked up at Anna Marie, caught her eyes, and said, "Thank you."

"You are welcome. The door is open anytime."

"The pudding is nice, what did you add to it?" Chris asked.

"Nutmeg, sort of spices it up."

"Yes, it does."

"Tell me, do your parents own both sides of the duplex?"

"What do you mean?"

"Well, I saw the other entrance and I just assumed this was a duplex."

Chris had been pondering in his heart if he should share, thinking she would be curious anyway, so he decided to go ahead and show her 'The Haven.'

"Anna Marie Koch, it is time for a tour. Just leave the dishes, I'll get them later."

CHAPTER 2

The Almost Tour

"Follow me, please. This home is my childhood home and my father added to it several times. This last addition was two years ago and I headed the construction for Dad as I purchased the home at that time. Mom and Dad can stay here the rest of their lives or decide to move elsewhere if they so desire. My add-ons were extensive as you will see," Christopher pulled a hotel card from his pocket and swiped it in the lock of a door as they entered the first bedroom suite. "This is my sister Frances' suite. She is in Paris studying to be a chef."

"Wow. Why the hotel key?"

"You will understand that later. Frances is about your size, so you will be sleeping here tonight and you can go through her clothes and find something more comfortable and warmer than that dress, although I believe it does highlight your blue eyes nicely." Anna Marie blushed slightly and lowered her eyes.

"There are forty-two homes here in this development. There are an additional twenty-five families within a mile of the subdivision. Most of the residents have been here since I was a little boy. There was not a community center and we are far from Aiken, almost six miles from the city limits. There is no development this side of town, and I felt we needed a place for fun and also in case of disaster; a place for people to come if they lost electricity. We have actually lost electricity this side of Aiken many times in the ice storms over the years, and I am sure we will this weekend. I had a very sophisticated generator system installed, much like hospitals, so we should be warm."

They proceeded down the hall, passing several doors. The carpet turned to fine laminate wood. They reached an elevator door ahead of them and a stairway to the right. Anna Marie started to ask about the elevator when Christopher said, "Follow me, please," as he turned right and opened the glass door for her to follow. They turned left again and went up one short flight of stairs. Anna Marie was puzzled as they entered what appeared to be a very fine hotel lobby with a man at the desk.

"Good evening, Roger, this is Anna Marie. She will be staying in Frances' suite. May I have a family key for her, please?"

"Yes Sir. We already have several guests."

"Anticipation, I am sure."

"Yes Sir. Here you are ma'am."

"Thank you," Anna Marie said as she reached for the key.

"Follow me, if you will," Chris said. He led Anna Marie to a kiosk style map that showed the layout of where they were. "There are ten floors underground. The first four consist of a parking garage. The next two are shops, dining, a bowling alley, an infirmary, a church, a theatre, a ball room, and a conference room. The final four are hotel rooms. We can house up to 1,500 people; more if an emergency calls for it. Mostly only the neighborhood knows we are here, but word does get out and we have an occasional traveler."

"I really do not know what to say, Christopher. I am amazed and full of questions, but I am also really tired and think I should call for an early evening."

"That's okay, let's go back to the house."

They descended the stairs and as they turned left to go to the main house Anna Marie noticed a sign that said "No Entrance."

"So, if no one is supposed to come into the house, what keeps them out?"

"Anna Marie, hand me your key. Now back up. That should be fine. Let me go ahead a few feet to the carpet area, now try to follow me." Anna Marie stepped forward and stopped. She could not go beyond what appeared to be a wall pushing her.

"It's a force field, an invention of mine."

"I'm impressed."

Christopher came forward, reached for her hand and she easily followed him through the field. He handed her key to her and commented, "This room to the right is mine. See the sign that says 'Christopher.' You will notice yours says 'Frances.' Family keys open each door, so if you want to come see me, your key will work. Don't worry, the bedroom is separate from the sitting room, just like Frances'. Here is your door. Goodnight, Miss Koch. It is a pleasure to meet you."

"Goodnight, Christopher, and thank you for being my knight and saving me from the cold."

"You are welcome."

CHAPTER 3

Confusion

Later that evening as Christopher headed for his room after finishing the dishes, he hesitated as he passed Anna Marie's door, but kept walking to his room. As he entered, he let out a long sigh.

"I am not looking for anyone, Lord, and she is right; You are sovereign, even to the point of her car breaking down and my showing up when I did. For now, please give us Your safety through the night as well as for all of the emergency personnel working in this. Let those who need a 'Haven of Rest' find us this night, Amen."

After praying, Chris decided to call his office.

"WPPA help desk. Oh, Agent Beckett, I didn't expect your call; you are on leave."

"Yes, I am, Virginia. Can you check the weather satellite and report for North America, specifically South Carolina, and let me know what you find?"

"Sure, just a moment." After a few moments Virginia came back on the line. "The report does not look good. If the low front off the coast causes the current storm to stall you are in for several days of very cold weather and extreme road conditions. This is being called a once in a century event by many forecasters and meteorologists."

"Thank you, Virginia. Please tell Edna hello for me."

"Yes, Sir."

Back in her room, Anna Marie was on the phone with her father. "He has a hotel underground at his house, a shopping center, a bowling alley, a church, a theatre, and…"

"Anna Marie, slow down. I've been there and I have seen everything."

"You have? Why didn't you tell me? You have met him? I had no idea!"

"Hush, honey, and listen. I work with Christopher's dad here at the SRP and when Christopher built the underground city he needed someone to handle the ventilation. He contracted me to work out the details for the ventilation and the requirements for the system of heating and air conditioning. I didn't tell you because it was a secret when I was working with him. He asked me not to tell anyone. If I had told you I knew him you would have wanted to know the details. He is a very nice man and was easy to work with."

"You work with his dad?" she asked.

"Yes, and he and his family are very pleasant people to be around."

"Dad, I realize I have just met the man, but I have feelings about him. I have never felt like this around any man. He is very sweet and gentle and intelligent and prays like he is talking to God in the same room."

"Watch your heart, honey."

"I am trying, Dad. I am tired, I must go. Goodnight."

"Your mother and I send you our love. Goodnight."

Christopher did not sleep well. In fact, he didn't actually fall asleep until 3 a.m., about two hours before the time he would normally get up. He spent a lot of time writing in his journal and studying the Bible, seeking information about God's will. He also spent a considerable amount of time in prayer, arguing with God and explaining to Him why he was not interested in a relationship right now. It hurt too much to think of a relationship after Mary Adams, even after hearing what Anna Marie had to say on the subject. All he felt was God was saying, "This one is for you. You think I would not have someone for you? You and she have a mighty work to do for me!" He finally fell asleep, exhausted, but with a peaceful heart.

CHAPTER 4

Anna Marie had been up at 5 a.m. and had done her Bible study and prayer time. She had some pointed questions, yet she felt at peace as she prayed concerning the unsettling issues of her heart. She had searched through Frances' clothes and had selected designer jeans with a western style blue shirt and a boa tie. She even finished it out with a pair of western boots that fit perfectly. After styling her hair and looking in the mirror to check it all she heard and felt her stomach rumble. She left her room and knocked on Christopher's door, not knowing if he was in his room or somewhere else in the complex. Reasoning she had to find out, she used her key and opened the door. The first thing she saw was his Bible and journal on the floor by a recliner chair, so she picked them up and placed them on the end table. "I wonder what he wrote," she thought. "No, that would be snooping." She turned and knocked on the bedroom door. There was no answer so she knocked again, very hard. She heard a mumble, so she knew he was in there. About that time her stomach rumbled again. There was a protein bar on the counter, so she walked over, unwrapped it, and began to eat with gusto. She walked to his refrigerator and pulled out a bottle of water and sat down in his recliner, finished off the snack, and waited while reading his Bible and praying. Two hours later, the bedroom door opened and Christopher came out in his robe.

Anna Marie looked up and said, "Good morning, sleepyhead."

"I'm sorry, I didn't get to sleep until early this morning. How long have you been here?"

"About two hours."

"Aren't you hungry, or have you had breakfast?"

"I ate a protein bar I found on the counter."

"That's good. That's a very nice outfit, blue is indeed your color. Can you give me about fifteen minutes and we'll go to one of the restaurants for brunch?"

"Sure, I am ready for that tour as well."

It took Chris a little longer than he expected to get ready, so thirty minutes later, they were on the way to the elevator to go to brunch. Christopher had chosen an outfit very similar to Anna Marie's, except his shirt was maroon. His boa tie had an eagle to hold it together; hers had an onyx stone.

"I like your outfit, cowboy."

"I already told you I like yours, but I'll tell you again: you look very nice today. Not that you didn't look nice yesterday; you look nice!" Christopher's ears turned pink.

During the trip to the restaurant, Christopher had acknowledged several people who spoke to him and almost all of them looked at Anna Marie with curious surprise.

She asked Christopher, "Why the looks?"

"You are a stranger and they are only curious," was all he said, although he knew they were probably curious because he never brought anyone there.

Anna Marie took a look around as they passed several shops and finally reached a restaurant that was open. As they finished their brunch, an announcement came over the public-address system. "Christopher Beckett, please report to the clinic. We have an emergency."

"Care to come with me?" he asked Anna Marie.

"Sure," she replied.

As they walked deeper into the mall, Anna Marie saw the front of a hospital clinic.

"Wow, that looks contemporary, how is it staffed?"

"Normally it is not staffed, maybe just an RN or a PA, but at times like this, we have a doctor on hand, as well. Have you ever heard of Dr. Jeff McNealy?"

Anna Marie stopped in her tracks. "Yes, he saved my life once."

"That's interesting, he saved my life, also."

"We need to discuss this," they both said at the same time.

"Hi, Colleen, what's the emergency?" Chris asked.

"It's my sister, Kathy. I think she has appendicitis."

"Well, where is Dr. McNealy?"

"He is in Chicago in a conference, and he didn't get a replacement, because no one expected this storm."

"Where is she?" Anna Marie asked.

"Forgive me. Colleen Knight this is Dr. Anna Marie Koch. Dr Koch, meet our RN, Colleen Knight," introduced Chris.

"You're a doctor?" Colleen asked. "Will you come look at my sister?"

"I would be happy to," Anna Marie said.

"Right this way, Dr. Koch."

Colleen led Chris and Anna Marie to the room where her sister was. After a careful but quick examination, Anna Marie confirmed Kathy Knight needed an operation as soon as possible. "How can you get her to Aiken County hospital?"

Colleen looked at her with fear in her eyes and supplied the obvious information.

"With this weather and the road conditions I do not see how."

"Colleen, I am a surgeon, is there an operating room here?"

"Yes, there is," said Colleen.

"Could you assist me with the surgery?"

"Yes."

"Alright, that leaves the anesthesiologist. Is there one here?" Anna Marie asked.

"You are looking at him," Chris interjected.

"Christopher, I do not need jokes right now."

"He is, ma'am, fully trained and certified," Colleen confirmed.

"We'll also discuss that one later. Let's go."

The lights flickered just then and Anna Marie looked at Christopher with apprehension.

"That was the generators kicking in. We have secure electricity."

As Anna Marie prepared to make the incision, Christopher leaned toward her and indicated she should make a vertical rather than a lateral cut and at a slightly different location than she was accustomed. No X-ray or sonogram was taken, so she looked at Christopher with a puzzled look, but he just said, "Please, trust me, you will be making a smaller incision." Sure enough, he was right.

After the operation, they went to the exit at the waiting room and found several people there needing help of one kind or another.

Christopher did the paper work and dispensed the medication as Anna Marie saw the patients. Colleen was taking care of Kathy in recovery and then taking her to her hospital room. It was about 7 p.m. when they left to go to a restaurant. Chris took her to "Charlie's Place." They went over the menu and after they ordered, Anna Marie said, "How many talents do you have, Mr. Beckett?"

"Other than what you have seen, I am a licensed commercial pilot and…." Just then, someone dressed in a military uniform approached, saluted, and asked to speak with Christopher privately. He excused himself and went a few feet away. They discussed something that included the words 'medical unit' and as Christopher sat back down he told Anna Marie an Army Medical Corps Platoon had arrived and would be staffing the clinic.

"And he saluted you because…?"

"I may or may not be in the National Guard."

"As an officer?"

"Yes."

She started to ask more questions when Christopher asked, "Do you dance?"

"Yes, I do, but I need more questions answered," she replied. Then she made a decision they needed to be somewhere they wouldn't be interrupted, or she felt she would continually be put off. As soon as they finished the meal with no questions from Anna Marie, a fact which Christopher noticed but was puzzled by, she said "I need to go to my room."

"Alright, let's call it an early night. Today has been rather taxing."

CHAPTER 5

REALIZATION

They returned to the house. Anna Marie noticed as they returned to the elevator the place was a good bit more crowded than earlier. He attempted to drop her off at her door, but she would have none of that. She pulled him into the sitting room and directed him onto the recliner.

"Sit!" As he sat down with a surprised look on his face she said, "Okay, cowboy, talk! And don't stop until all of my questions are answered."

"It is a rather long and involved story."

"I have time."

"On June 5, 1963, I was the driver in a car that was involved in a very unusual accident. Our 1962 Oldsmobile F85 was struck from the left side at the driver's door by another car of the same make, color, and year model. In fact, when the state patrolman arrived, he noticed he was looking at twins of each driver and each passenger of the cars. Every detail was identical, except for the fact I was the only one injured. The other driver was actually taking care of my injuries as much as possible. I was struck unconscious and all of the following happened while I was unconscious, but I was told before the ambulances arrived, some five minutes after the accident the other car and all of the people from it disappeared, but not before my friend Kenny and our two dates could speak to them for a while. What we have determined is they were from a different reality."

"You are speaking science fiction now."

"No, this is true. There have been enough substantiated reports and interviews to ascertain indeed there are many dimensions. However, this is the only instance recorded where there has been an actual breech in physical dimension. We have this record top-secret, so we don't truly know if there have been other instances, but we have never heard of another report."

"And you expect me to believe this?" asked Anna Marie.

"No, you do not have to, but you just need to know I was in a severe accident and who or what I am now is a result of that accident.

"Kenny, Kenneth Knight, Colleen's brother and my best friend, had been recruited by WPPA. That agency has some very modern medical techniques and facilities not available elsewhere, and Kenny knew I needed immediate, acute medical treatment. He used his mobile phone to call WPPA, and they called Dr. Jeff McNealy, who also worked with WPPA and had designed the neural implant in my brain. He came to Aiken County Hospital and worked to stabilize me. The ambulance had taken me there and I was still unconscious and did not know what was happening."

"I know you said this, but no one else was injured?" asked Anna Marie in a rather shaky voice that didn't go unnoticed by Chris.

"No. Dr. McNealy determined I had severe head injuries and I needed to be in a more modern facility to have it handled correctly or I was going to die, or at the very least remain in a vegetable state the rest of my life. There was a tremendous loss of blood so they gave me several units to keep me alive. I was then transported to a military hospital in Alabama where some emergency surgeries took place to prepare me for long travel. From there I was taken to Liverpool, England, the headquarters for WPPA. Dr. McNealy went with me. What they did for me had never been attempted before, but the technology was there waiting for the proper time and need. About forty-two percent of my brain is bionic; that is about as close as I can get to the detail of what it is. The neural implant is such that some is electronic, some is biological, and it is powered by a unique power cell. To my knowledge there is only one other person like me and she had the similar operation in 1968. I do not know who she is."

"Chris, it was me," said Anna Marie. She was shaking. "I was injured when I found myself in the middle of a gang war I walked up on as I was leaving classes one night in Boston. I was hit with a baseball bat. My father has a high security clearance and knew of the operation you had. He never told me it was you. He was called by Boston Memorial and told he and my family needed to get to my bedside quickly if they wanted to see me before I passed. They saw no hope for me. On their way, he called Dr. McNealy and had him call WPPA and work out arrangements for my operation. I also have a mental capacity beyond what most humans ever hope to attain. They told me I had a mental link available to WPPA, but since I was not connected with them it could not be activated. Are you with WPPA?"

"In the interest of complete disclosure, yes I am."

"Okay, so you are a lawyer, an accountant, a business fixer, an architect, an anesthesiologist, a chef, and a pilot. You are in the military and at the same time a foreign agent; how can that be?"

"That's enough for now. We are both tired."

"My questions are not all answered, Captain!"

"It's General, and I'll see you in the morning."

"Don't change subjects on me, I have some more questions!"

"In light of what you have just told me I believe I can get all of your questions answered and more. Just give me until tomorrow. Are you going to church with me? The service starts at 12:30."

"Yes, I will, but we do need to talk some more. I am going to run by the clinic first thing in the morning to see Kathy and I'll meet you at the front of the clinic at 9 a.m.?"

"No, I'll pick up at your door at 8 a.m."

"Okay, that will give us plenty of time before services at 12:30. Goodnight, Chris, but you promise to answer all of my questions?"

"Yes ma'am, I do. Goodnight, Anna Marie."

❧ ❧ ❧

Back in the solitude of her own room, Anna Marie called her father again. "Dad, he is like me. He had the same operation."

"I know."

"You knew he was the other person operated on like me and you didn't tell me last night? Didn't you think that was important for me to know?"

"Yes, honey, I knew. And, no, it wasn't a story for me to tell."

"Do you know the circumstances of his accident?"

"No, I do not. My security clearance is not that high, but I have been told it is rather bizarre and is classified as super top-secret. If he told you then you must keep it as a secret; that is very important. And, if he told you, then he must care for you and trust you a lot. After all, he just met you a little over twenty-four hours ago."

"Well, he hasn't answered all of my questions yet."

"Did he tell you he would?"

"Yes."

"Then trust he will."

"Dad, this has been the strangest twenty-four hours of my life apart from the miracle of my operation. I do not know what God has for me in this. I am losing my heart to this man and I am full of questions. This day has left me whipped. Goodnight, Dad."

"I told you to be careful. Trust God, He will show you the way. Just trust Him and pray. Goodnight honey, your mom and I love you and are praying for you."

Anna Marie hung up the phone and dialed Palmetto Richland Hospital.

"May I have Pediatrics Surgery, please? Thank you."

"Pediatrics Surgery, Candi Stephens speaking, how may I help you?"

"Candi, it's me…."

"Annie, how are you? It's so good to hear your voice! How was the date with George?"

"I never made it home. My car broke down and…"

"Oh, Annie, your car broke down? Are you alright? If you are not home then where are you?"

"I was picked up by a very nice…."

"Annie, you were hitchhiking? You know better than that! Oh, Annie, were you kidnapped? Just say 'no' as the code you are in trouble…."

"No, Candi, I was not kidnapped. I am okay. I am at Christopher…."

"Okay, I got that, you have been kidnapped and a man named Christopher is holding you hostage for ransom…."

"No, Candi, I have not been kidnapped! Mr. Beckett is not holding me for ransom. Listen, I need to talk to you…."

"You are very good, I got his first and last name. Where is he holding you?"

"Candi, I am not being held hostage. I am at Mr. Beckett's house and I will be here through next week. I am calling you to let you know I am taking some time off. Do not expect me in the office before next Monday the 19th. And by the way, you watch too many soap operas."

"You never take any time off. Oh, Annie, you are so brave...."

"Candi, listen, I think I am falling in love...."

"With George? You haven't met him yet."

"Candi, have you heard a word I have said? Where is your mind today?"

"I've been on duty for forty-eight hours without any sleep and I feel as perky as if I just started my shift."

"Who else is there helping you?"

"No one, I am here all alone. The storm has shut everything down. Oh, Annie, I hope they find you before something bad happens."

"Goodbye, Candi. I love you, sweet sister, and please understand I am okay. In fact, apart from my operation, I have never been better!"

"Goodbye, sweet Annie."

☙ ☙ ☙

Chris was having a very similar conversation with Kenneth back in his own room.

"Kenny, I have never felt this way about a woman before and it scares me. I never had this feeling, even about Mary."

"Love is like that, Chris, it hits you in the gut and makes you weak at the knees. You don't know what to do with her and you can't be without her. You think of everything you want to say to her and then when the time comes you can't get a word out of your mouth."

"That is it exactly. What am I going to do? I just met her and I don't ever want to be without her."

"Well, right now you don't have to worry about her leaving. From what I see of the weather reports you are snowed and iced in at least until next Friday. Spend time with her and get to know her."

"If I can get my tongue untied I will."

"Carmen's calling me, I have to go help with the kids."

"And that's another thing, how can I take care of children with my job and other responsibilities?"

"Well, you don't marry with children and then it's at least nine months. Do what I did, Chris; I retired."

CHAPTER 6

PLANS

Using his link, Christopher paged Edna. *"Hello, Christopher, are you having a relaxing vacation?"*

"No, and I'm sure you know why."

"Well, I was hearing some interesting disclosures. Are you sure you want to be telling her all of your secrets?"

"I think you know the answer to that. You have been studying me for several years. However, my call is about something specific concerning the links and what their design was for. Tell me, from all I have read and understood there are two different links. Am I to understand you can activate both of them?"

"No, only the link to WPPA so she can receive phone calls. The link to you has to be instigated by the two of you and once it is turned on it will flood both of you with all memories, thoughts, and plans - good and bad; somewhat like an upgrade on a computer, but merging data rather than actually upgrading software."

"Can it be activated apart from the WPPA connection?"

"No, the WPPA connection must be activated first."

"Can that be done by you?"

"Only after your clearance, Agent Beckett."

"Will she notice anything?"

"No, not until a call is connected from me."

"Alright, please do so. Now, tell me how to activate our link."

"Chris, from everything we understand, it must be a chemical-magnetic-biological action. It is only activated by a kiss."

"A kiss? You have got to be kidding! So, this is supposed to be activated only if we met and fell in love?"

"*No, I am not kidding, and yes, you are right as to the possible implication of the two of you meeting and falling in love. The emotions of the kiss activate all areas instantly.*"

"*How do we stop the exchange?*"

"*We have no idea. This has never been done before, but we believe that once started it can never be stopped.*"

"*Okay. Would we go through the rest of our lives reading each other's private thoughts?*"

"*According to the blueprint it initially only works while you are touching after the kiss. Private thoughts can be limited, but it takes practice and something akin to firewalls have to be activated. Since it has never been done before I do not know how to tell you to accomplish it, and the scientists are not even sure the whole thing will work. You know the two of you are the only test subjects!*"

"*It sounds like it would be better to never activate the link. What were these designers and doctors thinking?*"

"*Christopher, only you can answer whether or not you want to activate it. As to what the doctors were thinking, you know the motivations of many men in power are not pure. Military power and world dominance come first.*"

"*Will the programming activate something else?*"

"*I do not think so, but I am not sure. I have seen the programming data and I do not see anything sinister in it.*"

"*Thank you, Edna. Goodnight.*"

"*Goodnight, Chris. I will be praying for you.*"

"*Thank you.*"

Anna Marie and Christopher, each on their knees in their own rooms, prayed.

"Heavenly Father, You are sovereign. You knew of this meeting before the worlds were formed. If we are meant for each other You will show us. Grant us wisdom and restraint; grant us comfort and strength as we seek Your will. Whatever the future holds, I know You hold the future. In Jesus Christ's name, amen."

CHAPTER 7

FEBRUARY 11, SUNDAY, 5 A.M.
GETTING TO KNOW YOU

Christopher and Anna Marie rose promptly at 5 a.m., had their Bible study and prayer, and finished by 7 a.m. They each chose their outfits for the day, and at precisely 8 a.m. Christopher knocked on Anna Marie's door. She looked striking in a teal dress and white sweater.

"Good morning. My, you look beautiful. I have never seen that outfit before."

"I am not surprised, your sister has a very large closet of many clothes. You look very dashing today as well. Your teal tie matches my dress perfectly. One would think we chose our outfits together. I love the black suit, by the way."

"Well, Miss Koch, please take my arm and we will stroll to the clinic and then to breakfast. After that, I have a surprise for you before church."

"Certainly, Mr. Beckett. Let's get this show on the road." She slipped her arm through his and off they went.

At the clinic, they saw Colonel Moffat from the medical aid platoon and Colleen in a heated conversation. "Hold on here. Colleen, what is wrong?"

"Chris, tell this, this, this...."

"Colonel?" suggested Chris.

"Yes, this *Colonel*, this is not a military base and he doesn't have to have every Standard Operating Procedure form filled out or whatever."

"Colonel, I thought I made it clear with headquarters Colleen was in charge and this is a civilian clinic where you are graciously helping during this emergency."

"I am sorry, Sir. Somehow I did not get the message as you are stating it. Please forgive me Ms. Knight. I will do whatever you need to rectify the situation."

Colleen's mouth dropped before she said humbly, "Thank you."

Anna Marie asked, "Colleen, how is Kathy this morning?"

"She is doing well. Want to see her?"

"Sure. Are you coming too, Chris?"

"I certainly am. Please lead the way."

Kathy's eyes beamed with excitement when she saw Chris and Anna Marie. "Wow, don't the two of you look spiffy? And you have matching colors too."

"Good morning, Kathy. Did you have a good night's rest?" asked Anna Marie.

"It was okay except for Colleen and the colonel at each other's throats all night."

"All night?" questioned Chris.

"Kathy, I am going to take a look at the incision and change the dressing. Chris would you wait in the hall, please?"

"Certainly. I'll be right outside."

As soon as Chris left Kathy turned to Anna Marie, "Well, do you like him?"

"Kathy, stop," said Colleen instantly.

Anna Marie blushed. "That's alright, Colleen."

"See, she does," said Kathy smugly.

"Actually, I do, very much."

"That is so wonderful, Dr. Koch. I can see by the way he looks at you, he likes you, too."

"You do, I mean, he does? Oh!" she exclaimed as she turned very pink and lowered her head. "Okay, let's take a look at that incision, young lady. Yes, it is looking good. I don't feel any fever. Do you think you can hold down some ice cream?"

"Yes, ma'am. I didn't mean to embarrass you."

"That's alright, Kathy."

"Are you ready in there? We need to get going," Chris called through the door.

"Coming, Christopher."

Anna Marie recovered the incision and then met Chris in the hall.

"Was everything alright with Kathy?"

"Yes, it was. Where are we headed?"

"You'll see."

They arrived at the ballroom and it was decorated in pink with a "Happy Birthday" sign in one corner above a finely decorated table filled with silver topped trays of food. "Here, have a seat. Let's pray. Heavenly Father, thank you for bringing Anna Marie here and thank you for the day of her birth. Thank you for her being here yesterday to help heal Kathy. Thank you for the circumstances that have brought us together. May we use godly wisdom in understanding where this is taking us. Bless this food to the nourishment of our bodies, I pray in Jesus' name, amen."

"Amen."

"Anna Marie, I understand blueberry pancakes are your favorite for breakfast. Am I correct?"

"Yes, you are, Christopher - topped with peanut butter?"

"And that they are!"

"Wow," Anna Marie said as she removed the cover from her place. Christopher removed his cover as well and picked up a smaller cover to reveal pancake syrup.

"May I?" he asked.

"Yes, you may."

As Christopher poured a generous helping across her pancakes, Anna Marie looked at his handsome face with those large brown eyes and wished she could have breakfast every day for the rest of her life with him. He was looking at her sparkling blue eyes and wishing the same.

After a few minutes of silent eating, Christopher laid down his fork and looked across the table at a very contented Anna Marie.

"Anna Marie, I told you I had a surprise for you, and this is not it, however, I want you to think the following phrase in your mind. Don't say the phrase, just think it: Edna Ryder this is Anna Marie calling."

Anna Marie did that and was suddenly startled when she heard a voice answering her back.

"Hello, Anna Marie, it is good to finally meet you. I knew of your operation, but was not given any information on you after that. It is good to know you and Christopher are getting to know one another."

Anna Marie's eyes went wide with fright and her mind went blank.

"Anna Marie, did you not hear me?" Edna called.

"*Yes ma'am, I did. I was so startled. This is surreal. You are in my head.*"

Edna chuckled. "*Yes, I am. I have been in Christopher's head for many years. I must go now, the two of you have a schedule to keep. I am going to keep the link open because you received a call. Christopher is on the line.*"

Anna Marie looked up and Christopher was standing at her chair. "*May I have this dance?*" she heard in her head. Startled again, all she could do was stare at him. Is he in my head?

"*Yes I am.*"

"*This is too much.*"

"*No, the too much part will come later. For now, we are just having a conversation. Let's dance.*"

The music started and a slow waltz was playing. Suddenly it felt as if she were dancing on air. "*You are,*" Christopher said as she looked down. They were literally two feet off the floor.

"*Another invention?*"

"*Not an invention, more like a talent or an ability.*"

They danced all kinds of dances for two hours. When they finished and floated to the ground, Anna Marie was beside herself with joy.

"*I cannot believe this.*"

"*Well, then don't pinch me because I do not ever want to wake up.*"

"*Neither do I, Chris, neither do I.*"

She went to kiss Chris, but he held her away.

Chris began by speaking aloud. "Not just yet, you need to know something first. I love you and I want to marry you. I know I need to ask your dad first, but I need to know if you feel the same way."

"I was wondering what all of these feelings were, but now I know. I love you, Chris, and yes, I do feel the same way you do. Believe me, I do."

"Now, here comes the hard part. There are two ways for us to link. One is through the earth's magnetic link we have been using, the other is through a chemical-magnetic-biological link. Once it is made, it cannot be broken. That link will merge all of our thoughts, plans, and ideas. All of the training we have ever had will be available to each other. I am told it is like upgrading your computer and having the data added to it from another computer."

"Okay, how is this activated?"

"I am told it is activated by a kiss, so before we kissed, I wanted you to know what would happen so you had a choice of not merging the link if you did not want to do so."

"So, let me get this straight. You will know all of my thoughts, past and present, and I will know yours as well. Chris, are you able to handle my past without being jealous or upset with me over the choices I have made? Can you go through the depression I felt after my surgery? Can you handle my rants and anger and my questions to God? Can I handle the feelings and thoughts you had for Mary?"

"Anna Marie, I have had some thoughts similar to all you have stated. Perhaps we do need to think about this, especially because of my relationship with Mary."

"Chris, would we ever be able to kiss without the link being activated?"

"From what I have been told, no."

CHAPTER 8

SURRENDER

"Let's pray." Christopher and Anna Marie knelt on the dance floor. They held each other's hands and prayed to God, asking for wisdom, discernment, grace, and the strength to walk away from each other if that was His will. They agonized in prayer for a good hour. Tears fell from both their faces, and if they didn't hear the call on the PA system for church services, they would have missed it and continued in prayer. As it was, they made it in time and sat on an aisle seat about one-third of the way back on the left side.

The song service was beautiful and uplifting, and the perfect way to start the service.

"Helping others as we glorify God," Pastor Scott began, "is what God has called us to do. If God had not laid it on his heart, Christopher would not have built this facility for us to be in safety and to enjoy today. If God had not chosen for Dr. Koch's car to break down where would Kathy Knight be today? Each of us has been given jobs to do and talents with which to do them. Sometimes it takes two working together to accomplish what God has requested." Thirty minutes later Pastor Scott was saying, "In closing, let me say this; Jesus took upon himself the form of a man and came and sacrificed Himself so you and I might live. What has God chosen for you? Oh, you may not know the full extent of it, but do not fear. He will carry you through whatever He asks of you. Our song leader will come now and...Yes, Christopher?"

Anna Marie and Christopher had been conversing on and off through their link, and as the sermon was concluding they had made a firm resolve.

"Anna Marie and I have song for all of us."

"Please, let's praise God together."

Christopher whispered to the pianist the name of the song and then he and Anna Marie each picked up a microphone and came to the center of the platform.

"Anna Marie and I met less than forty-eight hours ago, yet we both feel we know God wants to change the direction of our lives. I have to speak to someone first, but we hope and believe we will not receive any resistance to that change." No one could miss the look of love Anna Marie was giving Christopher as he was speaking. Having said that, Christopher and Anna Marie waited for the music to begin and then she in a beautiful tenor voice and Christopher in a beautiful alto voice began to sing. In their song, they proclaimed their love for Christ and their determination to give their lives fully to Him. As they sang the last lines they each lifted the microphones they were holding up toward the ceiling and said "Praise God" as they joined their other hands. The congregation resounded with exclamations of "Praise God," "Hallelujah," and "Amen."

Christopher looked at Anna Marie and said, "Are you thinking what I am thinking?"

"I think I am. We can do so much for Him together."

"I need to see your father and mother. I need to ask them."

Christopher didn't know the microphone was still on and the entire church was listening in and, there, coming down the aisle were Albert and Alyce Koch. As they came on stage Christopher shook their hands and said, "Mr. and Mrs. Koch, may I have your daughter's hand in marriage?"

Mr. Koch smiled as he said, "Which one?"

Anna Marie whispered in Christopher's ear, "I have a twin sister."

"Oh! Anna Marie, Sir."

"Yes, you may, Christopher. When?"

"First things first, Sir." Christopher turned to Anna Marie, got on one knee, pulled out a red jewelry box and said, "I do not want to spend any more time without you in my life. Will you, Anna Marie Koch, marry me?"

He opened the box to show a beautiful pink clustered diamond. He asked Edna to reconnect the link and then he told Anna Marie in her mind, "*I purchased this ring this morning, it is not a recycle.*"

She looked him straight in the eyes and said, "Yes!" In her mind, she asked him, *"Can we get married today?"*

"Are you sure?"

"Yes!"

Christopher turned to Mr. and Mrs. Koch and said, "Is today soon enough, Sir?"

"Today is fine, Chris," Mr. Koch agreed.

Christopher turned to Pastor Scott. "May we have an afternoon wedding? All of you are invited. 5 p.m." Pastor Scott nodded and the congregation went wild with clapping, cheers, and praise.

Christopher and Anna Marie walked over to the pastor and asked a couple of questions and made a couple of directions regarding the ceremony and then walked back to Mr. and Mrs. Koch and thanked them. They then determined the Koch's were brought in by Edna's direction in an WPPA 4-wheel drive vehicle. Christopher asked if they had checked in yet and found out they had not. The four of them walked to the elevators and went to the check in lobby.

"Roger, please give Mr. and Mrs. Koch a hotel key for guest room number two in the house."

Edna had severed the link between Christopher and Anna Marie after congratulating them both and Christopher then began making plans. Flowers were ordered, attire was ordered, and reception plans were begun.

"Anna Marie, I have ordered the flowers and my tux and your father's and Kenny's as well from stores here in the complex. Everything we need is here."

"Isn't Kenneth in Alabama?"

"He was. However, he is on the way to Columbia now on a F16. If you want Candi as your maid of honor I can make those plans as well and get someone to hold the fort for her at the hospital."

"Do I need to call her to have her get ready?"

"Yes, but she doesn't need to pack anything. We can figure all that out here. We just need to schedule her and Kenneth on the same helicopter. The weather has cleared enough to allow that to occur and we have a helipad topside."

"Wow, you have a lot of pull."

"Anna Marie, you will know it all after a while. Now, how about a dress for you?" They had reached Frances' suite and Chris went into the sitting room with her. "Anna Marie, I have never seen it, but my sister purchased a wedding dress and then changed her mind on the man she thought she wanted to spend the rest of her life with. It is hanging in the rear left of her walk-in closet in a bag. I have already called her and she said you could wear it."

"Wow, again. You certainly have taken care of everything."

"No, I have not. I just need to know; will you be there?"

Anna Marie looked into his eyes as she said, "Definitely!"

CHAPTER 9

THE WEDDING

A video link for the wedding had been set up to Chris's parents in Hawaii, his sister in Paris, and to Edna in England. High security was put in place around the complex. Chris wasn't able to see Anna Marie since he dropped her off at the suite. Kenneth and Candi made it with time to spare. Mrs. Koch assisted Anna Marie in getting ready, while Colleen helped Candi. A hair stylist was brought in from the salon. Chris and Kenneth, Christopher's best man, went to his suite and Mr. Koch was at the chapel. Kathy was to be in a wheel chair manned by Colonel Moffat in his dress uniform, as she was the flower girl. The wedding march played and all parties made it to the front except the bride. As the organist played the introduction, the back doors opened, and the crowd stood and turned as Christopher looked at the most beautiful sight he had ever seen; his bride prepared to come to meet him at the altar. Her wedding gown was exquisite. It had beads around a high collar and along the sleeves that went to the wrist. There was a high waist design and an A-line skirt to the ankles. There was no train and the veil was light and tiered to her waist. Her hair was flowing down her shoulders and curled. Tears flowed down Christopher's cheeks as he thought how God had brought him from despair to joy in a short forty-eight hours. Though he cried, the smile on his face was enormous. God had prepared and brought to him the woman with whom he would spend his life, his bride in Christ. Slowly she walked toward him with tears streaming down her cheeks and an immense smile on her face as well. She was not really looking, but God had sent to her the man of her dreams and her life-long partner, her husband in Christ.

CHAPTER 10

THE WEDDING NIGHT

The celebration that followed would be a difficult celebration to duplicate. Jesus had been glorified in the bringing of these two together, in the love they were beginning to know, in the ceremony, and in the song of commitment. The dinner and the toasts were no different. There was no alcohol served and you could hear comments praising the Lord throughout the evening.

It was 11:45 p.m. that night before Christopher carried Anna Marie across the threshold of his room. Anna Marie could not help but notice the redecoration of the sitting room. It was beautiful with a feminine touch.

"I hope you like it. I had Candi, Colleen, and Kathy do the redecorating after the wedding and before the dinner party."

"It's beautiful, Chris, I love it and appreciate the consideration you had of letting it be something new for you as well."

"Anna Marie, I love calling you by that name and hope it does not seem too formal. It was how you introduced yourself and I love the flow of it on my lips. I have thought of Annie as Candi calls you and Anna, but neither has the ring I like. Am I making sense to you?"

"Yes, you are, Chris, and I like the sound of it coming from your lips as well. I feel honored and cherished."

"You and I have not had any personal discussion concerning ourselves and you probably have many questions you wish answered. I have thought and prayed long and hard as this day has gone on and believe I have reached the correct decision concerning where we go from here. There are literally billions of bits of information in each of our brains.

Normal brain capacity is never fully used by human beings. We only use about fifteen to twenty-five percent. With the added brain capacity we have from our bionic upgrades, along with the fact it is a neural implant, we should be able to absorb the added information from each other with no adverse effects. However, in order to plan for possible difficulties, I have decided to fly in the teams that did the operations on us and have medical facilities available should something go wrong."

"Chris, what are you saying?"

"I am saying, I want us to have intravenous hook ups and medical personnel ready at our sides when we do this link process."

"So, there will be no privacy and intimacy involved? I would wish you to rethink this, please."

"Anna Marie, what would you suggest?"

"Why not have the teams available outside our room and our vitals monitored? Should something look amiss, then they can enter and proceed with caution. I would suggest Colleen, Candi, and Kenny to be first responders."

"That is a good suggestion. I'll go with your idea. We will be fully dressed and lying together, touching. From my understanding, we have to be touching each other throughout the entire download. I suggest we interlock our fingers on one hand and tie a band around those wrists."

"That is good as well."

"Anna Marie, I have never even kissed a girl, and I wish to walk slowly through the consummation of our marriage. I believe this hurdle of the mind meld may be very overwhelming for both of us, so for the physical, I want to see us walk slowly."

"Chris, I have never so much as kissed a man and I fully agree. Since it is late, let's just get to bed and sleep until later in the morning and do our devotionals together."

"I am in complete agreement with you."

After prayers, the two retired for the night.

CHAPTER 11

FEBRUARY 12, 1973, MONDAY MORNING, 9 A.M.
THE LINK

hristopher and Anna Marie woke around 6 a.m. Chris had had some of Frances' clothes brought over to his closet for Anna Marie and she had plenty to choose from. They ordered breakfast to be delivered to the room, had their quiet times, and prayed together. They set up a meeting for 11:30 a.m. with the operating team and their friends. When everyone arrived, Chris explained the situation to them.

"Thank you for coming. The medical team and Kenny know the circumstances of this meeting. Colleen, you and Candi do not. I will make a short explanation. Anna Marie and I would have lost our lives if it were not for the efforts of Dr. Jeff McNealy and the surgery team from WPPA. We each had accidents at different times and had to have extensive brain surgery. A byproduct of that brain surgery was if we ever met and were united in marriage then perhaps we could be joined through a link that would allow us to communicate with each other regardless of where we were through the earth's magnetic and gravitational fields. The joining of this link is electronic and biological. That link is instigated by a kiss. Once the link is made we need to stay joined physically until the downloads of data are complete. I know this sounds purely science fiction, but in our society often science fiction later becomes science. We make headways every year. We want our friends to be first responders if something goes wrong. This has never been done before, and to date there have been no other operations like ours. Are there any questions? Yes, Candi?"

"Connected by a kiss? How absurd!"

"We are not asking you to believe in the situation, just believe in us and the fact we don't want anything to go wrong. Okay?"

"Yes, Sir, Mr. Beckett."

It was decided to initiate the link at the house. Special hospital beds were wheeled to the first guest room and the necessary emergency equipment was placed in the sitting room. First responders were outfitted and given what was needed. Ports were installed on Christopher and Anna Marie and intravenous fluids were administered. The doors were closed and Christopher and Anna Marie were alone. The links through Edna to WPPA Communications were closed.

"You have taken tremendous precautions, Chris."

"Yes, I have, Anna Marie. I would rather be safe than sorry. I have just found you and do not want to be without you."

"Thank you, I appreciate that. I do not want to lose you either," she said as she squeezed his hand that was intertwined with hers."

"Are you ready, Anna Marie?"

"Yes, I am," she said as they leaned toward one another and kissed.

CHAPTER 12

It probably took five minutes, if that long. Christopher and Anna Marie were suddenly asleep with normal readings from the monitors. When they awoke the next morning, Anna Marie was the first to speak.

"That was a nice kiss. May I have another one?"

"You certainly may. I enjoyed it also."

"Wow, you can fly a B1 Bomber. Now I can, too!"

"Just remember it is a top-secret aircraft."

"Why are we talking? Can you understand my thoughts?"

"No, Anna Marie. I have a lot of information on how to cook various meals and more information concerning patient care and surgeries and how to ride a bike, but I am not able to read your thoughts. Are you directing them toward me?"

"You have filled my thoughts from the first moment I saw you attempting to make me come out of the snow, so, yes, I am directing my thoughts toward you, with as much love as I can muster."

Chris almost laughed, but just smiled. "I can certainly sense your love and I see it in your eyes, but as for the reading of each other's thoughts, I do not sense that. Well, let's get them in here and get these monitors off. I am ready for morning devotions and then a hardy breakfast together."

"It is 6 a.m., do you suppose they stayed awake all afternoon and all night waiting?"

"We'll soon find out."

Christopher and Anna Marie signaled their friends and they came in. Candi and Colleen disconnected the intravenous fluids bottles and removed the ports. They thanked their friends for their vigil, explained to the surgical teams what had happened, and went to their room. After showers and devotions, they settled in for breakfast.

"How should we prepare for marriage unity?" Anna Marie asked. "Do you think we should ask thirty questions, or what?"

"Anna Marie, there is an author named Wayne Mack. He has a premarital counseling manual. Would you like to study it with me?"

"I have heard of him. Yes, I would. What if we have questions?" she asked.

"Pastor Scott would always be available. Of course, we need to determine where we need to live and what we need to be doing about our careers as well."

"I have done rather well with investments. I found I was able to plan well after my operation. I have plenty of money, but now, even more so, I want to be useful for The Lord."

"I was also, Anna Marie, and with my business investments we could retire if we wanted to and go into some fulltime ministry."

They discussed their net worth and were so shocked with this information, all they could do was stare at one another.

Christopher was the first to break the silence. "You know, we would be perfect kidnapping targets if anyone knew, don't you?"

"I never considered that."

"There is something else you need to know, Anna Marie, and that is when you said yes to my marriage proposal you came under the protection of the largest and best security force in the world. You and I are protected by WPPA. I am the head of WPPA and the corporations that surround its operation. We have an army of over 200,000 men besides our security team and our Air Force is the best in the world, above even that of the USA. We have airplanes much better than the B1 and I am surprised you did not pick up on that. We are a well-kept secret."

"Is that the KLN32?"

"Yes."

"I guess I just slipped by it with all of the information that came in. Wow, I am accessing it now. An engine that does not use petrol as a fuel and that can fly six times the speed of sound?"

"That's it. I am proud of it as I helped design it."

"Christopher, just what did our operations open? I mean, there are procedures in the medical field I have instigated since my operation that are unheard of. I have designed a heart valve ten times better than any in existence before. I have thought of other things in other areas, but have never acted on them."

"Anna Marie, since my operation was in 1963, ten years ago, there has been much that has crossed my mind. It was little things at first, but now they are advancing more and more into my thoughts."

"Are we using more of our human brains or is it the neural implant?" asked Anna Marie.

"I believe it is a combination of both. Our understanding of the magnetic field of the earth and the gravity field are just two things no one can understand who speaks with me. The surgical team was telling me they felt the merge would open up a larger capacity for both of us."

"I guess they were wrong."

"Maybe so, or perhaps we have not found the key." With that statement, Chris changed the subject. "Anna Marie, would you like to go out for lunch?"

"Yes. Do you have a menu in mind?"

"Well, we both enjoy Italian, and there is a smaller restaurant here that has a romantic setting. I think you will enjoy it. They serve a delicious salad and pizza."

Chris and Anna Marie enjoyed their lunch, walked around the complex, and were back at the suite around 3 p.m. Edna called Chris with worry in her voice.

CHAPTER 13

Thrust forward

"Christopher?"

"Yes, Edna."

"I think you need to turn on the television."

Chris turned on the television as an alarming report played.

"Repeating what you have just heard, the United States of America has been hit with an unprecedented attack on Washington, DC. Four very large non-nuclear missiles exploded over the capitol less than ten minutes ago. They just appeared out of nowhere. Radar did not show any flight path. We do not know who launched them or how they were launched. These were concussion bombs. There is devastation everywhere over the capitol complex. Emergency personnel are having difficulty getting into the area. The President and Vice President have both been confirmed dead along with several who were in the line of succession. Congress was in session and all Secretaries were in Washington as well. By that we mean the Secretary of Defense and Secretary of Homeland Security, among others. I am sure someone will be letting us know who is in charge very soon. The entire military is on alert and there are to be no flights in or out of the Capitol. Everyone is urged to stay home and wait for further news…."

There was a series of four knocks at the door in a unique rhythm. "Come in Kenneth."

"Protocol 1345 has been established and you are on the air in fifteen minutes, Sir."

"I guess you have been recalled from retirement?"

"You are correct, Sir. I am your number one man."

Anna Marie searched her information from the download and found out Christopher is to take over as Protector then President of the United States should such an event like this occur. Her eyes grew wide as she read the material in her mind and she was awed at the protective procedure that had been worked out should such an attack take place. She smiled up at Chris with an understanding that allowed him to continue with the planning without being concerned over her reaction.

After a few moments of prayer together, Kenneth escorted Christopher and Anna Marie to guest room number three. There she found them in a television studio that was rapidly coming to life. She also saw men standing in various places, watching. No weapons were drawn, but she knew they were part of the security force Christopher had mentioned to her earlier. They set him in front of the cameras and moments later were preparing to broadcast.

"Three, two, one, you are on the air," said one of the WPPA agents.

"Good afternoon, my fellow citizens of the United States and our friends and neighbors worldwide. My name is Christopher Lee Beckett, Jr. My heart goes out to those who have lost loved ones because of this senseless attack. You have my condolences. Rest assured the emergency personnel are searching and identifying those in need of care as we speak.

"I will mention the hard part first and then begin the measures to be taken. I am now the acting President of the United States of America. I and your new Vice President, Kenneth M. Knight, will be sworn in during this broadcast. I am also the head of WPPA, The Worldwide People Protection Agency, an international police agency pledged to world peace. As your Protector, I am broadcasting to you on every known radio and television frequency. This signal is being broadcast and translated in every country worldwide.

"Exactly one year ago the current administration had signed an agreement with The Worldwide People Protection Agency to protect the United States and its citizens should such an attack as this occur. Various countries worldwide have also signed this agreement. This agreement places the USA and the world, as necessary, under martial law. The agreement is Protocol 1345 and a copy is being made available to all news agencies as I speak. All fulltime and reserve military personnel for the United States, you are being activated effective immediately. Each unit has a copy in the Emergency Packet Protocol and the Commanding Officer is to read the document section that affects their particular unit. Proper notification is being sent through normal channels. A protective security shield has been placed over all military units overseas and they are to wait for further instructions and not go on the offensive. A protective security shield has also been placed over our allies, our outlying states, and the continental US. WPPA has the most modern weapons and military hardware. The ability to activate these safety shields should give you some idea of our capabilities."

Chris paused as he heard Edna speaking. He placed his hand to one ear to act as if he were listening in an ear bud. "I have just been informed that other capitols have had attempted bombings. After the bombing of Washington, DC, WPPA launched in place the protection shields and the world was protected so no other bombs have caused any harm. My authority has just been authenticated. Shields have been secured over all countries worldwide. There will be no travel and no percussion weapons will operate, so don't even try. Please notice the film being broadcast alongside my image. You see a person firing a percussion weapon and what happens. Notice the bullet begins to melt and then the firearm is rendered useless. In the interest of public safety against possible third-degree burns, do not attempt to fire any weapon." Chris paused again to listen to Edna's report.

"ICBM's are firing up."

After instructing Edna to tell the teams to proceed as planned, Chris returned his attention to the broadcast. "I have just been informed missiles are being fired up around the world. Watch your televisions intently. What you are going to see is more technology never before applied. The white light beam is directed at the missile's electronics to render it useless. The blue light beam you see changes the molecular structure of the atomic material in the missile head; the bomb itself. The material left is not even radioactive. I am asking all governments to stand down and not attempt any more attacks on anyone. The attack on the US and the attack on your countries did not come from within our dimension. I will explain more of that at a later time.

"WPPA satellites are now engaging every missile and every nuclear warhead on the planet, even those under the sea in submarines. In a few minutes, there will be no atomic warheads in our reality and all ICBM's will be rendered useless, including those inside the USA. I meant what I said when I stated the WPPA is in charge and that is what we are doing. We are protecting the world from its destructive nature. Now that you understand the power of the Agency, let us get down to business.

"As your president, I will be asking all military units to perform the tasks outlined for them in the Protocol document. It is long and intensive and was meant to be used to help our nation recover its true mission of world peace. My teams and I will assist all countries in learning to live at peace with your neighbor. Further instructions will be forthcoming as available. To help you with questions concerning my identity, I am a born again Christian, serious about my Savior Jesus Christ receiving glory through my life. I wear many occupational hats. I am a pilot, able to fly any and all aircraft. I am a General in the South Carolina National Guard; a devoted patriot to my home nation, the United States of America. I served in the Vietnam conflict and Desert Storm. I am a Special Services Veteran. I was married just thirty-six hours ago to the talented and very lovely Dr. Anna Marie Koch. She will be by my side during this crisis and I value her input. You catch a glimpse of her on camera now. Yes, her lovely blue eyes took me in as well. I have contacted Federal Circuit Judge Jeremy Gadsden in Mobile, Alabama to do the swearing in of Mr. Knight and myself. Judge Gadsden, it is good to see you again."

They connected a video link into Judge Gadsden's office because he was still in Alabama.

"It is good to see you again also, Mr. Beckett. I had hoped a day like today would never happen. However, I believe the Protocol was the best measure for this nation and the world."

"Judge, I have a Bible and my wife is holding it for me."

"Good. I understand from our previous conversations you have the oath memorized. You may proceed."

Christopher raised his right hand and placed his left hand on the Holy Bible as he looked into the camera. "I, Christopher Lee Beckett, Jr., do solemnly affirm I will faithfully execute the Office of President of the United States, and will to the best of my ability, preserve, protect and defend the Constitution of the United States."

Judge Gadsden responded, "In light of your statement of affirmation and in accordance with the current law in effect of Protocol 1345, I pronounce you, Christopher Lee Beckett, Jr., President of the United States of America."

"Thank you, Judge. Kenneth, it is your turn. I will hold the Bible for you."

Kenneth placed his left hand on the Bible and raised his right hand as he looked into the camera. "I, Kenneth Marion Knight, do solemnly affirm I will faithfully execute the Office of Vice-President of the United States, and will to the best of my ability, preserve, protect and defend the Constitution of the United States."

"In light of your statement of affirmation and in accordance with the current law in effect of Protocol 1345, I pronounce you, Kenneth Marion Knight, Vice- President of the United States of America."

"Again, thank you Judge Gadsden. By the power invested in me from the constitution of the United States and Protocol 1345, I appoint you, Jeremy James Gadsden, Chief Justice of the Supreme Court of the United States of America."

"Thank you, Mr. President. I pledge to do honor to my God and Country."

"My fellow citizens of this planet, as President of the United States I pledge our resources in the direction of global peace. As CEO and Commanding General of The WPPA, The Worldwide People Protection Agency, I pledge the resources of this organization to the implementation of world peace and the protection of all peoples of this dimension."

"Thank you for your time and understanding. I do not want to lessen the tragedy that we have just had happen, but I want you to know that our Vice-President will be in charge in the US. I am seeking to close conflicts between nations world-wide. My first stop will be Korea. We have much to do and much to learn together. Pray to the King of the Universe, Jesus Christ, for wisdom and guidance for all of us in authority."

Anna Marie walked up to Christopher, took his hand and lead him out of the studio to their suite. Once there she directed him to a seat and sat next to him. "Okay, Cowboy, you have more explaining to do."

"About the document or the nanotechnology?"

"The nanotechnology."

"Did you read my whole report?"

"Yes, but most of it was conjecture on your part and this report is nowhere else. If I understand correctly, only you are in possession of this information and the documents you have from this other dimension are only in your head. Well, also in mine now. They told you this was coming and gave you plans to build certain safeguards so we would be safe."

"Safer, yes, we do not know yet if we will remain safe."

"So, I have these same nanorobots?"

"Yes, you do, once you kissed me."

Kenneth's knock rang out on the door. "Come in, Kenneth."

"Are you going to come clean with me or am I going to stay in the dark like some three billion other people?" Kenneth asked.

"I just told Anna Marie. You need to know, but I am not sure who else needs to know."

"Why not give him the basics, Christopher?" Anna Marie suggested.

"Okay, Anna Marie, let's see how you handle this one for me."

"Are you sure?"

"Yes, I am."

"Kenneth, when Christopher had the accident, he was injected with nanorobots that placed information in his brain that allowed him to help protect us against a dimension that would be trying to destroy other dimensions. For what reason we do not know, we haven't been told that yet. The programming in his neural implant also had information the nanorobots unlocked for him as time progressed. These nanorobots gave Chris the information and have now entered my blood stream. Dr. Jeff McNealy had been injected earlier by a visit from another reality so he could design the neural implant before Chris's accident."

"Wow, that was intense. Okay, now I know, that is sufficient. How can I help, Chris?"

"Okay?"

"Yes, okay. I have known you all my life and when we started this I didn't know why, but I trusted you. I still trust you. Where do we go from here?"

"I know you have not had a chance to read Protocol 1345 in its entirety, but as Vice-President you are going to need to know a lot more than you know now. Have a seat."

There was a knock at the door. "Is that you, Colleen?"

"Yes, it is, Mr. President."

"Okay. Come in, but don't go formal on me just yet."

"Why do you need this syringe and needle?"

"Colleen, please draw a syringe full of blood from me."

Colleen followed the proper procedure of cleaning the site, put the needle in, and drew the blood from Chris's left forearm. "Okay, now what?"

"Inject it in our Vice-President over here."

"What?" asked Colleen and Kenneth at the same time.

"Kenneth, you need the nanorobots in order to digest the Protocol document quickly."

"Do you and I even have the same type of blood?"

"Yes, we do; type O positive."

"Come here, brother dear, and, by the way, Chris, what are nanorobots?" Colleen said.

"Colleen, I'll let Kenneth explain that to you later. It is top-secret as far as we are concerned, so do not tell anyone else."

Colleen followed the same cleaning procedure as she injected the blood into Kenneth.

"Okay, that is handled. You should be feeling the effects within thirty minutes. Colleen, take him to a private place. He will go to sleep and awaken in twenty-four hours. Kenneth, you will know everything when you awaken. Oh, and Colleen, he will need hydration. Please keep an IV bag on him," requested Chris.

"Okay. Are you absolutely sure?"

"Yes, Colleen. Kenny will know what to share with you when he awakens."

"Colleen, take me to my suite. Have Colonel Moffat bring up three bottles of Ringer's Lactate solution with the necessary equipment and I will have a WPPA guard outside my door."

CHAPTER 14

PLANS AND MORE PLANS

"I plan on Anna Marie and me making a trip to Korea tomorrow morning."

"Is it wise for you to place yourself in such a vulnerable situation?"

"Kenneth, the world's population needs to see I do care about them and this helping of the people is not just a dream of mine, but a passion. By joining North and South Korea I will be making a great impact on the people. Besides, Anna Marie and I need a honeymoon."

"To a war-torn country?" Kenneth asked disbelievingly.

"To a country that needs compassion and healing."

"Kenneth, I am in agreement with what Christopher is saying. There are many orphans, battered children, and oppressed citizens who need love as well as to have their physical needs met," said Anna Marie.

"Kenneth, your family is traveling here. They can temporarily be housed and then you can share with Carmen what is going on when you wake up tomorrow afternoon. Colleen, you will be with Kenneth. Tell Colonel Moffat to greet the family and take them to Family Suite Six."

"Alright, Chris. I won't see you before you leave, but our prayers are with you," Kenneth responded as Colleen nodded her acknowledgement.

"Thank you, Kenneth. Now get going before the programming causes you to pass out. Anna Marie, are you ready for dinner?"

"Absolutely. How will that affect security, since you are now President Beckett?"

"We have had security at the Haven since it was built. I will be relying on the watch care of the WPPA personnel. I will have secret service personnel involved in the future, but my men will be watching them and we will weed out the ones we do not need or who are untrustworthy."

Over dinner Anna Marie and Chris discussed intimate plans for themselves and a desire to come together as one. She went shopping after dinner and they met at their suite later that evening. The two of them settled in with some Bible Study on Ephesians 5 and 1st Peter 3. Around 10 p.m. they retired in for the night, taking it slow, and with extreme care they became one.

CHAPTER 15

FEBRUARY, 14, 1973, WEDNESDAY
SPRICHST DU DUTCH?

hris, speaking to her in perfect Korean, was what Anna Marie heard in her mind the moment clarity returned to her the next morning at 7 a.m.

"Good morning, gorgeous."

Her eyes snapped open to see Christopher staring at her, laying on his side with his beautiful brown eyes sparkling. She grinned at him as she responded, also in perfect Korean, "Good morning, handsome."

In Hebrew, Chris said to Anna Marie, "Genesis 2:24 says, 'For this reason a man shall leave his father and his mother, and be joined to his wife; and they shall become one flesh.'"

"That is God's plans for all married couples, is it not, Christopher?"

"Yes, it is, my love. Becoming one flesh means what it says. It was more than a kiss."

"Yes, it does, absolutely! Do we share this information about our ability to speak to one another in our minds with anyone?"

"No, this will have to remain between the two of us."

They spoke to one another in their minds, marveling they understood and could speak every language and dialect on the planet. They were aware of where they were and could sense the groaning of the universe for perfect peace. Their minds and hearts were one! The joy and responsibility they felt was overwhelming.

They enjoyed the morning, had their quiet times and Bible Study times apart and together, and by 11 a.m. were dressed for travel after a breakfast of blueberry pancakes and bacon. Their luggage was placed on the KLN1 helicopter at the Haven compound and they were in their flight suits, taking off at 11:47 a.m. Christopher was the pilot and Anna Marie the co-pilot.

"I always heard there was a lot of noise in a helicopter."

"You are right, there is. However, you are flying in a WPPA helicopter. There is no internal combustion engine and no wind noise as the aircraft is perfectly designed. We are cleared to land at Ft. Gordon, Georgia in ten minutes."

"Why do you think no one else has harnessed the powers of the earth and sun as you have? It appears complicated, yet simple. I guess the combination is uniquely formed."

"I believe the pressure from the oil magnates thwarts the inventive process. Perhaps we would have invented this without outside intervention in another couple hundred years, but this information came with the nanorobots and the technology is needed now to help us to unite and fight the other dimension."

"Chris, just how much danger are we in?"

"It isn't the danger I am worried about, but the possibility of having to kill people and especially looking at myself and having to kill him. I do not want to do that. All of the technology I have received allows me to see even more that God's intentions of harmony for mankind and power in Christ have been totally suppressed by the world's system and Satan for thousands of years."

"Do you ever tire of hearing me say I'm impressed?"

"No, and I think I never will. However, remember God has allowed me to have this brain for a reason and I need to remember my life is not my own. It is for His glory and His control."

"It will take both of us, Chris, and I am not sure I understand it all yet from what I read throughout your brain waves."

CHAPTER 16

World Security Preparation

"So, I am reading but not understanding exactly what will happen ahead."

"Anna Marie, we will transfer to a KLN32 and travel straight to South Korea where we will pick up more passengers before heading to North Korea. We will be part of an invasion force that will take over North Korea in just a few hours."

"You are going to invade a country and expect them to allow that to happen?"

"Yes. There will be no bloodshed, and they will beg us to take over."

"I'll ignore that. Now, you say more passengers. You are speaking of our security detail?"

"Yes, as well as a detail of soldiers. We will have ten security personnel, two hundred soldiers, and Park Chung-hee, the Premier of South Korea, and his wife. We are also taking fifteen pediatricians and quite a bit of antibiotics and other medicines. We are also taking 2,000 Korean Bibles."

"We will be flying with twenty-four planes like ours with 250 soldiers each who will go to separate airports in North Korea and make those airports safe for the rest of the forces to enter and assist in ridding the country of all vestiges of the reign of Kim Il-sung. The Korean People's Army Air Force will also surrender without conflict."

"The South Korean's Premier's wife will work with me and the doctors."

"Yes, and you will each be protected with one of the personal protection shields."

"Chris, is it your power only that is maintaining these shields? I am not sure I am understanding all of this technology."

"The maintaining of everything is being done with the help of our security team and all of our personnel. There is a physical power source, but as you can see in our conversation its location is completely secret. Only you, Edna, myself, and a few others know about it."

"So, you've been preparing for this for almost ten years?"

"Yes, I have, but I didn't know everything I needed to know until this weekend when you showed up. I never put two and two together to understand that when you had your operation I should have looked you up then and we would have been together much sooner. God had prepared you for such a time as this and I blew it."

"But, aren't we catching up pretty fast?"

"Yes, we are, but we were supposed to have children by now," Christopher grinned as he faced Anna Marie.

"Christopher Beckett, are you teasing me?"

"You already know the answer to that."

ɤ   ɤ   ɤ

"Anna Marie, please just listen for awhile as I handle some current details of the pacifist policy with Edna."

"Sure, Chris."

"*Edna, this is Chris. How are the agents doing on having the planes out of the air?*"

"*Most everyone is complying with no problems; however, we do have a couple that appear to be loaded with explosives trying to head for populated areas. So far the agents have control of those planes and the pilots are going ballistic. They're really angry because they won't get to do the damage they felt they could do.*"

"*Okay, what about all ships?*"

"*We have some dead in the water due to arrogance from the Captains, but I believe all will end well.*"

"*So, better than the practice sessions?*"

"*Much better.*"

"*Are all North and South Korean planes out of the air?*"

"Just a couple more to land. Everyone will be on the ground by the time you arrive."

"Good. Is there anything I am leaving out just now?"

"Just your conversation with General Anna Marie."

"Thank you."

Chris ended his connection with Edna and turned to Anna Marie.

"I was wondering when we were going to discuss the uniforms," she said.

"The North Koreans are very conscious of uniforms and medals. You are a four-star general in WPPA. Our uniforms will be in our room on the plane. You will have an aide who is your personal body guard. She will be with you at all times. She cannot be dismissed for any reason. She will stick to you like glue. Her name is Captain Sarah Walker. I am sure you will like her."

"The design of the uniforms looks fairly familiar."

"Yes, do you catch the irony? Our dress blues are modern navy-blue Calvary uniforms similar to USA uniforms. Our soldiers are in combat fatigues similar to the US Army. USA uniforms are the most practical so we copied them and added some flair to the design. You will be wearing dress pants because of culture in many countries regarding the showing of legs and for your protection should physical force be needed."

"Okay. Now, what about medals?"

"Mostly for show, but each one has a reason should you be asked and you have those catalogued in your brain."

"Yes, I see that now."

"Alright, here we are. We are landing. Do you see that plane over there?"

"No, I do not," she replied.

"It takes practice. The plane is camouflaged. You should be able to see it with your 'implant eyes.' Think it through."

"Chris, I do see it. That plane is huge, and flies at six times the speed of sound? What is the camouflage?"

"Yes, it does, and the camouflage is light refraction. It also can be adjusted to where even the light refraction causes it to totally disappear. It is adjusted as it is now for show."

"I see some people waiting to see us."

"Yes, they are to take our luggage and become our body guards to get us on the plane."

As President Christopher Beckett and General Anna Marie Beckett left the helicopter they were saluted by the personnel and they returned the salutes.

President Beckett did the introductions. "General Beckett, this is Commander Jones, the Commander of Ft. Gordon; Commander Jones, General Anna Marie Beckett."

"It's nice to meet you ma'am, but not under these circumstances," said the commander.

"I understand, Commander."

"General Beckett, this is your aide, Captain Walker; Captain, please guard her with your life."

"I will, Sir. Come along with me, Ma'am," said Captain Walker.

"Commander, we will be taking off immediately. Please keep your base secure and on Defcon 1," Chris instructed.

"Yes, Sir, Mr. President."

President and General Beckett headed toward the plane along with their aides and security guards. Once on board, President Beckett went to the front of the plane and addressed those on board. "Men and women, we are in an unprecedented time in our world. We have an outside force threatening our very existence. We have no way of knowing when, how, or if they will arrive. I have been given technology through the sacrificial service of others. I pray it is enough. As we begin to unite our planet, we are at the same time honoring the God of the Bible who does not like us killing one another. I shall now lead us in prayer. Heavenly Father, You have brought us to this with much planning and education. May we go forth in love of our fellow man as we seek to reunite a country torn apart by war for over twenty years. Give us strength, protection, and Your grace. In Jesus' name, Amen."

Many throughout the plane said 'Amen' as well.

"Major Adams," said President Beckett.

"Yes, Mr. President."

"As General Beckett would say, let's get this steer moving."

"Ah, yes Sir. We will take off now."

Anna Marie gave a smile to Christopher.

CHAPTER 17

KOREAN UNIFICATION

Anna Marie and Chris were in their room preparing for the visit to Korea. A delicious dinner of grilled pork chops, broccoli, and baked potatoes had been prepared for them. After eating, they began changing clothes. Chris's uniform was the dress uniform for the Commander in Chief of the US and Anna Marie's was that of a four-star general for WPPA. They each looked sharp in their uniforms. Since the travel time to Korea was about three hours, Chris took that time to fully explain to Anna Marie what was about to happen.

"The drones will arrive about an hour before we do. They will seem like a large cloud over the entire nation. Can you imagine almost five hundred thousand 6" diameter drones over the entire nation? One for each square mile."

"Chris, I still do not understand. You expect these drones to get the gospel to each and every person alive. I mean, children will not understand what it is about, and many adults will be so hardened they will only swat at them or try to damage them."

"Yes, I know. However, the drones are not only to present the gospel they are also to be able to answer questions and to provide education in many ways as to what to expect in the future. They are also here to protect people and keep them in line. Even though some of us have individual shields, people can think of ways to hurt one another."

"And you do not expect there to be a panic?"

"No, they will stay at 45,000 feet attitude for several hours, and then start to descend only several at a time. It will be weeks before they are all in place. However, when we arrive they will drop to within 500 feet all over Korea and play the Korean National Anthem, the one that was in effect before the split. Then they will ascend back up to 45,000 feet. Yes, they will be out of the way for our planes. That was another reason we had all planes out of the sky."

"Christopher, I just don't know about you."

"Did I do something wrong?"

"No, it's just the way you think. You are not talking about shooting people and having a war, you are talking about playing music and presenting the Gospel. Just who are you?" she said.

"I love God, you, my brothers and sisters in Christ, my country, and my fellow human beings. That is about who I am."

Anna Marie moved over to him on the couch in their room on the plane and gave him a long, loving kiss. "I pray God will honor all of your plans and we will give Him glory in everything."

"They are His plans, I hope, because all of the schematics and ideas came with the nanorobots and the expanded brain. I hope the Chris who did this work gave me everything I need to know, and if not, I pray God will show me the way. He has never steered me wrong."

President Beckett and his team landed in North Korea on time. The North Korean Premiere was at the end of the Tarmac. A red carpet was between him and the plane and many soldiers lined both sides of the carpet. As Chris stepped from the plane he set a shield between him and all soldiers with an opening only to the Premier. The front line of soldiers on each side attempted to attack Chris only to find the shield blocking them. He and his wife and the Premier from South Korea moved forward to the Premier of North Korea. President Beckett greeted the Premier in Korean and wished him a long life. The North Korean Premier returned the greeting. President Beckett and the entourage followed him into the Palace at the edge of the airport.

Once inside President Beckett requested a private interview with the North Korean Premier. He explained to him the power of the WPPA. Then he said, "There is One who is above the power I have demonstrated, and One who is to be honored more than any human being. I have in my hand a copy of the truth of God's Word, the Holy Bible, and I would like to tell you about Jesus. It will not take long for you to see and hear the correct message about life. May I tell you?"

The Premier thought and then told President Beckett he would listen. They spoke together for over an hour. The premier did not make a decision for Christ, but seemed open to listen again. During the next few days there were several discussions between the two premiers and finally an agreement was made. The two Koreas were reunited.

CHAPTER 18

FEBRUARY 24, 1973, SATURDAY EVENING
THE MISSION

The trip was nearing ten days in length and there had been many meetings, reviews of troops, and a few incidents of anger. However, all the personnel had been fully protected and no lives had been lost.

On this night, Chris and Anna Marie were invited to stay in another palace. After they were in their rooms for a short period of time the air crackled and a man who looked just like Chris appeared. It was Joshua who was standing in front of them.

"It is time, we must leave now," said Joshua.

"We can't leave now, it will look like we've been kidnapped. How much time do we really have?"

"Twenty-four hours at the most."

"Okay. Anna Marie, pack our things. Joshua, teleport us from the jet once we are in the air and after I have instructed the pilot and Kenneth."

President Beckett moved to the door as Joshua disappeared. He spoke in Korean. "An emergency has arisen back in the United States and my wife and I must leave immediately. Please arrange for a limo to the airport."

Once they were at the airport and the pilot was on board the plane took off. Chris spoke to the pilot. "I am changing your clearance to the same as mine. My wife and I are debarking on a mission to the origin of the concussion bombs that fell on Washington, DC. We will disappear once you reach altitude. You are to take the plane to the base in Augusta, Georgia, and park it at the hanger where we left the helicopter and put on the stealth program. Should anyone request to enter, tell them you are waiting for the Vice-President. He will use the code name "Joshua" to let you know it is okay. Understand?"

"Yes, Sir."

Chris activated his link with Edna and began to speak with her through his mind link. *"Edna, get Kenneth on the phone now."*

"Yes, Sir."

Kenneth sounded groggy when he answered the phone.

"Mr. President, do you know what time it is here?"

"Never mind that, Kenny, Code Joshua. The plane will be at the Augusta, Georgia Army Base. You have read my plan because of the nanorobots, now you must tell the world. This will be the last you hear from me until we return."

"May the Lord be with you, my brother and sister."

Joshua and his plane came alongside the jet and Chris and Anna Marie #4 were now on their way to Joanne's reality after they picked up Chris #3 and his wife.

BOOK 5
IN THE NICK OF TIME

CHAPTER 1

Chris was in the control room. He had changed the periodic table value for gold and silver, so, worldwide, gold and silver were worthless. In his mind, he felt justified because of the one-sided control the rich had over the poor. By doing this, all gold and silver jewelry was worthless as well. He had also taken processed uranium, the type used in atomic bombs, and changed its value. As a result, atomic warheads would not explode and cause worldwide damage and death from the radiation, for there was no radiation. Chris was messing where he ought not to be messing. Playing God was only going to cause trouble, and trouble he received. The governments of the world formed an alliance and battle cruisers were surrounding the island. These cruisers were bombarding the island with concussion bombs around the clock. The bombing had been going on for over twenty-four hours and the shields were holding, but weakening.

"Why have they attacked me? Don't they know what I did was for their own good? All this just because I took away their gold and silver? They are such a wicked people. I'll show them." Chris waved his hand and four of the concussion bombs aimed at the retreat disappeared. His intent was to teleport them to Washington, DC, as a show of strength and power but they disappeared from his reality. "What have I done; where did they go? Who have I killed, and only because of my own stupidity?" About thirty minutes later when more bombs came toward him he waved his hand again and several more bombs disappeared. "What am I doing? I must be teleporting them somewhere. I don't understand."

CHAPTER 2

"Anna Marie, where are you? It has been over ten years. I know I blocked your coming back, but that was in anger, as was what happened the other day. You could have operated on me. This tumor is going to kill me. You spoke to me once of John 3. If any man be born again…. In all of my studies and encounters I have heard it all," Chris dropped to his knees. "Dear Jesus, I do not deserve Your forgiveness, but You did die for me. I am a sinner. Please forgive me. Please come into my heart. Please take over my life and be my Lord." Chris wept and fell asleep, the first calm sleep in over ten years.

CHAPTER 3

FEBRUARY 26, 1973, MONDAY
MIDNIGHT ON THE ISLAND

" I cannot keep up the pace; the shields are failing because my strength is failing. They will destroy me if I don't do something. I'll remove the blocks which have taken up too much of my energy. Now I will have more energy for the shields. I opened up communication with Washington, DC, this morning and they refused to talk to me unless I remove all my shields and return their silver and gold. I cannot let my technology get into the wrong hands. I would rather it die with me than for them to have it."

CHAPTER 4

Joshua was speaking: "Chris and Anna Marie from 437267, you are to stop the bombs and encapsulate the carriers all around the perimeter of the island. Just leave the bombs in mid-air. That will get a lot of world attention as they have reporters all over the place. I will place a shield just on top of Chris's shield to fortify and strengthen the integrity of the retreat, as his is failing. The design of his computer is wrong and it can only draw extra strength from him. He just removed the blocks; let's go."

The plane, under stealth mode, flew into the reality of 437269. Chris and Anna Marie from 437267 teleported in stealth mode to ship after ship, stopping bombs from being launched and also stopping all bombs in the air. Each launcher was encapsulated and no further bombs could be launched. The people on the cruisers couldn't figure out what was going on. They just watched and waited.

"Okay, Anna Marie from 437266. Do you see where the surgery suite is?"

"Yes, Joshua, I do."

"Alright, teleport all of the surgical equipment and supplies and yourself to the suite and start setting up. Just as soon as Joanne can reach Chris, she will kiss him to get the codes from his mind. She will then teleport him and herself to the suite. She will be searching for passwords and giving those to me, so you will have to put him under ASAP."

"Yes, Sir."

"Joanne, do you see Chris yet?"

"Yes, I do."

"Okay, you have practiced 'exact location' teleporting and you have to come directly in front of him and kiss him immediately. Otherwise, we will not be able to obtain the passwords and get into the systems and find out if there is a failsafe system. You have the most important assignment. Do you understand?"

"Yes, Sir, I do."

"Alright, Joanne, get to it."

Joanne teleported herself to the main control room directly in front of Chris. She did not give him a chance to react. She kissed him immediately, placed a shield around the two of them, and teleported both to the surgical suite. Anna Marie 437266 was there and she immediately placed an anesthesia mask on his face as Joanne removed the shield from his face. He had not taken two breaths before he looked at Joanne and said, "I prayed to receive Christ," just as he went under.

Joanne's hands went to her face and she began to cry. "Okay," said Anna Marie 437266, "you'll have to cry later, the clock is ticking."

"Joshua, this is the craziest password," Joanne said. "All of his passwords are the same. 'AnnaMariepleasecomehome' with no spaces and only the 'A' and 'M' in 'Anna Marie' are capitalized."

"Okay, got it. You get to the operation. Chris 437266, you are left in control of the plane. Keep it here with its computer running, as it has control of the main shield. We need that in operation until I stabilize his computer."

"Understood, Joshua."

Joshua teleported into the main control room.

"Computer, password 'AnnaMariepleasecomehome.' Do you understand me?"

"I understand you Christopher Beckett, what are your commands?"

"Please strengthen the shields all around and downward to maximum power."

"I cannot do so. My strength comes from Chris and he is in surgery," said the computer.

"Okay, first things first. Do you have a failsafe system?"

"Yes, I do."

"Will you please let me know what the parameters are?" asked Chris.

"I am to start the countdown when Chris is fully incapacitated or when another Chris attempts to take control," said the computer.

"But I am Chris."

"Not my Chris."

"How long is the countdown?" Chris asked.

"Thirty minutes."

"Does it have a turn off password?"

"Yes, it does," said the computer.

"Please turn it off, 'AnnaMariepleasecomehome.'"

"That is not the password."

"Joanne, I need a password for the failsafe system. We only have twenty-four minutes left," said Chris.

After a few moments, which seemed like hours to Joanne and Joshua, Joanne said, "Joshua, the password is 'AnnaMariewhydidyouleaveme?' The 'A' and 'M' are capitalized and there is a question mark. It has to be entered at the computer key pad with a login identity of 'ChrisandAnnaMarie.' 'C' and 'A' and 'M' are capitalized. Ask the computer to display the Destroy Me program login."

"Computer, please display the login for the Destroy Me program," Joshua requested.

The computer displayed the login and Joshua entered the necessary information. The question then appeared on the screen 'Cease countdown? Yes or no' Chris entered 'yes' and the screen flashed 'Program Terminated.'

"Chris from Reality 437268, what are your commands?" the computer asked.

"I need to reprogram you so your strength comes directly from your power supply and not through Chris. I have here a flash drive with the new programming that will allow you to operate even if Chris is incapacitated."

"Is that wise? What about loss of integrity?" replied the computer.

"All of that will be addressed by the program."

"Okay, the USB port is below the keypad on the left side."

"Inserting now. I am hitting the 'Program' button, are you with me? This will take only a few seconds. Okay, done," said Chris.

"Computer, maximum power on the shields, please," said Chris from 437268.

"Maximum power, what about the shield outside mine?" asked the computer.

"Being taken care of now," said Joshua.

"Chris 437266, you may turn off the shields and land the plane in the field behind the retreat."

"Computer, how many realities did Chris attack?"

"Only one, 437266, but it was a mistake as he intended to attack our Washington, DC."

"Alright, I understand now. Anna Marie from this reality told me he had lost the ability to teleport due to the tumor, but apparently he tried to teleport objects in his agitated state and teleported the bombs to another reality instead."

"Chris and Anna Marie 436341, please teleport to the control room. Computer, are all of the blocks off of all the realities?"

"Yes."

"Where are the Anna Marie's and are they shielded?"

"They are on the fourth level and yes, they are shielded by me and by another Anna Marie. I believe she is from your reality."

"Please open communications to my Anna Marie."

The computer opened a line of a communication and Joshua spoke to his Anna Marie.

"Hello, Cutie Pie, are you hearing me?"

"Cut the smart talk, what took you so long? I mean ten years, really?"

"It's good to hear you, too. Before I cut the shielding, I wanted to be sure I would not be zapped."

"Take your chances, big boy, this girl's itching for a fight."

"Not with me, I hope."

"We'll discuss that later. For now, I need to get these girls home."

"Will you need the computer or do you want to do it yourself?"

"Since when did I ever ask for help from anyone?"

"Understood. All shielding is being removed as we speak. I am also sending to you a Chris and Anna Marie who are Christian counselors. I am certain some of the ladies may need some spiritual support."

"That is a good idea. Have them teleport up to the fourth level."

"Okay, Chris and Anna Marie 436341. My wife will introduce herself and you can assist her. Cutie Pie, I'll see you in the control room when you are finished. Computer, allow outgoing teleporting whenever needed, please."

"Yes, Chris, 437268. Are you sure your wife is trustworthy? That exchange was rather confrontational," said the computer.

"Yes, Computer. You see, she loves me."

"You humans never cease to amaze me."

CHAPTER 5

After several hours had passed, Chris from 437268 was in the television studio adjacent to the control room. He set the controls and began speaking as the other Chris's and Anna Marie's stood behind him. Anna Marie from 437269, and Anna Marie from 437266 were still in the surgical suite operating on Chris 437269.

"To all citizens of this reality: My name is Christopher Beckett and I am from Dimension 437268. You live in Dimension 437269. I and the team behind me are from various realities and were recruited to assist Anna Marie Koch of this reality to stabilize the situation here before you virtually destroyed your way of life as well as compromise other realities. There are two Anna Marie's missing from the group. They are in the Surgical Suite of the retreat operating on the Chris of this reality as he had a brain tumor and that tumor is what has produced this situation, along with some actions that occurred over ten years ago.

"I am asking all world governments to cease their attack on this island. We have arrived to stabilize this reality and your assistance in that matter will be appreciated. Chris had attempted to return gold and silver to their original atomic numbers. I have completed that task for him. You will notice your concussion planes and bombs are frozen in place. I will return them to you at a later time without injury to you or damage to the planes. I am sure Chris will offer you an apology once he recovers from the surgery. I will be staying here until he has fully recovered and we have had an opportunity to discuss the future of this reality. There will be no question and answer period at this time."

"What you do need to know is it is because of my faith in the Lord Jesus Christ and the faith of the people behind me that we were able to pool together our strengths to accomplish this particular task. The world would not have been destroyed by the actions of the Chris from this reality, but you would have destroyed your way of life if you had continued in the path you were taking. I leave you now with these words: 'I will lift up my eyes to the hills—From whence comes my help? My help comes from the Lord, who made heaven and earth.'"

Chris then turned off the monitor and turned to the group behind him. "Reality 437267 and 436341, you are welcome to return home if you so desire. I can take you there or if you wish to wait and meet Chris 437269, you may do so. Chris 437266, your Anna Marie will be ready when they finish surgery."

Chris 436341 spoke, "I think I speak for everyone when I say we would like to see Chris's reaction to what has happened before we go home. I understand there is a large dormitory where he had housed the other Anna Marie's. Perhaps we can manage until he is ready to accept visitors. Also, don't you need a little help in returning those concussion planes and their remains to the proper owners?"

"Yes, I could use the help, so let's get to it. But before we do, I have missed my wife for over ten years. Please give us some time together before we begin. Say, tomorrow morning?"

With that, Joshua took his wife's hand and the two teleported to the plane in the field beyond the trees and to his suite on the plane. Joshua began speaking to his wife.

"Before we kiss, you need to know I was tempted over these past ten years, but I did bring every thought captive to the obedience of Jesus Christ and I remained true to you."

"I'll be the judge of that. Now quit talking and kiss me."

CHAPTER 6

Anna Marie 437266 had taken charge of the operation. Joanne assisted. She was too shaken by Chris's words to be of any use as the chief surgeon. She was also shaken by the information she found in Chris's mind that showed how much he loved her. She did, however, buckle down and assist with great capability. The operation was long and arduous. A transfusion had to be started at the beginning of the operation to replace some new style nanorobots that were protecting the tumor. Apparently, Chris had invented them to stay alive in his body, but they had a reverse affect on what he needed. Rather than helping him they allowed the tumor to grow. The new nanorobots had to eradicate the old nanorobots before the surgery could begin, and that took about two hours to accomplish. Using special detecting instruments, they received the signal when the new nanorobots were in place. Anna Marie 437266 then opened Chris's skull and began to remove the tumor. The nanorobots then began removing the tentacles that were throughout the brain, but the body of the tumor had to be physically removed so the implant could be inserted. Chris lost about thirty percent of his brain, but the implant would more than make up for that loss; that is, if it properly merged with the rest of his brain. They would need to wait another forty-eight hours after the twenty-six-hour surgery to find that out.

As the surgery ended, Anna Marie from 437266 asked her husband where he was and she then teleported to his location on the fourth floor, while Joanne collapsed on the bed that had been wheeled in next to Chris's bed.

CHAPTER 7

MARCH 3, 1973, 8 A.M.
THE SURGICAL SUITE

Joanne had awakened earlier, gone to her suite, and showered and dressed. She made breakfast for Chris. He woke at 8 a.m. and saw her in her pink dress with matching accessories. He looked at her left hand which she had strategically hooked under her chin. There was the engagement ring. "I am so sorry for all the misery I caused you and so many others, Chris. Please forgive me for running away."

"I forgive you Anna Marie. Will you forgive me for my heavy-handed attitude before you left?"

"I forgive you, Chris. How about some blueberry pancakes?"

"Before I accept the pancakes, am I seeing clearly? You have the ring on your left hand?"

"Yes, you are Chris, and that is based on three things. First, is it true you accepted Christ? Second, do you still want me as your wife? And third, will you ask my dad for my hand in marriage?"

"Yes, it is true. I asked Him to save me in my desperation. I had nowhere to turn. I know He is living in my heart. I felt Him drawing me these past few weeks. I could resist no longer. Yes, I do want you as my wife if you want to marry me. Frankly, I do not know if your dad would ever say it was okay for you to marry me after what has happened, but I will ask."

"Let's not worry about that just now. Have some pancakes."

After breakfast, Anna Marie was clearing away the dishes when the team started popping in. Joshua spoke first. "There are many people who have much against you, and most of it is justified. You took away my wife a little over ten years ago and other realities had lost their wives as well. What do you have to say for yourself?"

"I know there is no way I could repay you for the grief and suffering I have caused you. All I can offer you is my regret and ask for your forgiveness for all I have done to each of you. For you who have trained and given up much for me, I am thankful and humbly say, will you please forgive me?"

"Yes," was echoed around the room.

"I know I need to do two things in particular. I need to offer my regrets and ask for forgiveness from this reality and I need to go to four different realities and ask the Chris's and Anna Marie's of those realities for their forgiveness as well. Chris 437268, would you take me to each one? I do not trust myself to be able to teleport correctly."

"I need to go as well, since it was my leaving that precipitated all of this," Anna Marie added.

"Actually, you do not need to leave. I have programmed the computer to access each reality for a conference call in four hours. We will go to the control room and each reality will be seen on a separate part of the main screen. You can say it once and find out your answers right away. In the meantime, before that call, Chris, I understand you need to ask a certain man a question?" Joshua said.

"Yes, I do, but I need to get cleaned up first."

With that admission, Chris 437269 found himself in his own suite with Joshua.

"Go to it; get yourself ready. I'll wait in the sitting room here."

After only thirty minutes Chris was showered and dressed in a black suit and tie with a white shirt. He had chosen a tie that was hued in lavenders and purples. Anna Marie 437268 and Joanne were in the sitting room as well.

"My, you look handsome. Are you ready to meet my dad?" Joanne asked.

"How? Are you going to transport me?" Chris responded.

"That will not be necessary, Chris. Much behind the scenes work has gone on since we arrived here. My dad and my mother, along with my brother, his wife, and three children are all here in the dormitory upstairs. You and I are walking into the living area of our home first. Dad will be there. I will tell you the rest after we receive his answer. Are you ready to meet my dad?"

Chris looked into his Anna Marie's beautiful blue eyes and said, "Let's go, gorgeous."

Mr. Koch was standing by the window looking out over the forest and ocean. He turned to face Chris and Anna Marie when they walked in. Anna Marie had discretely taken off the ring before she met her dad, and she had given it to Chris in the sitting room. Her dad's stern look was unmistakable.

"I never did properly thank you for saving my daughter's life. There is no way I could ever repay you for that. Thank you," Mr. Koch said.

"You are welcome, Sir. I need to ask your forgiveness for all the grief I have caused you over these past ten years. Please forgive me. I cannot enumerate all of the sins I have committed. I have asked God for His forgiveness and He has granted that through His Son, my Lord, Jesus Christ. Now I ask for yours as well."

"You have my forgiveness, Chris. Mine and that of my family. Now I believe you have something you wish to ask me?"

Very nervously Chris replied, "Yes, Sir. I do not deserve her, but with your permission, I would like to marry Anna Marie. May I have that permission, Sir?"

Anna Marie's father looked sternly into Chris's eyes as he said, "Chris, much has happened since that first time you sat in my home to ask to be able to date Anna Marie. I understand you have learned much and I know you have much more to learn. You have, however, made a commitment to Christ and that was my criteria, not only to be able to date her, but also to marry her. Yes, you have my permission to marry my daughter."

Chris was beside himself with joy as he shook Mr. Koch's hand, perhaps a little too vigorously. "Thank you, Sir, I promise to love and cherish her, I really do."

Chris then turned to Anna Marie and got down on one knee. "I do not deserve you, Anna Marie. I pushed you away because I had found you were smarter than me, but I never stopped loving you. I cannot live my life without you. With God's help, I want to be the husband you need. Anna Marie Koch, will you marry me?"

"Yes, I will marry you, Christopher Beckett, but only on one condition; you marry me today," Anna Marie responded.

Chris was suddenly confused. He looked at Mr. Koch and noticed the smile on his face and noticed then the room was full of people who had slipped in unnoticed by him. He looked back at Anna Marie and saw the love in her eyes and the smile on her face as he responded, "Yes, yes, yes, absolutely." He stood and hugged her, picked her up, and twirled her around.

"Chris, you are squeezing me too tightly! Where is my ring?"

Chris suddenly remembered he had forgotten to slip the ring on her finger. He got back down on his knee and slipped the ring on her finger as he said, "Thank you, Lord Jesus, for such a precious woman. She is indeed a perfect lady in the Lord."

CHAPTER 8

Suddenly everyone was in the dormitory above which was now a wedding chapel. All of the team had worked on making it perfect. The missionary couple were the preacher and Anna Marie's maid of honor. The Chris's from reality 437266 and 437267 were groomsmen. Their wives, along with Anna Marie 437268 were bridesmaids. Joshua had carried on a quick conversation silently with Chris and found Chris's parents had still not forgiven Chris for many transgressions over the years even before the incidents of the past ten years. Edna Ryder was going to sit in the mother's place for Chris. Chris asked Joshua to be his best man. Everyone was in the room except Anna Marie and her parents. The elevator door opened, the wedding march began playing on the speakers, and Anna Marie's mom was ushered to a seat. The doors closed and opened again and there stood Anna Marie. She was dressed in a beautiful white gown that was similar in design of the pink and blue dresses Chris had seen her in earlier. He had to be told in his head by Anna Marie, "Close your mouth and smile," for he was literally shocked to the core. He smiled and she was escorted to the front by her dad. The ceremony began and it was a beautiful ceremony. Each Chris and Anna Marie reflected on their own ceremonies and the joy they shared with their mates.

BOOK 6
EPILOGUE

REALITY: 436341

The missionaries returned to their huts in the South Pacific. They used all of the money given to them by Joshua and Joanne to wipe out poverty in their reality. As more and more people were educated and more and more came to Jesus Christ, more were able to go to college. Many different men worldwide went to college to become preachers. The reality became over seventy-six percent Christian by the year 2016. Chris and Anna Marie had three children; James, Cassandra, and Cedric. Each of them grew up and honored Jesus Christ as both boys became preachers and Cassandra became a nurse and married a missionary.

REALITY: 437267

Chris and Anna Marie went back to fighting against human traffickers. They used a new tool. They located Dr. McNealy and asked him to engineer more nanorobots for different blood types. They then went worldwide and located many women and young girls who were abused or in compromising situations, rescued them, spoke to them about their need for a savior, and when possible led the women and girls to Christ. Then they injected the women who were saved with the nanorobots, trained them as WPPA agents and educated them in the Scriptures. They then returned to their home towns, districts, and neighborhoods to confront the bullies and traffickers and bring them to justice. WPPA had to build a much larger prison, but soon the problem of human trafficking worldwide was stopped. Women were freed from the stigma of slavery. In 1975, Chris and Anna Marie had twin girls, Laurel Ann and Abigail Rose, and twin boys, James Nathan and Christopher Luke, in 1977. The boys went to law school and seminary and became traveling evangelists. The girls became nurses and married surgeons.

REALITIES: 437266, 427268, AND 437269 HAD COMPLICATIONS.

437266 was the reality that had been attacked. Many of the victims' families requested there be retribution. Chris and Anna Marie 437269 gave heartfelt regrets and apologies and sent billions of dollars to be used for rebuilding and for the families of the victims. Many people, however, asked for the death penalty for Chris 437269. Chris agreed to be tried and pled insanity due to the tumor. Anna Marie, his wife, volunteered to be his attorney, as well as Joshua. They requested a jury trial and it took forever for a jury to be approved. The trial lasted three days. Chris 437269 was sentenced to death. Reality 437266 would take no bargaining. Their president stepped in and gave Chris 437269 a Presidential pardon; citing insanity at the time of the incident. Many people didn't like it and again would not accept Chris 437269's apology. He and Anna Marie did not take too well to this and disappeared from the reality, and Joshua could not find them anywhere. The bay on the island where his compound had been was empty. It was as if a compound had never been there.

Reality 437266 finally calmed down and rebuilt, and conflicts were cleared as nations were not torn apart by war. Christopher and Kenneth served for twelve years under the WPPA Protocol. They appointed many competent leaders worldwide and then stepped down after a national election they engineered. Chris and Anna Marie retired back to The Haven. They had three children by this time; Christopher III, Anissa, and Jamie. The family decided to tour the world incognito and did a lot of philanthropy in the process.

Chris and Anna Marie 437268 settled and were the proud parents of triplets; Joseph, Mary, and Abigail. They lived on their island, but toured throughout their reality. They monitored other realities, and gave their money away to various Christian organizations and churches.

So, what happened to Chris and Anna Marie 437269? From the time he received his implant to the time after the Presidential Pardon, Chris 437269 was not using his powers. Anna Marie would teleport him, protect him with her shield, and initiate their private conversations. When they went home in between court dates and before the trial he would strengthen his compound on the island and bring in stores of food, water and supplies from the rocket planes. When they disappeared they took the compound with them. He destroyed his satellites before he left. Calls to Edna Ryder were met with a disconnect signal. They had a boy and a girl; Carl and Carleigh. Their Nana was Mrs. Edna Ryder. But where were they?

ABOUT THE AUTHOR
CHARLES BRACKETT

Charles L. Brackett, Jr. was born in April of 1945 in Anderson, South Carolina. He graduated from high school in Aiken, SC in 1963 and was married in Aiken in December 1967. He has a two-year business management degree and a four-year degree in Pastoral Counseling. Charles and his wife, Patricia, have two children and six grandchildren.

His first career of thirty-seven years was in automotive parts and service management and ended in 1999. His fourteen-year career as a business manager for an entrepreneur who was involved in parking lot maintenance and as a restaurant owner ended in 2015 when he retired at the age of seventy.

Charles began writing in March of 2015. It took over two years to bring this book to the marketplace. Charles adds, "I have enjoyed working with Warren Publishing and I hope you will enjoy and appreciate our efforts."

www.ingramcontent.com/pod-product-compliance
Lightning Source LLC
Chambersburg PA
CBHW020558260626
47157CB00003B/761